Where Once We Loved

by

G. Gordon Long

Dedication

To my Mother and Father –
A True Love Story

To Aunt Shirley –
For the candle in the window, always kept lit to
guide us all home.

To Diane –
Always

Chapter 1

Though the war in Europe and the Pacific raged on during the summer of 1944, for Mercy Daniels, her own *personal* involvement had ended with the arrival of a single telegram from the United States War Department.

"The President of the United States regrets to inform you that Lieutenant Henry Gates has been reported lost along with the crew of the U.S.S. Perry as a result of an enemy attack. There were no reported survivors. We offer our sincere condolences and regret we are unable to provide further details due to national security. The President of the United States and the Offices of Naval Command extend their heartfelt sympathy."

The telegram had been like all the other thousands that had been sent that year alone, the same that all those sent since the beginning of the war. Telegrams received by families now without a son, without a husband. Families with loved ones who would not be returning. For many of these families they would take down their blue stars hanging in their windows to show they had someone away serving in the war. In their place, gold stars now hung a painful reminder of a war death for that family.

And in the little village of Wellfleet, Massachusetts, on the remote windswept stretches of Cape Cod, just as was so in many small towns, all too many gold stars now were displayed.

But life among the fisherman and oystermen who plied their trade off the waters surrounding the narrow spit of land jutting out into the often unforgiving Atlantic Ocean went on. Centuries of inhabitants, clinging to the land, scratching out a meager living, simply endured. These families were forever linked with those of their pilgrim fathers, who had landed there in 1620 in search of a new life and who often found only hardship, disease, and death. Yet somehow, they managed to survive that early first winter and went on with living, just as Mercy Daniel knew she had to now do.

Her family and friends had all come together to comfort her, surrounding her with love and caring. Softly whispered words of sympathy and condolences were offered. Visitors bringing meals to provide comfort and substance in a familiar ritual that extended back to forever times. Those first few days it was as if there was a funeral wake being observed, the grieving young fiancé at the center, the once to have been bride now alone. But there was no departed loved one laid out before them to pass by with quiet words and last visitations.

Perhaps it was this, more than anything, that sparked the slow burning ambers of anger deep within her. She would not accept the words so carefully crafted in the now crumbled telegram that still lay in the corner of her bedroom where she had retreated the day of its arrival to tear at the envelop with trembling fingers. She wouldn't accept those words. To do so, so quickly, all too easily, would be to simply let go of a love for a man that was the very definition of her existence. She could not commit such an act of betrayal.

So, she sat obligingly, listening to them and nodding mechanically at their good intentions, accepting their charity and goodwill. But after a while she no longer heard their words as she moved numbly amongst them. Though the dark night of her soul seemed to close in around her, there, in the distance, she saw a faint light, just out of reach and she would just have to move ahead, guided by the pale flame of hope amidst all the darkness that now surrounded her would somehow lead her back to the living. She would endure, survive, as all others before her had.

In the days and weeks that followed, Mercy not only sensed a change in herself but in the village itself. Not so much by any particular and tangible event but more in the way others looked at her as she made her way along the narrow streets of town or out along the docks where the fisherman sold their catch. She felt she had somehow become an object of pity, the diverted eyes of her neighbors that would not hold contact with hers when they greeted her in passing telling more than any words they might exchange. That certain glance between women locked in conversation across a street or the aisles of the market whenever Mercy approached. She wasn't imagining it. She knew it was pity they were now expressing and she understood, perhaps even expected it. She had become the town's newest "*pitiful thing*" as the women often said of those among them who had suffered misfortune. But she felt there was a sense of something else, something more; it was *fear*. For they had begun to see in Mercy that thing they feared and dreaded the most; the specter of more death to come, more telegrams with greetings no one wanted to receive.

As the months wore on, she started to keep more to herself, working at her loom, weaving fine cloth for sale to the villagers. Her artistry had become well known, not just around Wellfleet but towns and hamlets further up and down the Cape. Though it didn't bring the money a husband would earn working the sea, it was enough to keep her fed, clothed, and the roof of her small house in the meadow just outside of town over her head. And she could keep her pride by not having to depend on the charity of her Aunt Emily. Even though Mercy truly loved her and knew her Aunt Emily would never let her go without it was through her own sense of independence and pride that she wanted, needed to fend for herself. For Mercy Daniels and for the others of Wellfleet, life moved forever slowly on.

Chapter 2

As with the arrival of anyone new from the outside, word quickly spread that in the late Summer of 1944, the small village of Wellfleet was to have a new doctor taking up residence among them. Old Doc Harrington, a man who it was said had overseen the birth of nearly half the population of Wellfleet and most certainly all of those under the age of fifty, was getting on in years and his retirement was not far off. After half a century of practice, he had decided it was time to turn the reigns over to a younger man. Such a man as his own nephew, Garrett Harrington.

Though Salem born and Boston educated, the *young* Doctor Harrington was no stranger to Wellfleet, having often summered there in his childhood while his father, a businessman involved in the import trade, and Garrett's mother, who frequently accompanied her husband on his travels, left the young boy in the care of family in Wellfleet. In fact, it was this long association with his Uncle that many in the family believed had led the younger man to pursue the field of medicine himself.

But his frequent summers in the care of the old village doctor aside, Garrett Harrington was still, in many ways, a stranger to the inhabitants of Wellfleet. As was true with any close-knit community, the young doctor was a person largely unknown to them and as such needed time to be examined, to be accepted. This would have been true for any newcomer. But for a *doctor*, a man who would know more about them than anyone might dare, acceptance would be a slow and guarded process. All the more so if such a new arrival was to be taking the place of a long-trusted friend and near father-like personage as Old Doc Harrington, nephew or not.

***

As the mild weather of summer began to pass and signs of the coming Fall appeared with the turning color of leaves and the morning chill, the town grew busy in preparation for the change in seasons. The fisheries along the Wellfleet wharf extended their hours to keep pace with the increasing boat loads of incoming fish that would need to be dried and salted for winter consumption up and down the mainland. Bushels upon bushels of freshly harvested oysters and newly dug clams streamed in for processing in the local cannery. Most of the revenue the town took in each year would soon slow as ice and snow began to choke the harbor and passage to the sea grew more dangerous.

Mercy also busied herself making the rounds to the farms that dotted the interior of the Cape. She would purchase as much wool for her loom as she could afford and barter for the rest in exchange for weaving cloth for those who favored her woven fabric for garments. Her weaving was considered by many to be some of the finest. Her goods much sought after. It provided her the income she needed to make ends meet.

Her small, three room cottage, out along the bluffs of Nauset Beach, had belonged to her Aunt Emily's family. Her adoptive father had been an oysterman as many of the inhabitants of Wellfleet had been for generations. Her adoptive mother a weaver as she herself was now. But tragedy and the sea had taken them both at far too early an age. They had died together, lost when an island packet running between Nantucket Island and the Cape had floundered in a sudden summer squall that took the lives of all aboard. Mercy was barely eighteen.

Forced to move from the home she had grown up in when the Bank foreclosed on her parent's house, her Aunt Emily had insisted Mercy come to live with her at Halcroft House, a stately white columned mansion perched atop the hill overlooking Wellfleet. It had been in Miss Emily's family for several generations. But the fiercely independent Mercy had politely declined, preferring to make do as best she good. It was then that her Aunt had insisted that Mercy move into the small cottage that Mercy lived in now.

It was a tiny house, barely three rooms, not far from the village, in a spot known as Goody Hallet Meadow, a mostly barren landscape of scrub pines and windswept dunes. In the summer, small patches of beach plum flowers dotted the bluffs overlooking the sea. In the winters the wind beat hard at the soil and clouds of snow swirled up to sting the face with a mixture of sleet and sand.

On such winter days and nights, especially in the pitch-black darkness of moonless nights, the tiny cottage always seemed on the verge of flying away across the dunes and into the sea itself. But it had been built of sturdy oak, some said gathered from the wooden frames of the many skeletons of shipwrecks that washed ashore during storms. The tiny house's pilings and foundation were driven deep into the sandy soil. It had stood there in the meadow for two hundred and more years in one form or another, pieces torn down and others added until it came to its current form. But more than just a weathered cabin on a spit of desolate sand, the cottage had its own legend, its own tale deep within the history of Cape Cod. Some said it had once been inhabited by a witch.

Chapter 3

The rushing wind outside her cottage rose and fell as the sounds of the gale hurling in from the dark sea came at the land with ever increasing force. Mercy had heard these sounds many times before when the storms of October moved north along the coast, led by hurricanes from the south. But this night, as she sat in front of her fireplace, the sound outside her door was not merely the turbulent roar of wind and rain battering against her windows.

There was something else mixed in with the rattling of her house shutters and thumping doors. It was barely noticeable and she only seemed to detect it when the wind died down between the gusts assaulting the world beyond her windows. It was a separate, wailing sort of sound, almost as if it were the cry of an injured animal. As the wind rose it would become nearly undetectable, momentarily drowned out as the small house creaked and groaned against the storm outside.

But if Mercy strained her ears to hear, the sound would again come to her. It seemed to her to be a tortured sound, distinct from all others, coming from off in the distance.

After listening for a while longer, Mercy took her woolen coat from the hook near the door, tossed it around her shoulders and unlatched the bolt holding the door to the cottage fast against the beating winds outside. She inched the door open, a cold blast of wet wind and rain catching her face and hair. She waited, cocking her ear in the direction she thought the sound had come from. Below her, beyond the edge of the cliffs of Wellfleet, down along the surf battered Nauset beach, the waves broke hard again the rocks of the shoreline, dragging the flotsam of storm churned debris in and out with the water's ebb and flow. She studied the sounds of the beating surf, trying to divide it from the other sound she could still make out a little more clearly now further away, up the path that led away from in front of her small stone cottage. It seemed to be coming from up near the old stone ruins of the outermost house that overlooked the dunes and flatlands between the ocean and the safety of Wellfleet town laying snug on the bay side of the Cape.

Mercy pulled her coat tightly around her, blocking the wind that threatened to pull it off her shoulders as she stepped outside beyond her doorway. She peered into the darkness, her eyes following in the direction the sound seemed to come from. Occasionally, a sudden flash of lightening would illuminate the distant horizon, casting a brief, bluish glow over the dark silhouette of the ghostly ruins, its roofless stone walls jutting up above the saw grass and scrub pines. The ancient remains were the only profile of man-made lines in a landscape of jagged and twisted forms of natural growth.

And then again came the distinct sound. A cry she thought. A painful sorrowful utterance was all she could describe it as, like a small child or an injured animal, calling out in misery. She stared hard into the black abyss, waiting for another flash from the night skies to cast its glow on the horizon. Twice more the lightning cracked, ever so briefly pushing back the blackness. No, she thought, it was just the storm, nothing more. No child, not even an animal, would wander out from hearth or burrow on such a night. It was nothing more than the punishing roar of the northeaster coming in from the sea she told herself.

She chided herself for being so easily tricked. Here she was, a perfectly mature woman, she thought, standing outside in the cold blackness of a night not fit for man nor creature, straining to hear what no one would hear. But as she turned to step back into the warmth of the cottage, her eye caught something off in that blackness that until now she had not seen. There, in the midst of the ruins, she could make out an ever so dim light. A yellowish glow, framed in the opening of the stone wall where once a window had been. She paused, watched, studied it. For a moment, it just seemed to float there, motionless. It was just a trick her eyes were playing on her, she thought. Perhaps a reflection of something further away, maybe a ray of light from further down the coast line. Maybe even the Chatham Lighthouse, piercing the dark night skies with its slowly rotating beam of light.

But then the tiny speck of light began to move. It disappeared from the opening in the wall and then reemerged at the next window opening in the foundation. It wasn't just floating. It moved with deliberate direction, until it became visible outside of the ruins, between the house and the very edge of the bluffs not more than a yard or so from the drop below.

Mercy stood transfixed, mesmerized by the tiny point of light. It was no bigger than the light of a candle at such a distance away. Staring hard at the light, she realized that in fact it had to be a candle, or the light of a lantern. It seemed to flicker as it moved, swinging back and forth. As she continued to watch, the small point of light moved closer and closer to what she knew had to be mere feet from the edge of the bluffs. She stared into the pitch dark, frozen with both a growing fear and a hypnotic interest as to the source of the phantom light.

Then, as if it had gone over the very edge of the distant bluffs, it seemed to sputter and go out, the darkness swallowing up any trace of it ever having been there. Mercy stood still, her eyes trying to retrain themselves on the spot where the light had last been. But there was nothing now. Only the wind from the sea returning to fill any void left by the other sound.

She returned to the safety of her cottage, bolting the door behind her again. She busied herself with a few chores before turning in for the night. But she didn't drift off as quickly as on other nights. Her sleep was troubled, images of the storm and the floating light came to her. It was nothing but a dream she told herself upon waking in the morning, nothing more. And she wondered if she had really seen the light, seen anything, heard anything but the wind and the storm.

Chapter 4

Wellfleet was indeed a small town. In fact, many said it was nothing more than a village. From one end of Main Street to the other and the length of Commercial St to the town's wharf, there were but a few dozen houses, shops, and common buildings. In such a place, local news travelled quickly. Rumors and gossip even faster. So, upon the day of his arrival, the new doctor, even for one who was not a complete stranger such as Old Doc Harrington's nephew, word of young Garrett Harrington's coming had already been well circulated.

Among the women of Wellfleet in particular, he had been the subject of great discussion. It was said he was tall, short, thin, heavy set, blond, dark haired, and had deep brown, crystal blue eyes. Of that they were all most certain. But where they may have all differed in exact details, they were right about he being young, certainly would be handsome if he bore any resemblance to Doc Harrington in his early days, and no doubt a gentleman if he was in any way associated with the Harrington family. And of all these attributes, the most important was, he was a *bachelor.* Just the sort of man that any eligible young girl among their unmarried daughters would find a good catch when other prospects at the moment appeared so limited. Any of the town's eligible young man had long ago shipped off to the war and those that remained were either of questionable health or character having lagged behind or been turned down by the service.

Every day, as old Doc Harrington made his rounds or saw his patients at his office, people asked questions. So frequent were the inquiries that Doc had even begun to think it might just be simpler if he printed up a broadsheet, listing all his nephew's qualifications, both physical and educational, and had it posted in front of Jacob's General Mercantile store for all to see. He envisioned it should read, *To All Good People, be it known that my nephew, Garrett Harrington, Doctor, Boston educated, age twenty-nine years, an eligible person of all status, shall be taking my practice upon my pending retirement.* But as tempting as the thought, it was no more than wishful thinking. Doc knew only too well that such departure from decorum would hardly be taken for the tongue in cheek humor intended. So, Doc simply tolerated the curious, kept his answers to a minimum as well as the date of his nephew's arrival to himself until the day Garrett showed up at his doorstep, luggage in hand, and with youthful eagerness to begin.

That morning, as Doc Harrington opened his door to greet his only brother's son, Garrett extended his arm and took the older man's hand in a firm grip.

"Uncle, I am so glad to see you again. I do so appreciate your having asked me to come. I owe you a debt of gratitude," Garrett assured him in what had been a well-practiced speech.

"Nonsense, my boy. Tis you who do me the honor. Please, come in won't you. Here, let me help you with your bags," Doc Harrington offered, pushing the front door open wider and stepping out to gather up one of the leather satchels. Garrett took the larger of the two and followed Doc into the darkened, slightly musty smelling, interior of the house. The odor of cigars mixed with the smell of antiseptic fluids was thick. But he noticed that the house was in well-kept order though the window curtains were mostly drawn shut, keeping out the sunlight.

Doc Harrington preferred it that way. Even though he had a housekeeper to help him manage ever since his beloved wife Mary had passed a few years back now, he hadn't found the bright sunlight that once streamed through the lace curtain windows quite as cheerful and welcoming as he once had. He knew it wasn't depression. No need to call it that he had told himself. More just a case of *melancholy*, as the old folks once called it, and a sense of absence for the feminine spirit that had once filled the home and forged his better half.

But as he stood looking Garrett over, amazed how he had seemed to even grow taller, grow more into a man than the young boy he had been all those summers long ago, he felt at peace again. He had something to look forward to again. Theirs would be a partnership for the days he had remaining and all would be as it should be.

"Come, let me show you to your room. I think you will be pleased. The view of the harbor is a good one. You can see the boats going out in the morning and returning at night. I remember how you used to love to watch them. Mary and I had a devil of time with your father when you kept insisting as a boy that you wanted to be a fisherman." Doc Harrington smiled, shaking his head at the thought.

"And would that have been so terrible, Uncle?" Garrett asked.

"I suppose not but your father always wanted something more for you than hard labor with little to show for it after a long life of toil."

"Well, he got his wish, even if I didn't, I guess," Garrett grinned. He had to admit, if even only to himself, that so far, he found being a doctor more to his liking than he had even thought he would back when he was struggling through college and then all those additional years in medical school.

The pair climbed the stairs of the great house with its many rooms, as Doc Harrington led the younger man down a long hallway towards a door at the very end. He had chosen this corner room at the end of the hall for his nephew to provide him privacy away from his own room and any distraction that might come from the living quarters below. Doc opened the door to reveal a brightly lit interior, windows on three sides of the room, one with a view facing the harbor off in the distance from one side of the room and a view of the bluffs of Wellfleet overlooking the great expanse of ocean from the other set of windows. It was far more than Garrett had expected, far different than the confines of his parents' house or the tight dorm quarters he had shared with his college roommate.

"I hope you will find this to your satisfaction?" Doc said.

Garrett turned, facing him, the smile on his face the only answer the old man needed.

"This is way too generous Uncle. Surely there is something a little smaller to offer in such a beautiful house as this. This is far more than I need."

"No, I won't hear of it. I've been a bit lost in all this space since your Aunt Mary passed and frankly, the house will benefit from someone else sharing its walls. There is a small bathroom adjoining this bedroom so we will never need to worry about schedules," Doc grinned.

Garrett rested his hand on Doc's shoulder. It was a genuine expression of gratitude and Doc sensed it for what it was.

"You need say nothing nephew. You are like the son I never had and it is I that is grateful. Some of the happiest days Mary and I had were those summers when you came to stay. Besides, my days of doctoring these people is closer to an end than when it began and I'm just glad we will transition that within the family. They are a small community, not given easy to change and it will be a comfort to both them and I that there will not be a major break in things."

Garrett could see a sadness in his Uncle's eyes. He knew it must not be an easy thing to face one's own looming finality. His uncle had been born among these people, never left his origins longer than to complete his studies, and been their caregiver for over half a century of births, deaths, sickness, and injuries. And now, he was one of the few that remained from those early days. They were all gone. His brother and sisters. His wife. Even his daughter taken by the fever so many years ago when no medicine could prevent such a tragedy.

Doc Harrington stood a moment, staring out the window at the town below. Garrett sensed his uncle was seeing a different scene than the one he, himself, presently saw. Perhaps images from the past. Of horses and buggies. A time when no automobiles and trucks made their way down Main St. No telephone poles and street lamps.

"Uncle?" Garrett finally said, breaking the long silence. Doc Harrington turned, facing the young man, realizing he had been caught day dreaming again.

"So exactly what should I expect?" Garrett asked. Doc didn't need clarification.

"This is a good town, good people. Hard working. The sea is their business, their trade. If not fishermen, then there are those that make their living in support of those who work the sea. Shop keepers, the ship yard, everything centers around itself here. Not many come and go from the outside."

"But I'm someone new," Garrett reminded him.

"That's why I suppose you can expect some natural resistance at first. Anything unknown gives them pause. They are a cautious people. And more than that, they are a superstitious lot. I suppose the sea does that to them. Weather turns stormy, bad omen. A few days with little catch, bad omen. A ship runs aground, bad omen. Doesn't take much to start a little fear that quickly turns to a commotion. I've seen it. I've heard the stories. There are more legends abounding in these parts than there ought to be. More ghosts to haunt us than a body should have cause to believe," Doc shook his head.

"Certainly, you uncle, a man of science, don't hold with such things as ghosts?"

"Well, I like to think that Mark Twain, a wise man if there ever was one, had it right. He said he didn't believe in ghosts but he still had enough common sense to be afraid of them anyway!"

Doc Harrington took his nephew by the arm, smiling at his own joke.

"Come, you must be hungry after your long journey. Let's go downstairs and see what Elizabeth has cooked up for us. She may not be as good a housekeeper as my Mary was but she certainly makes up for it at the stove!"

Chapter 5

By the time Garrett had risen, dressed, and made his way downstairs the following morning to the small office and examination room Doc Harrington managed as part of the house, his Uncle was already seeing his first patients for the day. Though Doc Harrington still kept his practice of making house calls every Tuesday and Thursday afternoons, he also maintained office hours for those that either preferred to stop in or had but a few brief moments in the early morning hours before they shoved off from the Wellfleet wharf, heading out to make their daily catch.

As Garrett stepped into the small vestibule that served as a waiting room, he was surprised to find it quite full for so early an hour as seven in the morning. He realized that his days of laying around until nine or so as he may have done in college or even on limited intern hours were certainly over. If he expected to keep pace with his uncle, a man nearly fifty years his senior, he would obviously have to set his alarm clock.

Doc Harrington didn't have any assistant. No nurse or office clerk to check in patients. When he was done seeing one patient, he would just lead the next in through the door from the waiting room into the examination room or his office. There were no appointments and thus in his mind no confusion. He had always worked on a first come, first serve basis and other than for emergency cases, of which there were seldom if any, everyone abided by Doc's peculiar system. Everyone waited their turn. Everyone minded their place in line. It was just like Elmer Boyd's local barbershop down on Commercial Street. One chair, one barber, and you waited your turn.

As Doc Harrington opened the door to let Joe Barnes leave, with a bandage on the side of his neck from a freshly lanced boil and in a hurry to get back to his fishing boat the Dodie-Lea, he smiled at seeing his nephew who had finally made it to work. He nodded his head and motioned for Garrett to join him in the office. As he did so, he also offered a morning greeting to Miss Emily Wescott, an elderly friend who made regular visits to his office. Miss Emily, as her young school children called her right up to the day she retired some ten years ago, and the townspeople still called her even now, was one of Doc's "special cases." They had played as children together and he liked to think he knew her better than anyone in Wellfleet.

Miss Emily seemed to suffer from all manner of illnesses; most of them, Doc knew only too well, were largely of her own imagination and he kept a particular brand of medicine that appeared to be the only fix for what ailed her, Saccharin tablets. Nothing more and nothing less than a placebo of sugar pills. Perhaps it was having little to do after having spent a lifetime of rearing hundreds of children or fears of her own impending mortality, but Emily had succumbed to what many an aged person will lean on; attention through a catalog of ailments and a need to find company with others in misery. But Doc and her had been friends since childhood when they had both attended what had in the early days been the town's small one room schoolhouse. So, a few times a month, if not more, Miss Emily camped out in Doc Harrington's waiting room, biding her time with the others. It was as if she had come to a point where her presence there was a means of holding court among the other Wellfleet elderly, especially the women.

For Miss Emily was a figure of some renown in the village of Wellfleet. She was a member of the "old money class" though every year brought the count of its members to less and less. Founders of businesses, sea captains, and well-established merchants. All the families that had settled the area and over time, built businesses and stately homes high atop the hill overlooking the town. What Miss Emily thought, what she said, what she did was watched carefully and mimicked when it came to others wishing to stay astride of the social fabric of the community.

Miss Emily pulled herself up slowly, leaning on the cane she carried for support, and made her way at a slow but deliberate pace towards the door that Doc Harrington held open for her. As she stepped slowly forward, Garrett came up alongside her and offered his arm to assist her. But she quickly demonstrated an agility that surprised both men, jerking her arm free.

"Never you mind young man, I'll do just fine on my own," she said curtly.

Doc Harrington smiled, giving a wink to his nephew, his eyes telling Garrett everything was fine.

"Now you go on in and have seat by my examination table young lady and we'll be with you in just a moment to see what's wrong this morning," Doc Harrington assured her.

Emily kept moving forward though she continued to cast a suspicious eye on Garrett. Doc Harrington knew there wasn't likely to be anything wrong with the woman this day. She had come more or less as a *representative* of the wagging tongue committee, that unofficial organization of the elder women of any small town that would gather facts, compare notes, and ultimately hand down their verdict on any new arrival, especially someone about to enter their personal and intimate midst as a doctor would. As far as Miss Emily was concerned, Garrett was an unknown quantity and still a long way from formal acceptance, notwithstanding being Doc Harrington's nephew. She knew from experience that life was full of families where the character of one didn't live up to the character of another.

As Doc watched Miss Emily take her seat in his examining room, he ushered Garrett into his office away from the ears of the older woman.

"Ready to get started?" Doc asked.

"Well, I suppose though I had actually thought you'd expect me to go through some sort of period of ...well...simply observing?" Garrett confided. Doc shook his head.

"Nonsense. No reason for that. You did your time as an intern in one of the busiest hospitals in Boston. Probably saw more patients, with a wider range of problems, in a single day than you are likely to see here in a month. If I didn't think you were up to the task, I wouldn't have sent for you. As for the people? Well, you best jump in feet first and start to get to know them. As I said, for the most part, they are all a good lot and those that need special handling, like our friend Miss Emily there, I'll steer you through."

"I suppose you know best. But I'll admit I am a bit surprised to see so many people here in the waiting room for you so early. Is it always like this?" Garrett asked.

"Oh, not at all. And they aren't here to see *me*," Doc grinned, "They are here to see *you*."

"*Me?* I don't understand?"

"Oh, it's simple. You are a curiosity. Something new. Something to be observed. Well, at least the fine ladies of Wellfleet think so. As for the men? They couldn't care less. As far as they're concerned, anything that distracts their women from finding fault with them, and keeps them busy studying other prey, is just fine by them," Doc grinned.

Garrett thought about it, tried to take it all in. It was true, he knew little, if nothing, about small towns and people sheltered from the wider world he had grown up in. But to think he was somehow the object of inspection, a person of special interest, was somehow a little unsettling.

"And what if I don't meet with their approval?" Garrett ventured.

"No, I dare say that's not hardly to be the case. Let them have their little drama. Some intrigue. Certainly, no harm in that. Gives them something beyond the drudgery of the lives many lead here. Something to gossip about around the shops in town and during the ladies teas in the houses up on the hill," Doc assured him.

"Still, a bit unnerving all the same,"

"Oh, it won't last long. They'll make up their minds soon enough. It's all going to be fine and it starts with that lady sitting right in there in my examination room. She's the Queen Bee. We get her buzzing around with good things to say and the others in the hive will follow suit. Trust me on that. Besides that's only step one," Doc insisted.

"Step one? There's more?" Garrett asked.

"By all means my young boy. You see you are what they'll see as a *prospect*. That rare combination of young man, with good looks, and a clear means of support. And doctors come at a special premium around here," Doc laughed.

"I don't understand"

"Well if you ponder on it a while, I think you will. Now let's get to work. We have a patient waiting for us and the sooner we get her fixed up, and on her way, the sooner your approval ratings will go up!"

Again, Garrett could only offer a confused look, not following. Doc Harrington smiled at him, his youth, realizing he still had to explain.

"You see that small, frail looking woman sitting there? Miss Emily Wescott? Well, never was the saying truer that looks are deceiving. Make no mistake about it. That sweet old woman is a force to be reckoned with. She holds the pulse of this community politically more than I ever have literally."

"But she has to be in her seventies," Garrett offered, as though in his young mind, age certainly had to be a factor in who ran things.

"Trust me nephew, such assumptions as far as her age having even the slightest thing to do with it would be a mistake. And to support what I'm saying, did you not notice how fairly packed our waiting room was when you came in? Hardly a chair available. And perhaps you further noticed that the majority of those patients in waiting were women?

"Now that you mention it, I did find it a bit unusual that so many people would have appointments all at once at so early an hour," Garrett confessed.

"Oh, I don't give out appointments nephew. Never had much cause for that. It's a small place we have here. Not too much daily business that scheduling of the sort you might find in the city is called for. No, they just arrive here on their own but I dare say sometimes not without an agenda."

"An agenda?" Garrett asked.

"Yes, and you are that agenda," Doc Harrington smiled.

"Me?"

"It's really not all that confusing. There needs to be an *inspection*. They just can't have a stranger come in their midst and not have an inspection, a consensus, as to whether you meet the criteria. You see, I'm a long-established commodity. Hell, I helped bring half of the people that live here into the world. But that's about to change and they know that. Such things take time even in the best of circumstances but something as personal to them as a man who will share their illnesses, poke and prod their very bodies, know their most intimate physical conditions, now that's a horse of a completely different color."

"So, I'm to be *inspected* then, is that it?"

"That's it. But no worries. You will do fine. You come with my personal seal of approval. For some, they remember you as a child, a young boy coming to spend his summers here amongst them. And then you also have your Aunt's, my dear Mary's, endorsement, though sadly she's no longer here to give it herself."

Garrett thought back for a moment, recalling those summers. His parents allowed him to leave the heat and noise of Boston and spend a few weeks out in the open spaces of the Cape. Swimming in the ocean, playing in the tidal pools of the marshes, fishing off the Wellfleet wharf beside his Uncle. Lazy days and star filled nights, chasing down fireflies and night wings. That was all before his father had grown ill and died so quickly without much time to accept the loss. Before his mother had also seemed to age overnight from the loss and became gray haired and frail, years ago when life just seemed to be so less a struggle. And now, here he was, in an old and familiar place that somehow was all so new. Here in a place he knew so well but would have to again gain their acceptance.

"Believe me son, she's much more than a simple retired schoolteacher. She has the ear of just about every woman in this town. Not only those of her own generation but generations of younger ones who she taught and has earned the benefit of their respect. And as you will find out in life, when you have the ear of the women folk, you have a certain amount of control on the husbands of those women. Despite all the rhetoric about it being a man's world, there is one absolute about marriage. To pretty near every married man's way of thinking, a happy wife is a happy life and there is no profit in rowing against the current when just floating down stream is so much less work!"

Garrett looked at his uncle, could see the wisdom he had always seen in the older man's face and took notes in his head as he listened. Schoolbooks and classrooms, he had known much of, but life's lessons were still not so firmly in his grasp.

"So, you see nephew, if you win the vote of that fine old woman sitting out there, you gather more votes than you will probably ever need to win acceptance by this town as their next doctor. And that, my son, will make your old uncle here grateful and pleased."

Chapter 6

Had the incident during the night of the past storm been the only such one, Mercy might have just thought of it as nothing more than the peculiar sounds and phantom lights of a New England Nor'easter. Many a time, living along the ocean bluffs of Wellfleet, she had heard and seen what many others might swear to be ghostly spirits, cloaked in the darkness or the gray mist of a night perched between the edge of land and sea. But for two nights now following that storm, as she sat quietly in the evening, working at her loom inside the cottage, the soft, distant sound of a creature's tormented cry again came to her, riding on the winds blowing just outside her door. And twice now, she had left the warmth of her small house to stand just outside the threshold, peering with a focused gaze into the blackness. There, once more, off in the distance, coming from the stone ruins of the cliff house, the moans of an unseen specter could be heard. No distant light or flame flickered between the window openings of the stone walls as had previously accompanied the sound. But the soft wailing of the disembodied soul so pitifully alone in the darkness sent more than a simple cold night's chill up and down Mercy's body.

Each time the sound came to her in the late hours of the evening, she thought about going in search of its origins. But she found herself remaining motionless, frozen in that place between the darkness out there and the safety of the warm fire in her hearth behind her that only served to illuminate a few feet out beyond her doorway. She had long ago heard of the stories, of the tales that had affixed themselves to this particular piece of land above the jagged rocky shoreline below the bluffs of Wellfleet and the seas below.

When Mercy was but a child, she remembered how the elders of the village spoke of Goody Hallet the Witch of Eastham and her pirate lover, Black Sam Bellamy. They would tell the story of how a young girl, a mere teenager, had fallen in love with a man some years older than herself. The man, Samuel Bellamy, had a dream of going off to sea to find his fortune in distant lands. He would beguile the young girl with stories of adventure and of the riches he would obtain in faraway lands across the seas. He promised her he would return a wealthy man able to seek her father's permission for her hand in marriage.

And with such a promise, she soon fell in love with him, giving herself to him freely. He set out to sea in search of his fortune, leaving her behind to wait with nothing more than a promise of his eventual return and the baby in her womb he knew nothing of when he departed.

As the days drifted into months, Samuel Bellamy did not return. And as the child grew inside her, she soon found it harder to conceal it from her father. When at last she could no longer do so, her father cast her out into the streets, believing she had disgraced the family. She was marked a harlot and sent to the Barnstable jail miles from her home. But she only escaped from its confines time and time again, returning to her family, pleading to be allowed into her home. She would also stand night after night on the bluffs of Wellfleet, gazing out into the open expanse, waiting for signs of her lover Sam Bellamy's return. Many a villager spoke of having seen her motionless silhouette etched against the moonlit night sky. And even the most righteous and pious of them took pity on the wayward girl though none would go so far as to take her in when her family had cast her out.

When her time came, Goody Hallet gave birth to the child, though the story tellers do not say if it were boy or girl. But what is told is that the baby died shortly thereafter, some say from sheer exposure to the elements, others tell of the child having smothered in the bed of straw the newborn lay in inside Goody Hallet's jail cell. Whatever the cause, Goody Hallet was soon thereafter branded as a witch by the townspeople, their only possible explanation for the acts of so wanton a creature.

Eventually her father, despite the stain his daughter had caused to the family name, relented and asked the Constable to release her from the Barnstable jail. She was then allowed to live outside the village in a small stone cottage he agreed to build for her on the barren plain along the bluffs of Wellfleet. Here, Goody Hallet would live out her days, existing on the fringe of a community that largely shunned her.

And as for legend that remained after she no longer did it was believed that on nights when the moon was brightest her shadowy figure could still be seen on the Wellfleet bluffs, high above the sea, looking out in search of her lover Samuel Bellamy. That was the *legend* of Goody Hallet the Witch of Eastham.

Yet Mercy knew there was an element of truth to the legend all the same. It was not merely an old wives' tale. There had indeed been a pirate, his name *Black Sam Bellamy*, his ship the *Wyndah*. He did sail the seas in search of plunder. And he did return to Wellfleet during the stormy month of December in the year 1717, only to be caught up in a violent Nor'easter that claimed his ship and the lives of all aboard, save four men. As the story is told, they were taken to Boston to be hanged.

Though as there often is with legends, there is always the hope of the happy ever after ending. Some say Black Sam Bellamy did not go down with his ship that stormy December night but survived to find his beloved Goody Hallet waiting for him on the bluffs of Wellfleet where together, they disappeared into history to live out their lives in peace, far from prying eyes.

But this was a legend and Mercy wasn't given to believing such stories were behind the sounds and lights she saw coming from the ruins near the bluffs. She decided to return to the security and warmth of her cottage. When daylight returned, she could go have a better look for herself. Whatever was up there was either human or animal and traces would be left of its lingering.

Chapter 7

During his summers in Wellfleet, Garrett remembered hearing of the autumn festival the locals called the *Harvest Moon*.   Every village and town celebrated such festivals each year in October before the coming winter. But Garrett had never actually attended the festivities. He would always be back home in Boston by early September, his summer Wellfleet visits with his uncle and aunt long over by the time of the Harvest Moon.

But he knew it to be a long-observed tradition, a time when the community brought a close to the summer growing and fishing season. It was a time when the people came together to help bring in the harvest from the fields, cart them off to market, dry and salt the fish along the shore line in the waning summer heat, and prepare for the harsh New England winter's snows that would make them all soon enough long for the return once again of Spring. But it was also a time for friends, old and not so old, to share memories, to share food, and enjoy a brief rest from their labors. It would be a time when the elders would retell stories of their own youth as they sat in the churches, the barns, the wharf houses festooned with handcrafted decorations and watch the young engage in that ancient ritual of discovering the opposite sex. Young girls in dresses made of something other than broadcloth covered in aprons. Young boys dressed in their Sunday *go-to-meeting* suits, normally reserved for only that once a week occasion. There were only a handful of social events throughout the year that served to bring the young and the old of both sexes together and Harvest Home was such a time.

Garrett Harrington had not planned to attend any of the gatherings. He still thought of himself as merely a newly arrived outsider. But his uncle had insisted he give it some thought and persuaded him it would not be wise to avoid all of them. It wouldn't be seen as respectful. And so, reluctantly, he accepted an invitation to Miss Emily Wescott's home up on the hill overlooking all of Wellfleet, a rather grand mansion left to her by her grandfather, a ship's captain and eventually a fleet owner of some renown. The mansion was a truly imposing white edifice with grand columns and a wraparound porch, a long circular driveway where carriages once arrived to deposit visitors and family.

Unlike most of the other Harvest Home gatherings held in barns and wharf houses by the harbor, Miss Emily Wescott's Harvest Home was a social event of significant grandeur as well as importance. It was reserved for a different social set. Bankers, merchants, lawyers, people of prominence and standing. And of course, Doc Harrington among its annual attendees. It was considered the event above all others. And although Miss Emily herself had earned only a modest sum as the town's only grade school teacher, she was all the same rather comfortable in terms of ancestral fortune. Her grandfather, Captain Orpheus Darcy Wescott had once amassed a fleet of whaling ships, which journeyed to the far corners of the world bringing back the richest of riches; whale oil. It lit the homes of a fledgling country, greased the machinery of an industrial revolution and until the discovery and refinement of petroleum, formed the basis of a nation's economy. And it took courageous seafaring hunters to find it, process it, and bring home their ships laden with barrels of it for sale.

Attending Miss Emily's Harvest Home was by invitation only. It wasn't considered the same as all the other festivals that were more or less "*come and stop by if you wish*" affairs. Miss Emily's social gathering was more an annual Harvest *Ball.* Her finely engraved *carte de invitations* were anxiously awaited by those lucky enough to receive one. They were delivered by special messenger, never left to chance by mere postal delivery. To be invited was an honor not to be refused.

***

By late afternoon, after the last patient had gone, Garrett found his uncle in his office, busy filling out the patient reports for the day. Garrett knocked as he always did, even when the door was not closed. His uncle looked up, pleased to see him, and waved him in. The older man put down his pen, pushing himself away from the desk to turn in his chair towards his nephew.

"So, it's been nearly a month now and we really haven't had much time to talk. I'm sorry about that Garrett. I tend to get lost in my work. I'm afraid you will find it to be the same when you are the head man around here," Doc Harrington apologized.

"No worry, Uncle. Though I must say I've watched you work and honestly don't know how you've managed all these years by yourself. This town only keeps growing. Even I have seen the change since those summers I spent here so many years ago," Garrett said. He toyed with the envelop in his hand.

"What have you there?" Doc asked.

Garrett held the envelop up, grinning.

"Oh, I think you know only too well what this is. As if you had nothing to do with it."

43

Indeed, Doc did have something to do with it. He had not merely left it to chance that his nephew received an invitation. It, like so many other things, was an important part of the young man's acclimation to the life he was suiting up for. Attending Miss Emily Wescott's Harvest Home Ball would be a strategic part of that plan.

"So, are you going?" Doc asked.

"Do I have a choice?"

"Not if you want to be accepted here. To turn an invitation down like that, one that many wait years for and never see, would be a social blunder. Besides, you might even have fun. Many a lovely young lady attend I'm told,"

"You're told? Haven't you ever attended?"

"Oh, yes, every year. But I never had eyes for anyone but your Aunt Mary so I wouldn't be considered much of an expert on who the current beauties are. I will leave that up to the younger gentlemen such as yourself."

"Well, I certainly would not wish to appear rude so I suppose I will have to attend, if for no other reason than that. But I assure you Uncle, discovering the *beauty*, as you put it, of this town is of no real interest to me. I have seen what the affairs of the heart can do to people and it's of no real interest to me. A mate in life? Certainly, for all the practical and logical reasons. A partnership is always stronger than a lone existence. But beyond that? I watched my father's drinking destroy any love my mother had in her life. And when the drink finally did kill him, it killed her way too early as well," Garrett said sadly. His eyes seemed to be focused on something far away as images of the past, his past, flooded in. There, amongst happier times, remained the darker shadow of his youth.

"He was my brother and we all lost something when he was taken by that disease, and a disease it is as I'm sure one day will be recognized. But nephew, that is not you. That should not mean you can't find that someone who will come into your life and make it all the richer. Just like my Mary did."

Garrett considered his uncle's words. He had always respected his wisdom. Maybe he was willing to keep an open mind. But for now, he wasn't in search of anything more than the work he had before him.

"Perhaps you are right, Uncle. Anyway, growing up as a boy here in the summers I have often wondered what it was like inside that grand house on the bluff. At least now I will have a chance to see for myself,"

Chapter 8

There were many events that took place each year in Wellfleet. Fourth of July picnics, the annual Spring Blessing of the fleet ritual, local dances and church socials but none was awaited with as much anticipation and excitement as the Harvest Home festivals. And of all of those, none more so than Miss Emily Wescott's Harvest Ball. Although she was herself now in her eighties, and so many that attended were likewise part of the older generation of the town, the largest number of her invitations found their way into the eager hands of the young men and women in the area. For it was well known that Miss Emily's Harvest Ball had long proven to be the spawning ground for more than its fair share of young romances, romances that often led to marriages and lifelong unions.

So as the young ladies arrived in their festive dresses, their hair adorned with ribbons and hats, the young men in their best Sunday church suits, with polished dress shoes and neatly combed hair, the evening took on all the importance of a mating ritual that had been playing out since the early days of the oldest New England's families.

The elegant horse drawn carriages of a bygone era had long ago been replaced by sleek, shiny automobiles, some it seemed near the length of small sailing yachts. A steady entourage of arriving guests streamed up the gray granite steps leading up to the grand portico of the Federal style home once built by old New England money.

Though she had chosen to be a schoolteacher, Miss Emily still could not escape the simple fact that her parents, and their parents, and the many Wescott's before her had pulled themselves up from the hard conditions of working the sea to a place of notable prominence. She had chosen to be a teacher. Not out of any need to earn a living to survive but more to enjoy the pleasure of being able to give back to the children of the very families who had labored under the control of *her* ancestors. Many Wescotts had grown wealthy on the labor of others. It wasn't that it had been wrong that they had done so. She understood how things worked in the world. She believed that on their way to the social levels they had obtained, her family had always been fair in their dealings with others, had provided a means by which other families could earn wages and in time had also bettered themselves.

But being a teacher had meant that she could live among them again, the people her family had once been a part of. In that, she found contentment. Just as she now found pleasure in providing an evening of entertainment to the young and the old. But especially the young. Love had alluded her all her life. Her parents had perhaps been too strict she thought about what was and more importantly *who* was a proper match and she had followed along, always the dutiful daughter. But time had slipped through her fingers and marriage had as well.

"Why Miss Mercy, how wonderful to see you this evening," Miss Emily smiled, as she greeted her guest in the reception lie forming just inside the door of the house. "I am so very glad you decided to join us. It would have been a shame to have one of my past star pupils miss this evening."

Mercy took her Aunt's hand and squeezed it lovingly. She always enjoyed how the older woman referred to her merely as just one of her former students though they shared a much stronger tie than others might have ever imagined existed. Mercy had always felt they shared a special bond. Something deeper than merely the fact that Miss Emily and Mercy's own adoptive mother had been childhood friends.

Though tonight, for Miss Emily it was more than just mere pleasantry. She, herself, had been so terribly saddened of the news of Henry Gates' death in the war. She had felt such great pleasure in having shared a part in Mercy and Henry's introduction to each other. She had cared for Mercy all her life, being a constant part in her growing up. More than just being one of her students, Mercy had always held a special place in Miss Emily's heart like no other child.

"It pleases me Mercy to have you here. Could I perhaps impose upon you to be of some help to me tonight with all of my guests? Everyone enjoys conversations with you and I'm certain there will be some newcomers that just need a little coaxing to join the fun if you know what I mean," Miss Emily suggested.

Mercy knew exactly what she meant. She knew her Aunt Emily was well known as the town's spinster matchmaker, finding the joy she perhaps might never have known for herself through finding matches for others. The list of happily married former students of hers was a long one. Even for Mercy, having found her fiancé, Henry, had the earmark of a Wescott engineered connection. And she believed that few had come to grieve as much as herself at the loss of Mercy's young man than her Aunt Emily did. They shared many things, these two women, none so much as that loss.

"I would be glad to lend a hand. I'm always delighted to be invited and pleased to be of help," Mercy assured her.

"Good, then perhaps you would be so kind to join me on the receiving line. You know how important I feel it is to greet everyone as they come through the door, welcoming them. And you can help direct them to the coat room down the hall and to take a name tag from the hall table so everyone will know each other."

Mercy smiled to herself. She knew there would be but few guests who didn't already know the process, each having been to Miss Emily's Harvest Ball any number of times. And in what was still so small a little town, hardly was there much need of name tags. But it remained a habit of Miss Emily's school teaching days when she made all her students wear them on the first day of class. The sense of ritual continued was just how the older woman thought, learned from years of herding young students in and out of their days at the old school house.

Mercy dutifully took her station by the front door, next to Miss Emily, smiling warmly, kissing the cheek of every woman who stepped through the line, offering her hand ever so daintily to each gentleman, young and old. Mercy knew just about everyone. There were few strangers in a town the size of Wellfleet. One or two of the youngest guests she had to study a moment, until she recognized a once shy young girl that before her very eyes seemed to have blossomed into a young woman or a gangly freckled boy grown into a taller, sturdy, young man.

As each guest arrived and passed down the line, Mercy repeated the same instructions. Please hang your wrap or coat in the cloakroom down the hall, take your name tag from the table as you pass it, help yourself to the food and drink in the dining room, and above all have a great evening. Miss Emily is so pleased you could join her.

There was Mr. Laird Jonson, the town's one banker, Martin and Rebekah Jacobs who owned the General Mercantile Store, Nate Simons the Wharf Master, Bartholomew Bendix who owned the town's only gas station and repair shop, and dozens of others. Even Doc Harrington arrived, the absence of his wife Mary still so keenly felt by many who had always known them as a couple, inseparable, one name; the Harringtons. And, of course, the scores of students who had passed through Wellfleet Grade School, arriving filled with excitement and anticipation of having been among Miss Emily's *chosen*.

Mercy was pleased to finally see that before long the arrival line began to thin. She was looking forward to taking a seat for a moment and having a glass of wine. It seemed like she had been standing for well over an hour as the rooms within the great house filled with guests.

But as she was about to turn and step away, Miss Emily caught her arm and motioned with her eyes at the arrival of yet one more guest. He was not a familiar face to Mercy. A tall man with boyish features, clean shaven, and though standing erect, seemed somehow uncomfortable in what appeared to her to be his not so neatly pressed suit and his slightly oversized shirt with its loose-fitting collar. Even the hems of his trouser legs appeared rigged high above his ankles for chance floods.

As he made his way cautiously through the door and down the landing steps, Mercy got a better look at this stranger. The thing she seemed to notice most, beyond his ill-fitting suit and slightly disheveled black hair falling over his forehead, were his eyes. They were a crystal blue-gray, like deep pools of water and were, it seemed to her, his most distinct feature.

Mercy watched as Miss Emily took his hand and noticed how she greeted this stranger as though they were long acquainted.

"Doctor Harrington, I am very pleased you were able to join us this evening. I wasn't certain if you would be able to pull yourself away from your work for just one evening, though your Uncle did mention he would insist you take some time from your busy schedule to do so," Miss Emily said.

Mercy was now even more curious. *Doctor Harrington?*

Miss Emily could see the puzzled look on the young woman's face. She smiled to herself, pleased in having succeeded in the surprise she had hoped to provide her.

"Oh, my dear. I certainly must apologize. This is Doctor *Garrett* Harrington. He is the nephew of our own beloved Doc Harrington. The young doctor is newly arrived and hasn't really been properly introduced. But I can assure you his office manners are most satisfactory. I have already had the pleasure," Emily confirmed, smiling coyly back at the young man, noticing the slight tint of red coming over his boyish face.

"And if I may, Doctor Harrington, I would like to introduce you to Mercy Daniels. Though I have no children of my own, having never had the pleasure of marriage, Mercy is to me my own daughter in all manners and ways," Miss Emily offered.

Mercy was delighted by such a sincere compliment. She felt the same way. Her Aunt Emily had always seemed to be part of her life as far back as her memory could recall. And since her own parents had been lost at sea, Miss Emily had truly become even more so her guardian.

"Well, it is indeed my pleasure," Garrett said, taking her hand in a gentle embrace. Mercy noticed the softness of his skin, so unlike other men from the area who used them in hard labor.

"It is a pleasure to welcome you here to Wellfleet. I do hope you are finding it to your liking," Mercy asked.

"Indeed, I am. Even more so now it would seem," Garrett suggested, immediately realizing the forwardness of his comment. "I mean... now that I have seen how wonderful a celebration our host has prepared for us all," Garrett quickly amended.

Mercy pretended to have not noticed his comment or his quick correction, paying no mind to his intention one way or the other. But it was Miss Emily that had made note of the young man's words all the same, pleased that the two young people had met. It had been nearly a year since word of the loss of Henry Gates had been received and there had been far too much weary news of war. Miss Emily hoped that at least for a few hours this evening those who gathered to celebrate the end of a bountiful summer harvest could forget their worries ever so briefly.

"Well, Doctor Harrington, I do hope you enjoy yourself this evening. Perhaps we can talk again a little later. But now, you must excuse me. I need to lend a hand to our hostess," Mercy said, bowing her head slightly to take her leave. Garrett promptly nodded his head, acknowledging her wishes. As instructed, he continued down the hallway to deposit his overcoat in the guest cloakroom and began to search for his uncle. He suspected he would be found wherever the older men had gathered to share a glass of spirits.

Garrett walked through the dining room, crowded with people eagerly sampling a rich smorgasbord of delights from seafood to savory meats, various baked cakes and pies, and a punchbowl brimming with ice chunks and floating fruit. On the far side of the dining room, Garrett saw a smaller room where he spotted an elegantly carved mahogany bar, behind which were shelves lined with an assortment of liquor and spirits. A neatly dressed bartender, hired for the evening, busied himself mixing drinks and pouring whiskey. Already the air within the room had become a dense fog of cigar and pipe smoke.

In the midst of these gentlemen, Garrett spotted his uncle, the older man's animated face and hands busy accentuating what Garrett knew could only be one of his uncle's fantastical tales of adventures long ago experienced. Garrett was well acquainted with the family stories of his uncle's escapades, from days well before the older man had settled down to marry and open a practice in Wellfleet. Uncle *Lee* had travelled to faraway places, had known some colorful characters, and as the rumors would suggest, chased his fair share of ladies. But that all came to an end the day he met Mary Kathleen McDonald. A fair skinned, curly haired blonde, a mere wisp of a girl, with eyes the green of Irish pastures, she was his match in every way.

"I figured I'd find you here," Garrett smiled, as he stepped up to greet his uncle. Doc Harrington turned to the sound of his nephew's voice, a broad grin erupting on his face. The older man's face showed he was truly pleased to see his nephew had decided to come after all though he never truly doubted the young man would not.

"Garrett, my son," Doc said. It was a term he often used with him, spoken it seemed to Garrett with even greater emphasis whenever Doc was with his friends.

"I'm so glad you came. Miss Emily would have been deeply disappointed as would I. Let me get you a drink. What will you be having?"

"Oh, nothing. I don't usual partake," Garrett admitted. But the expression on his uncle's face clearly suggested he wouldn't hear of it.

"Now, that won't do. No, that just won't do. You must join us for a least a little libation," Doc insisted, nodding toward the bartender, holding up his glass to signal another of the same.

Doc looked at the other men standing around him, pointing back towards his nephew.

"Gentlemen, may I have the pleasure of introducing you to my nephew, *Doctor* Garrett Harrington," the older doctor announced, the emphasis of his introduction now proudly on the word *Doctor*.

The small circle of men surrounding Garrett began extending their hands one by one, offering their greetings. They had all heard of his arrival they insisted and were glad to make his acquaintance.

"Studied in Boston, I hear?" Laird Jonson, the town banker, asked.

"Yes, at Boston University, my uncle's alma mater," Garrett replied.

"Doc, you actually went to medical school?" Nate Simons the wharf Master chided his old friend.

"Certainly, he did, Nate. Where do you think he learned how to bleed his patients to death," Laird Jonson quickly added.

"You should talk about bleeding people. How about those interest rates you squeeze out of the poor?" Doc insisted.

Garrett only smiled, understanding this good-natured ribbing of each other was all just part of the long, close friendship his uncle and these gentlemen shared.

"Well, I'm sure we are boring the pants off this young man," Nate Simons suggested, "You certainly don't need to waste your evening with a bunch of old, past their prime, men as we. You should circulate a bit, get to know some of the younger folks. Plenty enough pretty ladies to admire I dare say."

"Indeed, an excellent idea," Laird Jonson agreed. "So, tell us, what *do* you think of the fairer sex gathered here? Do they compare to the young ladies of Boston town?"

Garrett knew a trap when he was about to step into one. To admit he had given it any thought would suggest he was already considered his options. To say it hadn't occurred to him would not have been the total truth either. True, he had not come to the party with any designs other than to appear sociable as his uncle had suggested and not offend a person of such stature as Miss Emily Wescott. Nevertheless, he had been introduced, albeit ever so briefly, to a young lady that he had to admit, if only to himself, had indeed caught his attention.

"Gentlemen, you have me at a bit of a disadvantage. I would not dream of offering a comment on so delicate a subject when I have truly had no time as yet to survey the landscape. I will merely agree that, so far, my experience here in your delightful community has been a very satisfying one. I have much work ahead of me before I can be of value to my uncle and my attention to that has left me with little time to consider other pleasures," Garrett assured them. To that they all raised their glasses, again starting to poke fun at Doc Harrington.

"I see you have learned one thing already. You know how to avoid being cornered on a subject as well as this old scoundrel can be. It certainly must be a Harrington family trait," Nate Simon laughed, playfully jabbing his nearly empty whiskey glass into Doc Harrington's side.

Satisfied that he had put the matter to rest, or at least for the time being, Garrett begged his leave, taking his glass with him as he headed back through the dining room and into the larger salon room of the house that tonight served as the main gathering place. He nodded his greetings to several people he had previously met at his uncle's office, stopping every now and then to briefly speak with one, then another. As he made his way towards the far side of the room, he again spotted Mercy Daniels. She was stepping out through a set of French doors that led out to the veranda into the night air away from the crowded room, probably, he thought, to merely take a moment to herself. It had been a rather warm evening for late October and the lights from the distant harbor would draw anyone's attention.

Garrett studied her a moment, watching as she stood between the white columns bathed in moonlight. He felt himself indeed being drawn to the image. He wondered if there was a *Mister* Daniels and if so, why had he left his wife to attend the party all alone. Curiosity finally got the better of him and he made his way slowly towards the doors leading to the veranda. He stepped out into the star speckled night, the warm evening breeze, even for Fall, greeting him. He wasn't sure what had compelled him to follow her. As he had truthfully told his Uncle's friends, he certainly had no intention of following any romantic interests at the moment.

He didn't approach her directly at first but instead stood there looking up at the same night sky and moon Mercy had fixed her gaze on. Then after a while, not wanting to appear as though he was silently intruding unannounced, he purposely cleared his throat as if stifling a cough. Mercy turned to see who it was.

"Oh, Mr. Harrington, or should I say, *Doctor*. I didn't hear you coming out," Mercy lied, indeed having seen him out of the corner of her eye as he stepped through the French doors.

"My apologies, Mrs. Daniels I didn't mean to startle you," Garrett said, moving closer now that they had at least begun an exchange.

"Mrs.? Oh, no, I'm not married."

"Well, indeed, perhaps I misunderstood," Garrett again apologized, "I assumed the opposite since you wear a ring. Engaged then perhaps?"

Mercy looked down at her hand.

"No, I'm afraid I'm not. At least not any longer. He was lost in the war. Aboard a ship," Mercy's smile quickly faded. It was still painful and she had continued to wear the engagement ring Henry had placed on her finger as a reminder, as though removing it too soon might somehow be a betrayal to his memory.

"I'm sorry. My deepest sympathy," Garrett offered.

"Thank you. As this war goes on there are only the more at home left to grieve. If there be any solace in it, I know I'm not alone."

Garrett thought it best to change the subject.

"I was in Europe. Signed up right after Pearl Harbor," Garrett offered. He had always felt a need to volunteer the information, knowing that people would wonder why a young man, certainly one with his medical skills, had stayed behind while other young men were off fighting and dying.

"Europe?" Mercy said, indeed a little surprised that he nevertheless was home.

"Yes, I thought the Army Medical Corp would be the right place for me. They wanted to assign me to a hospital here in the States but I requested overseas duty. Then they wanted to assign me to a behind the lines hospital unit but I volunteered as a frontline medic. Thought I could be of more use there. That was until a

German sniper bullet wound me up in the very hospital I had tried to avoid. It also ended my service in the field. They said I had nerve damage, lost the feeling in my one leg, though after months of therapy I figured I was healed. I wanted to return to duty but they said there was too much risk of a relapse or some such nonsense. Anyway, they sent me home and I finished my enlistment stateside. Then they discharged me when I tried to re-up."

"How horrible, Doctor," Mercy said, envisioning the whole thing in her head. She had wondered why so strong a looking young man was indeed not in the service fighting, had even for a moment thought a little less of him when Miss Emily had first introduced him. Now she felt a twinge of guilt.

"Please, may I ask a favor," Garrett said, his eyes searching hers, "Might I ask if you would just call me Garrett. *Doctor* Harrington is my uncle," Garrett smiled.

Mercy nodded her head.

"But only if you agree to call me Mercy. I think we have become friends enough in just these past few minutes, wouldn't you agree?"

"I would certainly like to think so," Garrett admitted.

"Well then, it is settled Doctor Harrington, we are indeed *friends*," Mercy smiled.

"*Garrett*, remember?"

"Oh, yes, apologies...*Garrett*," Mercy smiled. It all seemed somehow pleasing to refer to him on such an informal basis. It pleased him as well.

"I suppose we should return to the others. It's a small town and we certainly don't want to help feed the rumor mill regarding our absence out here," Mercy suggested.

Garrett bowed gently, sweeping his arm in a gallant gesture towards the doors, back towards the party. Mercy nodded her head, acknowledging the offer and proceeded towards the house, the young doctor following close behind. The still sounds of the night faded behind them as the din of the party engulfed them upon their return. The ice had been broken.

Chapter 9

It was not but a week after her party that Miss Emily was again found waiting in Doc Harrington's office. As always, she had no appointment, no particular malady that needed immediate attention. But as had been the case with her last visit, she did have an agenda. When the older Doctor opened the door from his office to the waiting room, he was not all together surprised to see her sitting there. And he knew she would soon enough reveal the purpose of her visit. Perhaps some new ailment that she had encountered, one he knew could likely be remedied with the usual sugar pills. If there was one thing he knew about his old friend, it was that Miss Emily Wescott was among the healthiest of all of the inhabitants of Wellfleet. Though she frequently had her "complaints", those aches and pains that bewitch the elderly, she was certainly not one to let them get the better of her. Old age and the Devil himself tread lightly around her.

"It's good to see you Emily," Doc Harrington offered.

He was one of the few that referred to her simply as Emily. Not *Miss Emily* as most who even knew her well did and certainly nothing as formal as Miss Wescott. It was one of those little luxuries she *indulged* him in.

"What seems to be the trouble this morning," Doc continued, holding the door open for her.

"Is young Doctor Harrington in?" Emily asked.

"Yes, but he's with a patient now. May I help?" Doc offered, admittedly finding her question a bit unusual.

"That's fine then. I will wait," Emily said, repositioning herself in the chair as if to suggest she was settling in to wait for as long as it took.

Doc Harrington knew better than to probe any further. It would do no good and at the same time he suspected that whatever it was that brought her here this morning had little if anything to do with a physical complaint. His only concern was that it might somehow be a compliant of another nature. One that somehow involved his nephew.

He had observed Garrett off and on throughout the night of Miss Emily's Harvest Home Ball and other than for what only seemed a few minutes, he believed he hadn't ever really lost sight of Garrett. Not that he had any reason to think his young charge had acted in any other way than the most perfect gentlemen. He knew his nephew wasn't even given to imbibing strong drink.

"Certainly, if you insist. I will let him know you are here. Are you sure there is nothing I can assist you with?" Doc tried one more time. But Emily only shook her head, obviously intent on maintaining the very essence of secrecy.

Doc Harrington returned to his office, taking a seat behind his massive roll top desk to continue his paperwork. While he had always kept his own medical files and reports, the work of writing out bills and sending them to his patients had been handled mainly by his wife Mary. Among the other reasons he missed her, this was but yet another. But he would manage.

While he worked, he kept an eye on the examination room, wanting to speak with Garrett before he went back out to the waiting room. After about ten minutes, the door finally opened with his nephew leading Emmett Cotter, the town sheriff out. In light of Emily's odd behavior, insisting on seeing only his nephew, Doc now had reason for concern. While he had hoped and indeed expected Garrett to gain the trust of his patients, Doc hadn't expected Miss Emily to so soon succumb to his nephew's bedside manner.

"Now you just be sure to keep that bandage on your arm clean. Your shoulder may hurt in a day or two from the tetanus shot but you'll be fine. And next time, be more careful rounding up stray dogs. I'm sure you are fine but you never know what they carry," Garrett assured him.

"Doctor, do you have a moment?" Doc Harrington asked, always sure to refer to his nephew as *Doctor* in the presence of patients.

"Certainly," Garrett said, motioning to the waiting room door for the Sheriff to see himself out.

Doc Harrington waited for Sheriff Cotter to leave before he spoke to Garrett.

"Miss Emily is out in the waiting room. Said she wanted to have you see her. And just you."

"Me? I don't understand?"

"That's what I was hoping you could tell me. I mean I suppose I'm pleased she is so quickly accepting you as she has but she's been my patient for forty years and I just don't understand," Doc Harrington said, "You don't have any problem with her, do you?"

"Why of course not. Least ways none that I would know of. Haven't really ever spoken with her outside of the office other than having attended her party,"

"Well, you best tend to her. Lord knows she's not a woman who likes to be kept waiting!"

Garrett opened the door to the waiting room, finding Miss Emily sitting in the closest chair. He wasn't at all surprised to see her seated in that particular one as it would have been certain that no matter what time she arrived and how many others had been there before her, they would have risen promptly and demanded she take that spot. It was more than simply deference to her age but more out of respect for her social standing in the community. School teacher or not, elderly or not, she was a Wescott and all knew what that meant. Money. Influence. Both resulting in authority.

"My dear Miss Wescott, to what do I owe the pleasure? My uncle says you asked for me in particular. Indeed, I consider it an honor. Won't you please come in," Garrett offered, being extra careful to appear more pleased than curious.

The elderly women rose to her feet, gathering her coat, purse, and her always present, rain or shine, umbrella and stepped forward. She leaned slightly on the curved umbrella handle much as anyone else might rely on a cane. But she was too proud to surrender to such a thing as a cane though her arthritis in her knees demanded some form of walking aid.

Garrett followed her in to the examination room, waited for her to take a seat on the bench, and pulled up a small stool on wheels to sit next to her.

"Now what seems to be the problem," Garrett asked. He was already well-schooled by his uncle in regards to the woman's many, but mostly minor, aches and pains that the miracle drug of sugar tablet placebos, Doc Harrington often gave her, continued to produce a curative effect.

"Oh, nothing critical I assure you Doctor. Just felt a bit of a cough coming on and at this time of year, thought it best to get ahead of it. Perhaps some cough syrup and nothing more will do the trick. I would have normally just brewed up a patch of tea with honey but I first wanted to be sure it was nothing else," Miss Emily said, trying her best to sound convincing.

"I see. Fair enough then, let's have a look," the young doctor said, grabbing a wooden tongue depressor from a jar on the cupboard.

"Say aah, please," Garrett instructed, gently placing the wooden stick on her tongue to get a closer look. As he suspected, there wasn't even the slightest hint of any redness. Clearly, she had not come here to have a sore throat looked after. His uncle would have been more than capable of assisting her if that had been the only reason for her visit. Garrett grew even more intrigued.

"Well, I'm surprised. I assure you when I awoke this morning, I felt just ever so slight a scratchiness in my throat. Gargled with warm salt water right away but still, didn't want to leave things to chance. Even mentioned it to my niece Mercy earlier. I had asked her to come for breakfast," Miss Emily informed the young doctor.

The word *niece* caught the young doctor's attention. He certainly realized there were many things he had yet to learn about the inhabitants of Wellfleet but he hadn't realized that Mercy Daniels was actually related to Miss Emily.

"I believe you have met her, have you not Doctor?" Miss Emily asked, her tone suggesting she was stating more a fact than a question for both knew only too well that introductions had been made.

"I do indeed. Or perhaps I should say I have had the pleasure of making her recent acquittance," Garrett confirmed. But again, he found their conversation a bit odd. It was Miss Emily herself that had made the introduction that night at her party in the receiving line.

"Oh, that's right. At my party. I'm sure that's where you would have met her. She did mention something about that this morning when we were having breakfast. I dare say you seem to have made quite the impression the way she tells it."

"I'm glad to hear that. I think it's fair to say she made an impression on me as well. You must be very proud of her," Garrett suggested.

"Oh very. Sad though. You know she was engaged to be married? A wonderful young man," Miss Emily said, her voice trailing off into a whisper.

"Yes, she did mention it to me when we were chatting. I know it must have caused her immense sorrow," Garrett offered.

"Still does," Miss Emily assured him, "Though the dear child pretends she is over it. But I know better. I know life doesn't heal deep wounds so easily and time doesn't always allow us to move on as quickly as others believe. But she has me now. I'm her family."

Garrett nodded his head. He sensed there was an agenda in all her words. But again, he just listened.

"Well, enough of such sad things," Miss Emily said, suddenly throwing off the gloom, "And what of you, young man? Surely such an eligible and educated bachelor has a special someone waiting in the wings. Perhaps a sweetheart back in Boston who is hoping for word from you to join you," Miss Emily probed.

"No, I'm afraid not. Seems I've been a little too busy for affairs of the heart. First there was college and medical school and then the military. Well before I knew it, I was facing thirty and other then my internship at Boston General I never even had a chance to start a practice of my own."

"Well, I'm sure you will young man," Miss Emily suggested, as though his working with his uncle had not occurred to her as being the start of just such a practice.

Garrett sensed there was more. But whatever she had come here this morning to discuss, beyond merely having a sore throat looked at, was left unsaid. She rose, gathering here belongings, allowing Garrett to help her on with her coat. She headed back towards the waiting room door, stopping briefly to bid good morning to her old friend Doc Harrington. Then as quickly as she allowed herself to be ushered in, she was gone. Garrett returned to the office door opening.

"Must say that was a bit unusual," Garrett said.

The old man put his pen down and swiveled in his chair to face his nephew.

"Unusual? What is ailing our dear lady this morning,"

"That's just it. Not sure honestly. She complained of a sore throat but I've seldom seen a brighter pink. Not a thing wrong. And then she wanted to talk about Mercy Daniels. Referred to her as her *niece*? I wasn't aware they were related."

Doc Harrington smiled knowingly, as if he was in possession of a secret.

"Mercy's mother, Adele Foster, grew up here in Well Fleet. Adele's father, Josiah Foster, ran one of the fish packing factories down near the wharf. Adele married a man she met working for her father and they moved down to Yarmouth after they got married. Miss Emily would often go stay for extended visits with them during the summer when school was out."

"Mercy said she lost her parents on one of the packet ferries crossing from the islands," Garrett said.

"Yes, that's true. That's when Mercy came here to live. She took over the small cottage Miss Emily's grandfather had bought with the land in Goody Hallet's Meadow out by the bluffs. There had once been a few other small stone dwellings out there but they had long gone to ruin. Only the one cottage Mercy now lives in is all that remains. It is a rather barren bit of land if you ask me. Miss Emily wanted her to come stay with her in that big house but Mercy must have felt she wanted her independence. Doesn't stop Miss Emily from fretting over her like she was her own daughter," Doc Harrington said.

"I got that feeling myself," Garrett admitted.

"Oh, I'm sure you did. And I'm pretty certain what our friend's real purpose in coming here was."

"You do?"

"Sure, it was to get a sense of her own what may have transpired between you and her niece the night of the party." Doc said, a knowing grin forming at the edges of his mouth.

"I don't understand. Nothing *transpired*," Garrett assured his uncle.

"Look nephew, this isn't Boston. It's not a city filled with strangers. Everyone here pretty much knows everyone else. And more so, they pretty much know everyone's business. You stepped out on the veranda for a few minutes. And Mercy Daniels was out there as well. I saw you and if I did you can be sure many others took notice as well. Nothing all that unusual but around here wagging tongues need to be fed and what better a tale than two young people, one a young girl who many see as still being in mourning and a handsome young doctor sweeping into town to literally take hold of people's hands and hearts," Doc said.

It had never occurred to Garrett that anyone would see it as anything more than two guests at an evening's festivities enjoying a social conversation. Nothing the slightest clandestine in any of that.

"I certainly meant no harm uncle. And nothing was intended to spark gossip," Garrett said earnestly.

"Oh, pay it no mind, nephew. Mercy is a wonderful young lady. A fellow could do far worse. Not that I'm suggesting anything of the sort in your case," Doc assured him.

Garrett truly hadn't given such a situation any thought, though he did agree with his uncle, Mercy

Daniels had made an impression on him and he hoped to find himself in the presence of her company again sometime soon.

"But mindful, if the man Mercy Daniels was to *have* married was here to tell you, I think he'd say that getting through the walls that Miss Emily threw up as protection around that young girl was quite a challenge. Like I said, some people might think Mercy was like Miss Emily's own daughter when it comes to allowing even the most gallant of princes take her hand," Doc Harrington continued.

"I was certainly left with that impression as well," Garrett confessed, "Anyway, there's patients waiting. I really should attend to them."

"Indeed. Always a good way to keep one's mind focused on the moment," Doc grinned, picking up his pen to continue work on his files.

Chapter 10

As she had heard a few nights before, again from outside her cottage door came that same mournful sound. But now without the turbulence of a storm beating against her walls, it was much more distinct then before. This time Mercy had little doubt that it was the soft whimpering sound of crying. It reminded her of the pathetic tones a wounded animal makes, a pitiful, anguished sound, rising and falling as the night air carried it across the dunes from the east.

Mercy took her coat from the hook by the front door and gathered it around her shoulders. She stepped out into the pitch-black darkness of the night, the pale gray light of a quarter-moon the only light to see by. She stood still, her ears straining to get a better fix on the direction of the sound. It was the sound of sobbing, of that she was certain. But she could now tell it was not that of any animal. No, she thought, not at all like that. She stepped back into the cottage, quickly lighting the oil lantern she kept by the door.

Emerging back out into the darkness once again, she listened, took a few steps towards the sound. Just as on the first night she had heard it, it again came from the direction of the old stone ruins. It was all that remained of a small stone structure perched on the bluffs above the ocean were legend told of it having once belonged to the Witch of Eastham, Goody Hallet. Most locals gave the place a wide berth in their travels, all the more so at night.

Mercy ventured further away from her cottage door, holding the lantern out to find the sandy path that led towards the ruins. Every few feet she halted, lowered the lantern to allow the darkness to flow back in around her, watching for some hint of light ahead. The previous night she had seen a faint light passing between the openings in the walls of the ruins. But tonight, no such light appeared from within the gloomy stone edifice. There was nothing more than the strange moaning sound, sometimes falling off to a mere whimper and then returning with what Mercy felt was increased agony.

She stepped slowly along the sandy path, listening, peering hard into the frail dim light being cast down by a sliver of the ghostly moon hanging in the sky above. She approached the shadowy ruins of the ancient house from what had once been the rear entrance of the structure. There were remnants of doors and window sills. They were now little more than weathered, sun parched gray wood, the white painted window frames with glass and oak entrance door long ago having surrendered to time and the elements.

Mercy came to a halt just mere feet away from the entrance, her heart pounding deep within her chest. She could feel the fear swelling up within her but she wouldn't, couldn't, turn away and retreat to the safety of her cottage. She needed to confront whatever specter haunted this place. She lifted the pale light of her lamp higher as she stepped through the crumbling threshold of the structure. The dim oil light barely pushed the pitch-black darkness back a mere few feet beyond her eyes. She inched forward; her ears locked on to the sound that had drawn her there. She summoned up her courage, pushing back her fear, and called out to the disembodied soul.

"Who's there? I mean you no harm and hopefully you mean me none," Mercy spoke softly into the night.

But there was no reply. Nothing but silence and the steady crashing waves lapping at the beach far below the bluffs. In fact, even the crying sound had now ceased as Mercy's own voice broke the silence. Nothing moved in front of her. No person or even shadows shifted across her sight. The darkness only seemed to crowd in around her.

"I won't hurt you. Please, I just want to help," Mercy tried again, wondering if ghosts really ever did speak to the living. She took a few more steps, crossing over what had once been wooden floors, now a mere mix of broken pieces of oak and sand.

She inched forward, approaching the opposite end of the old ruins and the opening to the front door. And then, as the light of the cloud covered moon emerged from behind its celestial curtain, giving aid to her eyes, she saw it, a dark form, silhouetted against the sky and ground. It stood, motionless, huddled over, sheathed in black outline.

Mercy found herself powerless to move, her legs frozen in place. She watched as the form before her slowly turned, a pair of hauntingly sad eyes staring back at her from the depths of the hood pulled tightly over its head. The two of them, Mercy and the specter, stood unmoving for what seemed like an eternity, their eyes locked on each other just a few yards apart.

It was then that Mercy realized it was not a ghost she was confronted with but a young girl, cloaked in a ragged shawl. She brought the lantern back up, taking another step forward. When she did the girl appeared to turn abruptly as though to dart away but then hesitated like a timid animal trapped by its potential captor.

"Please, don't run. It's all right. My name is Mercy Daniels," she quickly offered, "I live over there, in that small cottage. What's your name?"

But the young girl remained as silent as the surrounding night that engulfed her.

"You must be cold. It is a chilly night and that thin shawl can't be of much comfort. Why don't you come with me and warm yourself by my fire? Are you hungry? I have hot broth simmering for soup."

The young girl studied Mercy, who sensed she was beginning to consider her offer.

"What is your name? You can at least tell me that, can't you?" Mercy asked.

"Addy," the shadow girl answered softly.

"Well, that's a very pretty name. Where are you from Addy?" Mercy continued, trying to gain her trust.

Addy just raised her hand and pointed east.

"Down the Cape? I see. Well, why don't you come with me and we can talk more in front of the fire. Surely you would like to warm up and maybe have something to eat," Mercy offered again, waiting a moment before turning toward the path back towards the cottage.

She stepped off in that direction, keeping an eye out as she did to see if the young girl would follow. She took a few more steps and noticed that she did indeed begin to slowly follow after her, though cautiously remaining at a distance. If Mercy stopped to wait for her, the girl stopped, advancing no further.

Finally, convinced that Addy might just follow if she kept walking, Mercy proceeded, not stopping again until she had arrived at her cottage door. She waited for the poor thing to catch up and then opened the door, stepping in to her house. Mercy left the door open behind her, hanging up her coat and stepping across the room with the fireplace into the kitchen. She began to take down two bowls while keeping an eye on the open door. In a little while, she saw Addy cautiously step through the door, the young girl's eyes darting back and forth, taking in the interior of the small cottage.

"Now just shut the door and take a seat by the fire to warm yourself. I'll get us some soup to help rid the chill in our bones," Mercy said as though she were welcoming the return of a longtime friend into her home.

Addy moved slowly towards the welcoming fire, all the while keeping a watchful eye on Mercy. It was obvious to Mercy that the timid little girl didn't appear to trust strangers, even those who seemed only to offer kindness. Mercy ladled out two bowls of scotch broth, its rich liquid filling the earthen bowls with steamy warmth. She took two spoons from the knife box on the kitchen table and brought the bowls out towards the fireplace. She handed one of the bowls to Addy, who reached up hesitantly before taking it, all the while her eyes studying Mercy. Finally, she seemed to slowly drop her guard enough to raise the bowl to her mouth to sip from the inviting soup, its heat burning her lips. She pulled her mouth away quickly.

"Here, take this," Mercy said, handing her a spoon. She was not all that surprised to find this frightened, ragged looking, girl somehow unaccustomed to spooning a bowl of broth. She knew many of the people who lived off the beaten path, deep in the bogs and marshes of the Cape, simply drank from their bowls. It told her something about the origins of her strange guest.

Mercy placed another log on the crackling fire before taking a seat next to the girl. She began to spoon out the broth. It did indeed help fight back the chill from her adventure across the dunes. They both sat a moment, facing the fire, neither speaking, simply sharing the communion of the food and the warming fire in the hearth.

Then, without looking directly at Addy, as if just speaking in idle conversation, she commented on how cold a night it was beyond the walls of her cottage, how her favorite time of night was to just sit before her fireplace. Addy didn't turn, but she seemed to be listening all the same. After a while, when Mercy was convinced Addy was warm enough, she again spoke.

"That shawl is damp from the night air. Why don't you let me take it and hang it up by the kitchen stove? It will dry out more quickly that way," Mercy suggested, putting down her bowl on the little table between their chairs and standing to help the young girl. But Addy only pulled it tighter around herself.

"It's okay sweetheart," Mercy assured her, choosing a term meant to show the young girl she was safe from whatever had brought her to those ruins and the stormy seas below on such a cold and unforgiving night.

Mercy reached down, ever so slowly touching the edges of the garment and begin to gently ease it off of the young girl. As she did, Addy let go of her tight hold on it, allowing Mercy to retrieve the shawl. As it pulled away, Mercy could see the small bulge in Addy's belly but she made no immediate mention of it. She took the shawl into the kitchen, hung it up on a drying rack next to the stove and came back into the room. She opened the doors of a small linen cupboard and took out a wool afghan throw. She returned to the fireplace.

"Here, lean forward so I can put this around you. It will keep you much warmer than that damp shawl."

Addy looked up, her frightened eyes now slowly welling up. She allowed herself to be wrapped in the warm blanket, allowed herself to feel the comfort being given to her. It had been a long time.

They sat quietly, Addy continuing to feed her famished stomach. The crackling fire mixed with the sounds of the rising and falling wind outside.

"So, Addy, your people, they are from down the Cape you said?" Mercy asked, still staring into the fire, as if just passing the time in idle conversation.

Addy remained silent. Mercy continued.

"I have lived my whole life here in Wellfleet. My mother and father, their parents and all the Daniels before them. Some even say my family came here with the others on the Mayflower and first stepped foot on the shores of Cape Cod before they sailed on to Plymouth. But I suspect that's perhaps a bit of ancestral fiction that serves the family name," Mercy confided with a smile.

"I'm a Hawthorne," Addy said in a low voice, almost a whisper. But loud enough for Mercy to hear her. Indeed, she knew the name or at least knew *of* the name.

"Hawthorne?" Mercy repeated. "That's a very old and well-known name around New England, isn't it?"

Addy slowly nodded her head, expecting the usual reaction whenever her surname was announced. For many people in New England and beyond, the name had an infamous history.

"Yes, the same. Some say witches or at least their curses have always been connected with my family," Addy said in a hushed voice.

Like any New Englander, Mercy knew the stories of the Salem witch trials and how at the center of much of that notorious past the Puritan Judge Jonathan Hawthorne had played a role. His writings on spectral evidence and the very existence of witchcraft, along with the published works of the now infamous Cotton Mathers, fanned the flames of the very hysteria that gripped Salem and all of New England in the late 1600s.

"Surely you don't believe in such things as family curses?" Mercy asked.

"I'm not so sure. The family stories say Jonathan Hawthorne's wife, two newborn twins, and his two-year-old daughter all died not many years after the trials. Disease they claimed though many believed it was more than that," Addy suggested, suddenly becoming more talkative.

"Addy, such things all have natural explanations. Besides, they have nothing to do with a young woman such as yourself," Mercy assured her.

"Still there are those that think differently," Addy said.

"Well, they would be wrong. That was centuries ago. No one believes in witches and such things anymore," Mercy said, wanting to put an end to such talk. She changed the subject.

"When are you due," Mercy asked, making no further effort to pretend she couldn't see Addy's condition. The girl fell quiet again, offering nothing.

"Then perhaps you can tell me about your husband?"

Addy only looked away. Her silence provided Mercy her answer. There was no husband. That's why the girl was alone every night standing by the cliffs, lost, without a home.

"Certainly, your family must know?" Mercy asked.

"Billy is at sea. Merchant Marines. He's been gone nearly six months. No word," Addy now volunteered.

"Is Billy your husband?"

Addy didn't answer. She only shook her head no.

"He doesn't know does he?" Mercy continued.

Addy lowered her head, again shaking it slowly.

"And your parents, do they know?"

"I left before I showed much," Addy answered, beginning to cry softly, her hands trembling in her lap.

"And you've been wandering the marches and dunes for how long now? Where have you slept, what have you been getting to eat?"

"I make myself a bed in some of the barns around here and took what I can now and then from the people's root cellars. A few jars of peaches or pears. Sometimes a portion of smoked meat from the smokehouses. I wouldn't steal but I can't go home and I can't let the baby starve. I figure God will forgive me."

"But your mother, your father, they must be so very worried," Mercy insisted. "You need to go home. You can't live out in the cold. It's not safe."

"My mother is dead. Died giving birth to me. And my father? He would only throw me out anyway if he knew. But Billy and I love each other. I'm nearly seventeen anyway. Once Billy comes back, we can go off on our own and have a life together."

"But no one knows when that might be. The young men won't return until it's all over," Mercy told her. She knew the rest of the truth. Some, like her fiancé Henry, wouldn't be returning at all. If the father of Addy's baby hadn't been in contact all these many months there might be a reason.

"Maybe I could stay here," Addy said, her face showing the first signs of hope since Mercy had found her.

"Oh, I'm not sure that's a good idea. Your people must be looking for you. You just ran off without telling them anything. They must be besides themselves with worry," Mercy again suggested.

"He thinks I ran off with Billy. My father doesn't like him. He forbids me to see him but we still continued doing so in secret."

"Still, you need to go home. I'm sure he may even have the local authorities looking for you."

Addy only shook her head. It would not be that way. She knew her father was a hard man. More than that, a proud man. She had disobeyed his orders, continued to meet with Billy Thames and now had left her father's home. There was no returning and certainly not with her child growing inside her.

"I better go then," Addy said, standing to leave, "Please may I have my shawl. You've been so very nice Miss Daniels but I have to go now."

"Go? Where?" Back out to where I found you," Mercy asked, certain the young girl couldn't be considering that.

"He is coming back. I know he is. He said to wait for him and that's what I'm doing. I can spot his ship coming in from the sea if I wait a top the bluffs," Addy told her, sounding as if she herself even believed that was possible.

It was then that Mercy realized she had no choice. She simply couldn't let the young girl leave. Not back out into the cold, dark night. And certainly not with her unborn child.

"I'll tell you what. How about I fix a cot for you to sleep in tonight inside my work room. There's not much space but we can make do, at least for tonight, and we'll see after that what's best," Mercy suggested.

She knew Garrett or Doc Harrington would know what to do about Addy. They could check her over at least. Maybe contact the girl's family. But she couldn't let the young girl go back to the ruins or another damp barn to sleep in. That simply wasn't an option.

"Please, I promise I won't be any trouble," Addy assured her, "You'll see, I can be a big help."

"Well, I appreciate that Addy. But let's not get ahead of ourselves just yet. I need to give this some more thought. This is a small village and people will ask questions if I have a house guest that stays too long. Your family is bound to find out anyway."

"Oh no, please, you can't let that happen," Addy pleaded, the hope in her face quickly vanishing.

"Let's not think about that for now. We'll set up the cot and I have some extra blankets in the cupboard. We can make you comfortable for the night and see to things tomorrow," Mercy said, shifting the subject to the present, leaving the future to be worked on tomorrow. For now, she had a house guest of sorts and to be honest, it was sort of a pleasant feeling. She had never gotten totally used to living alone and it was somehow comforting to have someone else to share a bowl of broth with in front of her fireplace. In the morning she would go over to the town and find Garrett or his Uncle. They could help.

Chapter 11

Early next morning Mercy knew she needed to reach out to the Doctor. But maybe not Doc Harrington. No, she thought, she couldn't risk getting him involved, not just yet. Older people might not understand. She realized there was probably no one else, no one better to help, then Doc Harrington's nephew, Garrett, the younger doctor. They were, after all, *friends* now. They both had said it was so.

But she had to somehow convince him to come to her. She obviously couldn't show up in town at Doc Harrington's office with a young, pregnant, sixteen-year-old in tow. But she also couldn't simply dial up the doctor's office and ask for a house call. There would be too much need of an explanation, especially if the older doctor was the first to pick up the phone.

So instead, she called Jacob's Mercantile Store. She would order some supplies and merely ask that they have their Italian delivery boy, Andy, bring them out as she was extremely busy with her work. Then she could pay the boy a quarter or two to take a message to the young doctor.

Within a few hours, her plan had worked. With a crate of groceries tied to the front of his bike, Andy arrived at her front door. She greeted him there at the door, not inviting him in, even though she had first been sure to see that her young ward was secreted away out of sight. She quickly offered him the money for payment and another small number of coins to take the sealed envelope with her note in it.

"Now Andy, I need you to take this to the new doctor. Doc Harrington's nephew. His name is Garrett. *No one else.* Not even old Doc Harrington. Do you understand me? It is very important that you go directly there before you go back to the store. Can I count on you to do that for me?" Mercy asked.

The young boy nodded his head, excitedly counting the extra coins. He would have done it without any payment he thought to himself. He liked Mercy Daniels. She was always nice to him. Not like some of the other girls from town his own age whose fathers had warned them to stay away from those *Italian* boys. But the extra money was appreciated. His family could use the money to add to that his father earned working on the scallop trawlers.

"You bet, Miss Daniels. You can count on me. No one gets this envelop but the new doctor. Met him already. I like him. He seems..."

"You best be on your way, now," Mercy cut him off in mid-sentence. She didn't want to appear as if there were any problem but she was anxious to have Garrett get here to look Addy over. It was already a miracle, she thought, that the young girl hadn't caught her death living out in the open as it was.

As noon came and went and the afternoon sun began to fade from its yellow glow, Mercy grew more anxious. She had thought Garrett Harrington would have been here by now. She became concerned that perhaps Andy had forgotten to deliver the message. She kept checking in on Addy, who had briefly been awake earlier during the day, long enough to take some more of the broth and a slice of homemade bread. But the girl was still exhausted and quickly fell back to sleep on the cot. Mercy covered her up and tried to go about her chores without disturbing the her. Soon she heard the sound of a car coming up the lane. She stepped outside, watching as the face of the driver grew clearer. It was Garrett Harrington.

He slowed the vehicle as he approached the cottage, seeing Mercy standing outside. He wasn't at all sure why he had been summoned. He had only met her the one time and was surprised she had needed a house call. There had been nothing to suggest at their first meeting a few nights ago that she was feeling any distress. And now, as he stepped out of the car, her expression seemed more a look of worry than of being anything else.

"Miss Daniels, I'm glad to see you again. I surely hope there isn't anything wrong. Your note was a little vague but I came just as soon as I could. We had quite a number of patients today. This change in weather is bringing in the colds. My apologies," Garrett offered.

"Doctor, are you a man who can keep a secret?" Mercy asked, skipping the customary pleasantries.

Garrett was certainly surprised by the directness of such a question. It was strange way to begin their second meeting.

"Well, I suppose it's all a part of being a doctor. So, yes, I certainly can keep a secret. Why, are we about to share one?" Garrett asked, trying to sound light hearted though he could see Mercy was anything but.

"Please come inside then," Mercy said, stepping back into the small cottage holding the door open behind her. Garrett followed, growing more curious by the second. As he entered, his eyes adjusted to the light of the interior of the little house. Immediately the homespun style of the room made him feel a sense of welcome. It was hard to explain but it was somehow as he had imagined a home that Mercy Daniels lived in would be. Comfortable. Simple. These were the thoughts that came to his mind. It said a lot about the woman. No pretense of any of the finer things that might have been bestowed on her by her Aunt Emily.

"Very nice Miss Daniels. I believe you must love it here," Garrett complimented her.

"Thank you, but honestly I need your help," Mercy said, leading him from the main room into the tiny kitchen. There, laying under a blanket on a cot by the stove, Garrett saw the sleeping form of a young girl. He looked at Mercy, eyes questioning, not sure who this was.

"I'm sorry. I don't understand. Is this your sister?" It was obvious to Garrett that the young girl was too old to be any child of Mercy's and besides, no such situation had ever come to his understanding by her or anyone else.

Mercy shook her head.

"A relative then," Garrett tried again.

"No, nothing like that."

"I'm sorry. I really am confused. Who is she then?"

"That's just it. I'm not sure," Mercy explained, "I found her last night wandering alone up by the old ruins near the bluffs. I had been hearing things at night for some time. A light moving among the old stone house and the sound of crying. At first, I just thought it was the moonlight reflecting off the water below and the wind rushing through the ruins. But last night there was no real wind to speak off and no full moon to play tricks on the eyes. And yet I could hear the same sound coming from outside my window, thought I even saw the same light drifting past the stone openings."

"And so, you went up there, all by yourself, alone?" Garrett asked, his voice etched with concern. "I know, probably not the best idea. But I just had to see what it was all about. And that's when I found her. I don't know how long she's been roaming around up there. She was freezing. Hadn't eaten as long as she could remember. She told me her name was Addy. But little more,"

"Addy what? What's her last name?" Garrett asked.

"She said she was a Hawthorne. That her people come from Down Cape. But I've never heard of any family by that name living anywhere near here."

"Well, it's something to at least start with," Garrett said.

Garrett went back out to the car, fetched his medical bag, and returned. He slowly pulled the blanket covering the girl down to examine her more closely. As soon as he eased the blanket back, he could see the young girl was with child, probably seven or maybe even eight months along he estimated based on the size of her belly.

He placed the end of the stethoscope over her heart and his hand on her forehead. Addy didn't stir, still fast asleep. Her breathing seemed only slightly elevated but her heart was strong and there was no fever. Yet it was obvious that she still had to be quite exhausted from her ordeal and only rest would help.

He looked up at Mercy, his eyes still showing a puzzled expression.

"Mercy, we have to find out where she comes from. Her people must be desperate with worry."

"I told her the same thing though she did share with me that her mother was dead and her father would only throw her out if he knew of her condition. I insisted that the authorities would be out looking for her. But still she wouldn't tell me more. She only said her boyfriend was in the Merchant Marines and had shipped out months ago without knowing of her condition," Mercy said.

"I'll have to report this. No choice. I can call the State Police and see where these Hawthornes might be living on the Cape." Garrett insisted.

"Certainly, if you think that's best," Mercy agreed though Garrett detected a hint of doubt.

"What else can we do? Surely you aren't suggesting she stay here? She's going to need medical attention of a whole other kind before long."

"I know, I know but...the *authorities*. If they can't find anyone other than her father who might indeed cast her out, they will only place her in a home for unwed mothers somewhere miles from here. I can't let that happen," Mercy insisted.

"You seriously don't believe you can take care of her by yourself?" Garrett questioned.

"But I wouldn't be by myself. You're a doctor. You make house calls. I'm sure with all that work you had in Boston you helped birth babies."

Garrett couldn't believe what he was hearing. It made no sense. None at all. This young girl had a family, of that both Mercy and he knew for sure. Surely, there had to be others looking for her. Of that he was also certain. But he could see Mercy had strong feelings about it as well.

"Okay, just tell me why you? One good reason. You aren't married. You don't have children of your own. You probably have a hard-enough time just making ends meet as it is. How could you take care of a young girl *and* her baby? It doesn't make sense. I'm just not sure you are looking at this right. It's not as if she is a stray puppy or kitten you found wandering outside."

Mercy didn't have an answer. At least none that she could readily offer him.

"I don't know. I just have this feeling there's more to it than we think. Maybe it's because I was adopted myself. Maybe it's because I lost someone and feel a need to take care of another. Oh, I don't know. I just have a feeling about all of it," Mercy insisted, frustrated by her own inability to answer Garrett.

Garrett looked into her eyes, could see she was serious, saw the tears welling up. He was already finding himself being further drawn towards her. That feeling that men often have of a need to be a protector. That much he knew.

"Tell you what. I agree that for now it would be best she stay here anyway. She needs rest, needs to get her strength back. And it may take a few days to find out more about her and who might indeed be looking for her. Maybe she's not being exactly truthful about her father throwing her out. Likely he's sick with worry as any father would be with a daughter who has run off," Garrett suggested.

Mercy smiled, giving him an impulsive hug. It was unexpected and he found himself responding by quickly wrapping his own arms around her. They stood there momentarily, lapsing into an awkward yet comfortable silence. Finally, he released her, stealing a last capture of her scent.

Garrett reached into his medical bag and produced a small bottle of liquid. He placed it in Mercy's hand and closed her fingers around it gently.

"Give her a few drops of this just before she goes to sleep tonight. You can put it in a glass of warm milk to help it go down. It will help her rest. I'll be back tomorrow to check up on you both. But I best go now. I told my uncle where I was going and don't want to have to explain why I stayed out here so late. Getting enough questions about you from him and your Aunt Emily as it is," Garrett smiled.

"Then we agree? She will stay here?"

"I'm not really in any position to make any promises. But certainly, for as long as it takes to find out where she is from and contact her family. I have no choice. Anything happens to her under my care, I would be held responsible, would feel responsible," Garrett said.

"I understand. I do. You see what you can find out. Meanwhile, I'll take care of her and no one needs to know," Mercy insisted.

"It's a small town, Mercy. People will find out."

"Only if one of us says something and I have a feeling you will keep *our* secret," Mercy said.

"I take it you must have a lot of trust in me?"

"I do," Mercy offered.

They stood a moment looking at each, not another word being said. Garrett studied her, hoping. For what he wasn't sure and yet he couldn't keep the truth from himself. Maybe he had felt something that very first night they had been introduced, though as a man of science he held little belief in anything as surreal as kismet.

"Mercy, I..." Garrett started but stopped before the words could escape.

Mercy felt the same need. Something somehow needing to be said. But it made no sense. Not now. It was too confusing.

"When can you come back?" Mercy asked, quickly returning to the situation of the moment. There would be time to talk of other things later.

"I have a rather busy schedule the next few days. My uncle has asked that I start picking up more of his house calls. So, unless you need me sooner, I can work my way back here by the end of the week. Friday towards evening? Is that okay?"

"Thank you, Garrett," Mercy said, remembering how he had asked her to call him by his first name. She reached out, placing her hand on his arm. She left it resting there, perhaps a little too long she thought. But it was a connection she wasn't eager to break.

"I will make us some dinner Friday," Mercy offered.

"Oh, I wouldn't want to put you to the trouble," Garrett said.

"It isn't any trouble. Besides, I have to make something for Addy and I anyway. One more at the table isn't any bother. How long has it been since you had a real home cooked meal anyway?"

Honestly, Garrett thought, his uncle's housekeeper was an excellent cook. But he knew better than to say so in the face of so gracious an invitation.

"It would indeed be my pleasure, thank you," Garrett accepted.

"No, truly Garrett, it is I who needs to thank you. I know this is all a bit unusual to say the least. But I just have a feeling it is the right thing we are doing. At least for now."

"Perhaps. Anyway, I best be going. My uncle will ask questions if I'm gone too long. You have been under his charge since you were quite young. He will want a full report as to what caused a need for me to come out here. I'm not sure what I'll tell him," Garrett said.

He took his bag and headed towards the front door. Mercy followed him, opening the door to let him out. As he stepped passed her, she impulsively leaned out and quickly kissed his cheek. It took Garrett by as much surprise as it

id Mercy. He paused, turning to look into her eyes, a question in his expression.

"Just to say thank you," Mercy answered him before he could say anything.

He smiled back at her, stepping outside towards his car, he felt a certain pleasant lightness in his step.

Chapter 12

As Garrett had said he would, the very next day he reached out to the State Police barracks down near Chatham Town. The officer on duty informed him they hadn't received any reports of a girl missing by that name or any other name for that matter. But he did say they would look into it and get back to him if anything turned up. The Sergeant he spoke with said while he was certain that he didn't know of any family by the name of Hawthorne, people came and went during the seasons without much notice. They seldom bothered to register their arrival or arrange for mail delivery if they weren't accustomed to staying in one particular location very long.

Garrett continued seeing patients and working with his uncle for the rest of the week. He was beginning to think there wasn't going to be any return call from the State Police and that the girl had simply made up a name to avoid further detection. But early Friday morning, the phone rang in his uncle's office. Doc Harrington was busy with a patient in the exam room so Garrett picked up. It was Sergeant Cramer again from the Chatham State Police barracks.

"Doctor Harrington, this is Sergeant Cramer. Seems we may have found the family related to your inquiry. Was a bit surprised honestly. I thought I knew pretty much everyone around here," the officer insisted.

"That's good news. Is the family from Chatham?" Garrett asked.

"No, a little further down cape, Yarmouth area. Or at least the father, Charlie Hawthorne, lives there. Seems his wife died quite a few years ago and it's just him. He told us he moved here a little while ago from the area just below Salem. Sort of a handyman. Does odd jobs here and there. That's really all I have on him. If he'd run into any trouble with us, I would have probably remembered the name sooner," Sergeant Cramer said.

"Well, that's a big help. I'm sure he's been worried sick," Garrett insisted.

There was no answer. Garrett thought maybe he had lost the connection.

"Sergeant are you still there?"

"Yes, I'm here,"

"When is he coming for her," Garrett asked, certain the father would be on his way already.

"Well, you see, here's the thing. He claims he doesn't have any daughter. Least ways, as he put it, none he's interested in bringing back home," Cramer said.

Garrett wasn't sure he had heard the officer correctly. What did he mean, none the father wanted returned home?

"I don't understand?"

"He claims he knows his daughter is with child. Told me she thought he didn't know, that she believed she was hiding it but he knew all the same. Said she made her bed and now needs to lay in it is how he put it. Doesn't want anything more to do with her. I tried talking some sense into him but he wouldn't have it."

"But he can't do that, she's just a child herself," Garrett insisted.

"Actually, according to Mr. Hawthorne, his daughter is over sixteen and in this State that makes her an adult. He can't legally be made to do anything," Sergeant Cramer said. There was a hint of regret in his voice.

Garrett didn't know what to say. He was dumbfounded. This was ridiculous. She was this man's own flesh and blood. He couldn't just turn his back on her. Sixteen or not she was still just a mere child and about to be a mother. He had a responsibility even if the law said otherwise.

"So, what do we do now?"

"Doctor, I'm afraid there's not much either of us *can* do. It's not a legal issue and the father isn't breaking any law. The only one who maybe really has is the boyfriend who I understand is twenty and out to sea somewhere. Probably doesn't even know about any of this to be honest."

"Well, can you at least give me Mr. Hawthorne's phone number?"

"He doesn't have a phone. I had to drive over there myself just to talk with him. One of our other patrol officers knew about him living out near the marshlands. That's how I came to know where to stop in."

"Then give me the address," Garrett insisted.

"Now listen Doctor, with all due respect, I don't want you stirring up any trouble over this now. Confronting this man probably isn't the best thing to do right now. Maybe best to give it some time. Maybe he'll change his mind."

"The one thing this girl doesn't have is *time!*"

"Still, I'd give it a couple of days. I'll give you his address. Let's just say it's because it's a medical situation. Normally can't give out such information to civilians. But you have to promise me no trouble. You want to talk to him? Fine. But if he tells you what he told us here, that's all anyone can do. If the girl can't take care of herself, let alone a new born, the baby will have to go to the child services agency. That's unfortunately just the way it is. That's the law. Understand," Sergeant Cramer, his tone changing.

"Yes, I understand. I will give it a few days then hopefully I can reason with him," Garrett promised.

"All right, then," Sergeant Cole relented, "Have a pen and paper handy?"

Garrett wrote the address down, thanking the Sergeant again for his help before hanging up. It wasn't the news he had hoped for. As far as he was concerned, Mercy, and likely himself, still had a problem.

Chapter 13

As soon as he made his last house call on Friday, just as the sun was beginning to set over Wellfleet Bay, Garrett drove the half mile out of town to Mercy's cottage along the shoreline of Nauset Beach. The November winds were already blowing up a steady gale in from the sea and the temperatures had been dropping more and more each evening. Approaching the house, he could see a wisp of smoke raising up from the fireplace chimney. Another smaller plume of smoke rose up from the flue pipe extending above the roof over the kitchen. Mercy was preparing dinner as she had promised and it made Garrett feel a little special. It had been a long time since another woman, his own mother, had fussed over him. He wouldn't deny that it pleased him more than just a little.

He pulled his car up alongside the house and got out. The aroma of a meal on the stove greeted him. He was a lucky man he thought. But he pulled himself up short, realizing that it was probably just Mercy showing her appreciation for his help. Mercy Daniels was merely extending the courtesy of a neighbor, nothing more he thought. Don't read anything into it he told himself though he realized he was already developing strong feeling towards her, an attachment that if he was honest had begun almost from the first time he met her at Miss Emily's Harvest Home Ball. He had considered bringing a bottle of wine but then thought better of it. Maybe she didn't drink spirits and he wasn't sure how it might look. So, he had settled on a bouquet of wild flowers he had seen on a stand just outside the Mercantile Store. Surely, they wouldn't appear presumptuous.

As he followed the walkway up to the cottage, he spotted Mercy smiling at him from just inside the front door.

"Well, there you are Doctor. I was beginning to think you had forgotten," Mercy grinned.

Believing she might be serious, Garrett became concerned.

"Oh no, I assure you I..."

Mercy raised her hand, stopping him from apologizing.

"I'm just teasing you. Actually, you are a little early," Mercy said, still holding the door open for him, "Dinner won't be ready for a while yet. Come in. Would you care to join me in a glass of wine? I'm afraid I don't have anything stronger."

Garrett smiled, stepping into the front room of the cottage, realizing he now had his answer about the wine.

"Yes, I would enjoy that. Wine is fine," he accepted the offer.

His eyes followed her as she moved towards the kitchen. That was when he saw Addy peering from around the corner, watching him carefully. Their eyes made contact. They studied each other for a long moment, both apparently measuring each other up. It was Garrett that finally broke the awkward silence of the young girl's stare.

"Hello, you're Addy are you not?" Garrett said, knowing full well her name. He now knew more about her than when he had first laid eyes on her sleeping form.

Addy nodded, still not sure if his presence was a good thing. She had grown to mistrust most older people, especially men.

"I'm Doctor Harrington, though you may call me Garrett if you like," Garrett suggested hoping that even though he was a doctor, his willingness to be addressed casually as Garrett might put her at ease.

The girl remained in the safety of her spot just inside the doorway to the small room, watching.

"I understand you come from down Yarmouth way," Garrett offered, hoping to draw her out. It had just the opposite effect. The young girl seemed to retreat further at the words. Clearly, he had revealed something she wasn't prepared to hear.

"How do you know that?" Addy finally spoke in a soft, almost inaudible voice.

By now, Mercy had returned to the main room, holding out a glass for Garrett. She was as curious as her young   charge.
"Yarmouth?" Mercy asked.

"Yes, seems Addy has family there. At least that's where her father lives. Isn't that right Addy?" Garrett said.

The girl nodded, offering nothing more. But she eased out from her hiding spot, slowly coming further into the room. The light of the fireplace illuminated her and Garrett could see he had been right. Her pregnancy was very much well along the way.

"So, you spoke to the authorities?" Mercy asked in a hushed tone, hoping Addy wouldn't hear her. Garrett nodded.

"Yes, State Police. Her father lives alone. Told them his wife had passed away."

"Well, it's good at least that you found him, right?" Mercy asked. The look on Garrett's face told her it might not be so.

"Her father told the officer he had no daughter, least none he was willing to claim," Garrett said, shaking his head.

Mercy's eyes opened wide in disbelief.

"He can't be serious! It's his daughter and she's carrying his grandchild. There must be some mistake," Mercy insisted

"Not from what Sergeant Cramer said. He told me he had gone to Mr. Hawthorne's house. Told him has daughter had been located. But the father said he wasn't interested," Garrett repeated.

Mercy looked over at Addy, who had come close enough now to hear what was being said. Both Mercy and Garrett noticed there really wasn't any change in the young girl's expression. No look of surprise or even hurt. Just the same vacant eyes she had shown most of the time she had been there.

"No...no that simply won't do!" Mercy insisted. "How can a father just turn out his own daughter like that. I'll go there myself."

"Perhaps in a few days. I promised Sergeant Cramer we'd wait a few days before trying again. Maybe her father will think it over a little more and will see things differently by then," Garrett suggested.

"No, he won't," Addy finally spoke. "You don't know him like I do. He's always blamed me for my mother's death giving birth to me. But it got worse between us after my older brother died and wasn't there to protect me."

Mercy and Garrett looked at each other. They were both a little surprised by the girl's sudden outburst. It was more words than she had spoken in the span of nearly five days. Now she suddenly seemed very animated and distressed.

"We'll talk with him, sweetheart. I promise. He'll change his mind," Mercy assured her, though the look on Garrett's face seemed a little less convincing.

Addy only shook her head. She had accepted her life as it was though she felt a sense of comfort with these strangers that she hadn't known with her own kin. She had her plans and they didn't include a father who had never shown her much love.

"It won't do much good. But I can't stop you. If you'd be kind enough to let me borrow a warm coat and some food, I can be on my way first thing in the morning. I've already been enough trouble as it is."

Garrett studied Mercy, waiting to hear her response. He knew what his obligation was. If the girl's father wouldn't take her back, he had to alert the authorities. Even if Addy herself was of questionable legal age to be on her own, she couldn't be let to wander around near full term. There was now two of them involved; mother and child.

"We'll take a ride down to Yarmouth on Sunday. It'll have been a few days by then and your father is liable to be home and not working being it's the Sabbath,"

Mercy nodded her head, approving of the suggestion. It was the next logical thing to do. What happened after could be decided then.

"I've got a nice chicken roasting in the oven. Plenty for everyone. How about we have some supper," Mercy suggested, changing the subject.

Garrett nodded his head, offering up an eager smile. Addy followed him as he stepped into the kitchen where he pulled out a chair for the young girl to take her seat like a gentleman offering help to his lady. She decided then and there that she just might have to like this *Doctor Garrett* after all. He reminded her of her older brother, always looking after her. But she knew it wouldn't last, this feeling of comfort and family. It never had.

Chapter 14

Mercy had seen her share of dilapidated and weather ravaged cabins up and down the towns of Cape Cod. Some hardly more than shacks with tar paper roofs and outhouses for bathrooms. But when Garrett finally pulled off the paved main Mid-Cape road down onto the backroads of Yarmouth, she was surprised to see how even the gravel road surface turned more and more into mere dirt ruts that passed through the increasingly denser thicket of scrub pines the farther in towards the bayside they drove.

As they made their way, the number of dwellings they encountered grew fewer and fewer. Every now and then they passed a carved out opening in the thick brush that appeared to trail off into the barren landscape, a wooden sign or plague with a name or house number nailed to a tree the only indication someone lived down those paths.

She had travelled the length of the Mid-Cape Highway many times coming or leaving the Cape on her way to places inland or back home to Wellfleet but she had not often explored the area on either side of the highway for any distance. To her, the bay side of the Cape, places where villages like Yarmouth, Brewster, or Dennis lay, were not well known to her. Most who made a living off the sea lived further out towards the end of the Cape where access to the ocean waters was easier.

Garrett cautiously steered the car down the dirt roads, maneuvering around mudholes that popped up every now and then, some large enough to sink the front end of the car into if he wasn't careful. As they made their way several more yards down the crude trail through the ghostly stand of crippled looking pines, they spotted a crude wooden sign nailed to a tree. *Hawthorne – Carpenter* was all it said.

Garrett turned off and followed the road as it narrowed to little more than a path cutting through the brush. Up ahead, a small shack sat in a clearing. It was constructed of roughly cut planks and pieces of driftwood to act as battens against the wind. The roof was little more than pieces of overlapping tarpaper covering more rough pine slats, a small piece of galvanized tubing serving as a stovepipe flue jutting up through one side of the roof. Hanging from a tree beside the cabin was the gutted carcass of a small deer and beyond that a crude wooden drying rack with rows of skinned fish curing in the sun.

Garrett turned off the car's engine, watching for signs of life. Mercy started to open the car door but he reached over and stopped her. He continued watching the front and sides of the house as though he were expecting something. It wasn't long before the front door of the cabin opened and a thin scarecrow of a man stepped cautiously out.

"What's your business here," the thin man said in a demanding and anything but friendly voice.

"Mr. Hawthorne? My name is Doctor Harrington," Garrett said, easing out from the driver seat and stepping a few feet closer, extending his hand.

Hawthorne made no effort to step down from the porch to accept it.

"Doctor? What for? Nobody here sick," Hawthorne challenged.

"No, we aren't here about someone being sick. We are here about Addy, your daughter." Garrett told him.

Mercy opened the door and stepped out. Hawthorne eyed her up and down, wondering what she had to do with any of this.

"Like I told that officer feller, I ain't got no daughter. Least ways, no more I don't," Hawthorne said, grim faced.

"Mr. Hawthorne, I understand how you feel, but..." Mercy started to speak but the older man quickly cut her off.

"With all due respect Missy, I don't think you do. I don't think you know a damn thing about me. That's what I think. So, if you and your feller here will just get back in your car and leave, I'd be obliged," Hawthorne said.

"Your daughter needs your help. She's going to have a child, *your* grandchild!" Mercy insisted.

"You mean a bastard child don't you. That white trash Billy Thames and her got to messing around. Got her in a fine way now. I told her no good would come of it. But that didn't stop her, now did it?" Hawthorne snapped back, his hands curling into fists by his side.

"Yes, she told us about Billy. They fell in love. The heart can't help that," Mercy continued.

"Love?! What the hell do those two know about love. Love only gets people in trouble. That's all I know about such things. I loved her mother too. But that didn't mean a damn thing when she up and died bringing a child into the world. Then my son. Said he had to do the right thing. Said that's what I did in the Great War. Had to go fight them Nazis he said. Save the God damn world he said. Never made it more than a few feet on that beach in Normandy. Couldn't even give him a proper burial back here with his people," Hawthorne said, his eyes looking off in the distance like he was seeing some terrible scene he had fixated on now for a long time.

Mercy could hear the pain in the man's voice. She wanted to reach out to him, take his hand, try to tell him it was okay. She started to take another step forward but again Garrett caught her arm, halted her.

"Mr. Hawthorne, I'm not going to tell you I understand. Because I don't. Yes, I've seen people hurt, in pain. I've seen them die. You and I both know that's just the way things are in this world. But I like to think there is some good also, maybe more than all the bad. Every time I've witnessed a child being born, I like to think it somehow cancels out that pain we feel at someone's death. Addy needs her family. She is scared of what the future holds," Garrett said, trying to make the older man see what mattered now.

"As we all are Doctor. But that don't change things, now does it. She disgraced the family, disgraced me, my name. I'm not a forgiving man anymore," Hawthorne insisted.

"But God wants us all to forgive," Mercy offered, hoping there was still some compassion left within this obviously broken man.

"God?! What God?" Hawthorne said, spitting out the words, an even darker mood coming over his face.

Hawthorne stepped down from the porch, moving towards Mercy. Garrett stepped in to block his further advance.

"You want to believe in God? That's your business. Me? I've seen what *your* God is capable of. You know they say there ain't no atheists in a fox hole cause every one's praying they get out of battle alive. Well, all I can say for certain is there ain't no God on a battlefield. Where was your God when my son got killed? And where was your God when death took my wife?" Hawthorne asked.

Mercy remained silent, no longer finding the words that would work.

"So, you and your Doctor friend here best be leaving and take your damn God with you. He ain't welcomed here."

He turned and headed back for the porch of the shack then spun around to face them again.

"You know, maybe you don't know about us Hawthornes. Been around a long time. Some going back to the time of those Salem trials. Jonathan Hawthorne, my own ancestor, done helped hang those people, all likely innocent they say. One of them victims cursed him and all the rest of us through times to come as she stood there on them gallows. Said there would be no rest, no peace for our family. Maybe she was right," Hawthorne said.

Mercy could see his eyes starting to well up in tears. He quickly turned and without another word disappeared behind the closing door.

***

For most of the ride back to Wellfleet, neither Mercy or Garrett spoke. It had not been as Mercy had hoped. She just couldn't understand how a father could turn his back on his child, a daughter with a child of her own on the way. What would happen to her now? It all seemed like a terrible circle of fate, knowing she, herself, had been adopted. But that was different she told herself. She had been told her birth mother had been forced to give her up. Her adoptive parents never had much detail to offer her beyond that but at least her real mother had no choice. She had not simply turned her back on her as Addy's father was doing.

After a few more miles, Mercy broke the silence, turning to look at Garrett.

"You aren't seriously going to have the authorities take her, are you?" Mercy asked. Garrett didn't reply.

"They won't let her keep that baby. You must realize that, don't you?!" Mercy insisted.

Again, Garrett remained silent, staring ahead at the road.

"Garrett, there has to be some alternative," Mercy pressed.

"Like what?" Garrett finally spoke, "Mercy, you can't support a young girl and a baby. You barely make enough to take care of yourself. Sewing dresses and such. Weaving. Selling things at the Mercantile."

"I know. But maybe I could teach her to sew also. We could sell more items," Mercy suggested, knowing full well that she was fortunate to have the few people that were buying her goods do so simply because they didn't sew for themselves and dress stores were scarce to none on the Cape.

"Mercy, you *have* to be reasonable. I know you want to help. I love you for that," Garrett offered, immediately realizing the words he had spoken were beyond the status of their relationship. He hoped perhaps she hadn't heard him or at least not taken it as being personal.

But she had heard him. The words gave her a sense of comfort just as when Henry had said them. Now there was an awkward pause in their conversation. They drove on along the Mid-Cape highway, watching the sun ahead begin to dip down below the horizon. Without saying anything, Mercy slowly inched her hand across the car seat, letting it come to rest near Garrett. He kept looking ahead, steering the car into the on-coming night. He reached forward with his right hand and pulled the knob for the headlights, switching them on. But instead of returning his hand to the steering wheel he let it fall on top of Mercy's outstretched hand next to him. She didn't pull back nor register any alarm as he thought she might. They just drove on, the only sound the smooth humming of the engine.

Chapter 15

Though he had promised Mercy, at least for the time being, he would not contact the authorities about Addy again, not immediately anyway, he did say he felt it best to at least speak with his uncle about the situation. Mercy was truly still his uncle's patient and Garrett knew how Doc thought of her as his own niece. He hadn't felt right about keeping the situation from his uncle.

As he had expected, his uncle had told him calling the authorities was the right thing to do, the only thing to do. The girl was of questionable age, even at sixteen, and clearly had no means by which to support herself let alone a newborn when the baby arrived. It wasn't Mercy's problem, even if she felt a need to stay involved and if Addy's father wouldn't or couldn't be made to look after the girl, someone who could had to, even if that was the State of Massachusetts.

Garrett was frankly not at all surprised by his uncle's advice. He knew him to be someone that had always adhered strictly to the law. But Garrett said he had not just come to his uncle for advice. He knew what the law required, that they report the matter. Instead, he said he had come to his uncle for help, though he was at a loss as to exactly what sort of help the older man could offer. Couldn't Hawthorne be made to take his daughter back in, he said. Wasn't the father bound to do so as her legal parent and guardian.

Doc Harrington listened, thinking it through. He understood how his nephew saw all this. Knew he would have probably felt the same way at the younger man's age. Still full of hope and promise, not so yet weathered by time and the storms of life that only seemed to replace idealism with wisdom; with surrender.

"Listen son, I understand you must have feelings for Mercy Daniels and she no doubt has feelings for this young girl she took in but you both have to be realistic. Mercy is but a young girl herself and she just isn't able to take on two more mouths to feed. I know for a fact that Miss Emily sees to it that Mercy's bank account has a little something extra put in it every few months even if Mercy hasn't noticed it herself, though I rather imagine she has long ago," Doc Harrington revealed, stopping himself from saying more. He was simply trying to make a point.

"I suppose that's because she sees her as family," Doc suggested.

"Is that why she sometimes refers to Mercy as her niece?" Garrett asked.

"Perhaps, though Mercy was adopted. Her adoptive mother and Miss Emily were finishing school friends, back before most women of society went to college like modern girls do now."

"But Mercy told me her mother died," Garrett said.

"True, her adoptive parents that is. Tragic thing that. But not much is known about Mercy's real mother. No records. She just was given to Mrs. Daniels who raised her until Mercy's adoptive father and mother were lost on the island ferry sinking. By then Mercy was a young woman and Miss Emily sort of took her under her wing. Got her set up in the home she has now. Covered the costs of getting it back to where it could be lived in again," Doc Harrington said, "Anyway, my point is that good intentions notwithstanding, it's just not something that would work."

"Well, I don't have any solution. Mercy isn't going to take kindly to me or anyone else turning that young girl over to the State and I'm not inclined to make that call myself," Garrett insisted, realizing he wasn't helping matters. But his uncle could see that continuing this conversation wasn't going to get them anywhere either.

"I'll tell you what. Let me think on this a little while. Not saying I'm going to have any better an answer tomorrow, the next day, or even next week but I'll think on it," Doc Harrington finally said, turning back to his paperwork.

"You see if we've got anyone else waiting out there and if not, why don't you knock off for the day. Get something to eat, maybe some sleep," Doc suggested, "It's been a long week and Monday will be rolling around again soon enough."

Chapter 16

Doc Harrington arrived at Halcroft House, Miss Emily's home sitting on the hill overlooking Wellfleet Bay, a little before noon the day after his conversation with Garrett. He had thought it important enough to meet with her as soon as possible. Things were evolving quickly around the matter of the girl Addy, her unborn child, and Mercy, so he knew Emily would want to know if she didn't already.

When he stepped up to the door of the great house, it opened before he could even reach for one of the massive, polished, brass knockers adorning each of the finely carved wooden doors. Expecting Aldon Barlow, the house man servant to let him in, Doc was a little surprised to find Miss Emily standing on the other side to greet him.

"Good to see you Lee," Miss Emily said, though her face suggested that wasn't completely so. They had both known each other long enough that when in private, she called him by his first name and he by hers.

"Please won't you come in. I've had some lunch prepared for us if you have the appetite."

Again, he noted a hint of concern in her voice. What did she know of the reason for his visit he thought? He had simply said he wanted to see her when he had called, nothing more. This was not a woman you took for granted. He knew that much.

Doc followed her into the house, down the long hallway towards the dining hall. As he stepped into the room behind her he noticed a few covered dishes, plates set, and silverware already awaiting them. She motioned for him to take a chair next to hers at the end of the long table. He pulled a chair out for her, sliding it gently in after she began to settle. Then he took a seat.

The house was unusually quiet he thought. Though only the middle of the day, there was no sign of the household help moving around managing their chores. Aldon Barlow, her man servant, had not been there to open the door as he normally did and now there was no wait staff standing ready to serve the meal. Emily could see the look on the doctor's face. Ever the intuitive one, she knew what was on his mind.

"I gave them the day off," Emily said, answering the question he had not asked, "I thought we might have a lovely visit just the two of us, old friends. But don't worry, Milly made the sandwiches and coffee just before she left for town to do a little shopping."

Doc smiled to himself. Miss Emily was known for many things in Wellfleet. But her cooking *wasn't* one of them. Though she had spent her life as a devoted school teacher, she had grown up in the luxury of a household only her father's money and her grandfather's before that could provide. Most everyone knew she had merely decided to become a teacher simply to show her family that their wealth was one thing but her independence was another and far more important to her.

Emily lifted the cover off the silver charger to reveal an assortment of petite sandwiches, neatly cut in crustless triangles. She motioned with her eyes for Doc to help himself which he obligingly did. Then she took hold of the slender carved handle of the silver teapot, pouring out two cups of tea in her fine china teacups. She always insisted, even when only among her most casual of friends, that the table be set with a touch of elegance. Life in a fishing village such as Wellfleet was drab enough without surrendering the finer things of entertaining company.

They sat quietly, enjoying the sandwiches, sipping their tea, exchanging the obligatory pleasantries about family, health, and local news, though neither were the type inclined to dwell on gossip. Women might, man as well, but rarely in mixed company. Just wasn't done. After a while, when Emily felt she had covered enough of the niceties of their social visit, she put her tea cup down, turning slightly in her chair to face her friend head on and asked *the* question that had been lingering in the air since Doc Harrington had first stepped through the door.

"Although I am always so very glad to have the pleasure of your company Lee, it is indeed a rare occasion when just the two of us can spend a moment together undistracted. So, I must ask you, what was of such importance that you took time from your practice to visit an old woman such as myself?"

Doc Harrington's first instinct was, of course, to insist she was anything but an *old* woman, but he knew she wasn't fishing for compliments. She was an old friend; one he knew only too well always came to the point and expected others to do the same.

"I suppose you have heard of the *visitor* Mercy has taken in?" Doc said.

"A *visitor* is it. Well, I dare say my dear friend, I believe you, more than anyone, knows full well that there is little that goes on in this town that I am ignorant of," Emily offered.

Doc nodded his head. There was no argument there, he thought.

"Then you no doubt understand that Mercy has said she intends to let her young charge remain with her," Doc added. He was surprised when he detected an ever so slight smile come across Emily's face.

"And perhaps given her past, it might be a little more than coincidence she feels this need," Doc added, instantly noticing the smile on his friend's face disappear. It was a nerve he knew he had struck. Cautious ground Doc thought.

"We were never to speak of Mercy's origins," Emily quickly replied.

"It is, in my opinion, an unworkable solution. Mercy is a strong woman. No doubt. But to take in a young girl with child? Well, I must say, even with your providing for her since her parents died, it's not a sustainable situation. Wouldn't you agree?" Doc asked, certain she did.

"Of course, we both realize that. What could she possibly be thinking?" Emily asked, knowing, however, what Mercy was indeed thinking. She had been adopted, and in Mercy's mind, abandoned by her own mother. Though she didn't know the reason, the truth, it was all she had to go by.

"Maybe it's time you talked with her," Doc suggested. "Maybe it's long overdue."

Emily thought about it. She had played out that scene in her own mind a hundred times or more over the years. Yes, Emily's best friend had raised her. Yes, Mercy's real mother had had no choice but to give the child away. As her *Aunt*, Emily had seen to it that she had helped raise the child, providing for her needs when her adoptive parents at times struggled to meet them and now could no longer. It was Emily that had helped with funds for Mercy's attending finishing school, helped her start her small business, gave her the family cottage to live in when the bank had no choice but to take her parent's mortgaged house. She had watched over Mercy from a young child to the woman she had become.

"Perhaps you are right. I suppose I've always known such a day might indeed come. But once she became a woman in her own right, there seemed less reason to disrupt the sense of family she already has. Mercy knows she is adopted. There are no secrets regarding that," Emily said, hoping Doc would see it that way.

"I understand. I really do Emily. But I also believe Mercy thinks she somehow owes it to this young girl and wants to ensure the girl doesn't have to give up her child as Mercy's mother was forced to do," Doc Harrington suggested, his eyes appealing to Emily to understand as well.

"Lee, you have been my friend for longer than I can remember. We grew up together, attended Miss Wilson's school and played in the tidal pools as children together. There are none I trust more than you," Emily confided.

"Then you must trust me now. Will you speak with Mercy?" Doc asked.

Miss Emily paused, at first saying nothing. Doc could see she was weighing things out in her mind. Finally, she answered him.

"I will though I'm not sure what I will say."

"I believe you do. She needs guidance on this matter. She will listen to you," Doc assured her.

"I will think on it. I may have a suggestion after all," Emily said, mulling over something in her mind. Something that she wasn't ready to discuss, even with someone as close to her as Lee.

The two spent a little more time just sitting, finishing their lunch together, talking only of times now long ago when they were younger, when the town was merely a remote outpost on a spit of land that jutted out into the sea. Finally, Doc stood, thanking his host for the meal. He waved her off when she had insisted she would see him out. No need, he said as he took his leave.

As he drove down the long driveway to Main St., he couldn't help feel some of the anguish he knew his dear friend, Emily, was dealing with. Families often had secrets. Secrets that in time, would be found out. He was certain the time had finally come for Emily Wescott.

Chapter 17

It had been slowly building up in him, a feeling of needing to make his desires known to Mercy. He felt that if he were honest with himself, they had started almost from their first meeting, that evening when he first took hold of her delicate hand in the reception line and introduced himself. He didn't believe in such things as kismet or fate. He was a man of science, of medicine, and believed that every feeling, every emotion, had a rationale human cause behind it. As shy as he often found himself in the company of the opposite sex when it came to matters of the heart, he would not have even considered her open to his advances if she had not given him a sign.

During the ride back from Yarmouth, he believed they had somehow grown closer from having both shared the experience with confronting Charlie Hawthorne. Her hand had ventured across the car seat as if communicating in a simply act what no words had expressed. He had dared to assume it was indeed an overture when he let his own hand come to rest atop hers. But his doubt, his own insecurity still troubled him. Had it merely been her way of looking for a friend's comfort over a troubling encounter with a man she couldn't understand, a father of young daughter who needed her family.

Garrett knew he was not well skilled in the affairs of the heart, had little experience in them. He was a practical man, not given to a false belief of his own attractiveness, certainly not by a creature as beautiful as he found Mercy to be. But he would have to find the inner courage to test the waters, thinking nothing could be gained without risk.

Garrett had sent an invitation to accompany him to dinner by the delivery boy Andy from the General Store. He realized he ought to have phoned her to ask but while he was willing to put himself out to face a polite decline, he hadn't the courage to receive such in person. If she wasn't interested, she could provide any number of excuses in her reply and no one would need to save face. He was elated when Andy returned with a simple handwritten response of yes, it would be her pleasure as well. For a moment the entire exchange seemed somehow childish of him. It reminded him of passing notes in school. But it mattered not now, he thought. The door had opened a little wider and he would act on his impulse.

Saturday seemed to drag on forever as he saw to his patients and counted the hours towards evening. When the last of them were cleared from the Waiting Room, Garrett quickly sought out his Uncle, who was, as it always seemed, deep in paperwork in his office.

"Uncle, that's the last patient we have for today," Garrett announced, anxious to be on his way. Doc Harrington looked up from his work, checked the old Seth Thomas wall clock ticking the minutes away, saw it was only four in the afternoon. He smiled at his nephew, pleased they might end the week a little early. But he also suspected Garrett had another *appointment* he was eager to keep. The opportunity to bedevil the young man a bit was simply too enticing for the old man to pass up. After all, he thought, he'd been young once himself.

"Well, that is a surprise. Good then. We have time to spare. Perhaps you can help me with this paperwork. I'm afraid I'm a bit behind on my filing. Shouldn't be but a couple hours and we can get all caught up," Doc suggested, barely able to suppress the grin trying to escape his face. Garrett's own expression sank in noticeable despair.

"Ah...certainly sir. I'd be only too glad to give you a hand," Garrett reluctantly answered, his tone, however, doing little to conceal his disappointment.

"Well, that would be of some help. Of course, that is if you don't have something else that needs your attention. After all, it is coming on Saturday night and I would understand. Perhaps you have some laundry to attend to or socks that need darning," Doc suggested.

Garrett realized he was being trifled with. His mood swung back.

"Since you asked, I do have plans. But only if I'm not needed here?" Garrett offered.

That was enough, Doc thought. He'd had his fun, his little joke. Time to let his young nephew off the hook.

"These plans. They wouldn't have anything to do with a certain young lady we both know, would they?" Doc asked, though they both knew the answer.

"I'm not sure I know who you mean," Garrett said, still trying to avoid committing to anything.

"The hell you don't boy and if I was your age, I'd be setting my sights on a fine young woman just like her, just like my Mary was," Doc insisted. "Now, be off with you and enjoy yourselves. Time goes by quickly. Waits for no man."

***

Garrett arrived at Mercy's cottage just a little before six o'clock. He wore a newly pressed suit and had a freshly laundered shirt on. A bit of hair cream to slick down his unruly strays atop his head and a slight touch of cologne to complete what he hoped was his best appearance. He held a boutique of fresh flowers out as he knocked on the door, waiting for Mercy to greet him. He was a bit surprised to see Addy instead, standing on the inside as the door opened. She smiled up at him, delighted to be involved in what she saw as the beginnings of a romantic encounter.

"Oh, Doctor you look swell. Please do come in. Miss Mercy will be along directly," Addy said, in what Garrett thought must have been a well-practiced greeting she and Mercy had worked on. Fine he thought. He could certainly play along, thinking it was all part of a plan on Mercy's part not to appear too eager.

"Well, young lady, I trust the mistress of the house isn't just yet ready to receive company?" Garrett said, falling into character.

Addy's smile seemed to brighten even more, seeing that Doctor Harrington was going along with the scene she saw her playing a role in.

"She will be out presently. Would you care to come in and wait?"

Garrett accepted the invitation, stepping through the doorway into the cottage.

"Oh, are they for Mercy?" Addy asked, pointing to the flowers Garrett held in his hand.

"Yes, they are indeed," he said, pulling out one of the flowers from the boutique and holding it out for Addy. "But I am sure she won't mind if I present you with one of your own."

Addy gingerly accepted the offering with what Garrett perceived to be ever so slight a curtsy. If she had enjoyed their little banter before, she was enthralled with it now. She had long had her fairytale dreams of gentlemen and princes charming a fair lady. But now, standing in front of her was the most handsome of men she believed there could ever be and he was delighting her with a special tribute of a single flower that no one, not even her Billy, had shared with her before. Her face turned to an even deeper shade of blushing red.

"Perhaps I can put them in a vase?" Addy finally said, becoming embarrassed by unfamiliar feelings welling up inside her for a second time in her young life.

Garrett handed her the bouquet of flowers and she was off quickly to the kitchen to fetch a vase. Her own flower she would be certain got its own glass to rest there on her nightstand next to her cot.

Just then, Mercy appeared in the doorway of her bedroom, off from the living room, and when Garrett caught sight of her he was dumbstruck. He had always thought her a handsome woman, but this vision before him was more than he had expected. Her dress accentuated every graceful curve of her statuesque body. Her hair was done up in perfect waves of delicate curls that flowed down around her shoulders and her face prepared with no more than just a hint of rouge and red lipstick. Yes, he thought, he had seen her nicely attired at Miss Emily's Harvest Ball, even knew how she could fill out a pair of simple women's slacks and a jacket, but this was altogether different. She was the prettiest thing he believed he had ever laid eyes on and having lived in Boston surrounded by all the fine women of the town, he knew he had seen much for comparison.

"Is something wrong?" Mercy asked, not sure why Garrett just stood there, staring, not a word, "I did my best to clean up. I know you are used to seeing me a little less...well, formal?"

Garrett quickly snapped to his senses, shaking his head with significant energy.

"No, nothing wrong. It's...my God you are just so beautiful," he finally blurted out.

Mercy smiled, feeling her face starting to heat up.

"Oh, you are far too kind sir," she replied, hoping her hint of humility was convincing. In truth, she felt her heart softening even more towards him. She had worried it might be too early to have such feelings again, somehow a betrayal of her fiancé only gone these some ten months. But many people had already lived a lifetime in the few short years the war had gone on.

Hearing Garrett's words now lifted her from the gray mist of emotion she sometimes still found herself lost in. She had been unsure of what the future might bring, unwilling to let the past slip from the tight hold she felt a need to keep on it.

By now, Addy had returned with the flowers in the vase, showing them to Mercy to see.

"Doctor Harrington brought us flowers. Aren't they beautiful? These are for you. He had one picked out special just for me," Addy grinned. She was finally feeling a part of things, her own place with Mercy.

Mercy looked at the flowers, admiring the many colors of the blossoms. So late into the Fall they still brought the summer's warmth into the house.

"They are indeed beautiful Addy. We are both very lucky ladies, aren't we?" Mercy smiled, being sure to include the young girl. Though it had only been a few short weeks since she discovered Addy among the stone ruins above the cliffs of Wellfleet, she was already growing quite attached to her; protective.

"Well, you two best be on your way. It's getting late. I'll be fine here. Have chores need looking after," Addy said, sounding like an older sister rushing off the couple.

"Perhaps we can bring you back some dessert?" Garrett suggested. Addy nodded her head.

"Oh, that would be wonderful. We can all share some together," Addy eagerly accepted. It would be the end of a perfect evening she thought.

***

The Wellfleet House was already doing a brisk business by the time Garrett and Mercy arrived. They were seated in a corner of the main dining room at a small table away from most of the noise and steady traffic of waiters and busboys crossing back and forth from kitchen to tables.

As they looked over their menus, Garrett continued to steal glances over the top of his at the beautiful woman seated before him. He slowly drank in every nuance of her being, silently congratulating himself on having at least enticed her to come this far with him. He knew she was no doubt still trying to deal with the emotions of having once fallen in love, of having had an engagement ring placed on her finger with the promise of a bright and happy future only to then have it vanish all so suddenly. He knew so many that had had their lives turned upside down by the war. But here was this precious young creature, so soon turned to an unmarried widow. It only served to draw him closer to her, to want to just hold her for a moment and tell her it would all be okay. And yet, in the midst of all that had befallen her, he realized how she had still found it within herself to give shelter to a young girl who had, but a few weeks prior, been but a stranger. It made him somehow embarrassed to feel he could do anything less. He realized now he could have no hand in taking Addy from her.

The waiter had given them a respectful length of time before approaching their table again to take their order. He brought with him a bottle of wine which he said was the pleasure of the house to offer them, this being their first visit with the establishment. After hearing of the house specials for the evening, Mercy and Garrett informed him of their selection. He bowed graciously, returning to the kitchen with their order.

Garrett reached for the bottle of wine resting in the chilling stand the waiter had placed beside the table, the cork already removed.

"May I?" Garrett asked, pointing the neck of the open bottle in the direction of Mercy's wine goblet.

"Yes, I would indeed love some. Thank you," Mercy smiled.

Garrett filled her glass and then his own. He lifted his glass and offered a toast.

"To the most beautiful woman I have ever had the pleasure of knowing," Garrett offered.

Mercy was surprised but flattered. Wasn't sure how to respond. In front of her sat a man she had only just begun to know, a man other than Henry, who she had. But she already felt so very comfortable being near Garrett.

"Thank you, Garrett. Though I'm sure you have spoken similar words to others no doubt," Mercy insisted, knowing it was likely the truth yet hoping she might be wrong.

"Then you would be mistaken Miss Mercy Daniels," Garrett assured her with a voice so earnest that she knew further objection, no matter how obligatory, would be thought of as an insult to him for doubting his sincerity.

They both fell into an awkward silence again, as they had when gasping hands in the car ride home from Yarmouth. It was a silence, however, that didn't need words to fill the void. They just sat a moment, taking each other in, breaking their gaze on each other only briefly now and then to look about the restaurant filled with patrons laughing, drinking, enjoying a brief moment from their troubles, from the news of the War.

"I received a note from my Aunt Emily. She asked me to come for a visit tomorrow," Mercy finally said, bringing them back from their thoughts, "The delivery boy, Andy from the mercantile store, brought it by this morning with the weekly delivery. My Aunt still believes in writing notes. She rarely, if ever, calls me on the phone," Mercy smiled.

"Did your aunt say what it was in regards to?" Garrett asked, though he suspected he might already know. His uncle had said he would give things regarding the young girl Addy some thought and no doubt that included a visit with Miss Emily since it involved her niece Mercy as well.

"No, but there isn't much that goes on in this town or for miles around for that matter that my Aunt doesn't know about. If the menfolk have the barber shop or mercantile as a communication center for gossip, my Aunt is surely the switchboard for the women's side of things," she smiled.

Mercy looked at Garrett, studying his face.

"I suppose you didn't happen to discuss Addy with her, did you?" Mercy asked, eying him suspiciously, though doubtful Garrett would have done so. Garrett quickly shook his head.

"No, you asked me to promise I'd hold off contacting the authorities and that is what I did. I've already come to realize in just these few months that your Aunt, Miss Emily, would easily be considered the very same thing," Garrett smiled, knowing also that he was avoiding her question. He was being honest, he thought, he had not *directly* reached out to Mercy's aunt.

"Well, it won't change anything. My mind is made up. Especially after our little visit with that wretched, horrible, man of a father she has. She's not going to be turned out by me and she certainly isn't going to be forced to give up her child if she doesn't want to. Certainly not by me. My own mother gave me up. Maybe for good reason. I suppose I'll never know. But I'll have nothing to do with the same," Mercy promised, her firm determined expression confirming her feelings on the matter.

Garrett knew he had to proceed with caution now, even if he still believed it was an impossible situation for Mercy.

"Won't be easy," Garrett said, "That young girl does have family, after all."

"You don't seriously mean that despicable man she calls her father, do you," Mercy protested.

"Well...no, but there must be others. Somewhere."

"If there are, she hasn't mentioned any and honestly, I'm convinced more than ever now that she's better off with us," Mercy insisted.

"Us?"

"You know what I mean. I can care for her and with me she has family. And you are her doctor are you not?" Mercy said.

Garrett thought about.

"Well sure, I guess so. I just hadn't really considered it like that."

Garrett reached across the table, letting his hand rest on hers. She felt the connection but was somehow afraid to look him in the eyes. It was a new feeling and yet an old one; one of comfort mixed with strange yet familiar emotion.

"Mercy, I..." Garrett started to speak but found himself stumbling.

"You must be starving. I wonder where that waiter is?" Mercy abruptly changed the talk, the mood. She sensed the coming words and wasn't sure she was ready to confront her own feelings. She still felt the need for the safety of the walls she had thrown up around herself.

As if on cue, the waiter appeared carrying a tray with their dinners. He placed each silver domed covered dish in front of them and lifted the tops to reveal their meals. They began to eat, making small talk about the weather, how it was beginning to get colder at night, about people they both knew in the small town, and his uncle's pending retirement. Nothing more was said about Addy or speculation on the reason Miss Emily had asked that Mercy visit her the next day. Neither needed to offer any opinion as to what that might be about. Without a word, they both knew.

After they finished their dinner at the Wellfleet House, Garrett suggested they drive the long way back, taking the coast road rather than the mid-Cape highway. It was a clear night and the stars filled the black night as if the unseen hand of the *artist* had flung the bristles of a paint brush of white to speckle the heavens above. The stillness of that frozen celestial picture was only interrupted now and then by the lonely beam of the Nauset Lighthouse off to the north as it rotated a thin line of yellow illumination out across the vast ocean, piercing through the darkness of the night sky.

Garrett pulled the car to a stop along the coast road near the bluffs of Wellfleet. He kept the motor running to keep the car's heater on and so as not to appear too bold. For the most part, only local teenagers and lovers came to the cliffs at night to spark and grope at each other in adolescent rituals of discovery. Garrett and Mercy were neither. So, he was himself a bit surprised when Mercy leaned over and turned the key off to silence the car's motor.

She could see the question in his eyes when she did so, felt a need to say something.

"It's such a beautiful night for star gazing. Thank you for thinking to do so but with all this gas rationing for the war, we hardly can just sit here wasting it," Mercy suggested, hoping it sounded like the correct thing to do and for no other reason.

Garrett smiled. She was always saying the right thing, he thought. An answer for every situation, for every occasion. He was discovering that she had the ability of taking the uneasiness off things that might otherwise be awkward.

"Oh, of course," Garrett quickly agreed. He reached back to the rear seat and fetched a woolen car blanket neatly folded there. He opened it, wrapping it around Mercy. She took the end nearest to him and insisted he wrap it around his own shoulder. He obliged her. They sat together watching the beam of the far away light come and go through the darkness. Above them the stars seemed to be everywhere, below them the sound of the rolling waves crashing in against the rocks provided a soft, lulling music to their ears.

She felt his warmth closing in on her. She had missed that feeling, the touch of a man. It was one she had only briefly begun to know with Henry. The strong scent of a man, the feeling of strength the muscles of theirs bodies gave off, all so new with Garrett yet familiar to her again.

She was content for the first time in what now seemed like years since Henry had left, though it had only been ten months. And here she was with a man she now was beginning to realize she wanted to be with; that excited feeling of the present seemed to clash with her memories of the past. Butterflies in her stomach competing with a dull ache in her heart. She knew she had to let go of the one if she was to embrace the other.

"Garrett, I want you to know, I understand," Mercy finally broke the silence.

"Understand?" Garrett asked.

"Yes. You and I, us," Mercy answered.

He didn't need more explanation. He *did* understand. He had wanted to say it, hoped *she* was the one who might understand. He turned his body towards hers, cupped her face in his hands, leaned in and kissed her tenderly, deeply, feeling the pleasure of her soft lips on his. She let it happen, surrendering to him, every muscle in her body going limp with his caress. Then he quickly pulled himself away, embarrassed by his impulsiveness.

"Oh, forgive me. That was uncalled for, Mercy. I didn't mean to take advantage," Garrett apologized, certain he had crossed a line.

Mercy reached up and without a word, kissed him again, long and full. Her response was her answer. No words needed. They sat a little while longer, his arm around her, she nestled contently in the hollow of his shoulder.

On the drive down from the bluffs, she sat close to him in the front seat, the blanket still wrapped around her. She rested her head on his shoulder, drawing in the scent of his skin, his shirt, feeling the comfort of his body so close to hers. She knew it was time to let what *might have* been go and welcome what *might now be* into her life.

Chapter 18

Mercy arrived at her Aunt Emily's house precisely at noon just as Miss Emily's invite had requested. She knew her Aunt's insistence on timeliness. Fifty years ruled by the schoolhouse clock had become a habit not soon to be broken by retirement, not by her Aunt or anyone else. The walk from the little cottage along the coast to the hilltop mansion in Wellfleet was little less than half a mile and the day was bright sunshine with a cloudless blue sky. Even with the chilled air of the approaching winter, it was a pleasant journey.

She loved the scenes that awaited her in the village, changing with the lingering days of Fall. Wagons loaded with goods coming in from the arriving ships at the wharf, crates of live turkeys squabbling noisily in front of the Mercantile store, awaiting pick-up to be fattened for Thanksgiving dinner in a few weeks, the newly dressed up store windows beginning to display items for the holidays. Before long the sound of the few cars in town would jingle with the ring of snow chains on tires and horse drawn sleds with snow runners would soon enough replace the sound of wagons wheels clicking along on cobblestone. But for now, in these waning days of Autumn, the air seemed charged with the coming season of holidays. Time didn't move as fast out on the Cape as it did in the cities. They were still somewhere between the way things had long been forever and the modern ways things were becoming.

Mercy heard so many of the elders lamenting about how it "once was" and how the world no longer made sense to them. Yet somehow, she believed that every generation since the beginning of time had felt the same way as the days moved on and she, too, would likely one day look back and say the same. But she pushed such thoughts from her young mind, preferring to look at the world not as one changing from good to worse but simply a world simply always in transition. Life didn't always have to make sense. Things weren't either right or wrong, they just were.

As she stepped up to the great doors of Hallcroft House, her Aunt's home a top the hills overlooking the town, she stood a moment, trying to calm her anxious heart. Any encounter with her Aunt could be challenging if the two women weren't in synch on a certain subject. She also knew that today the discussion that awaited her on the other side of those massive doors would be one they had never shared.

She reached up and took hold of the doorknocker, giving it three gentle raps. Within seconds, the brass doorknob turned and the door opened.

"Why Miss Mercy, it's indeed a pleasure, won't you please come in." Aldon Barlow, her Aunt's man servant greeted her. "You grow lovelier every time I see you. Your Aunt is waiting for you. Let me show you the way."

"Oh, please don't bother. Dining room?" Mercy asked.

Aldon nodded, and waited for her to hand him her coat. He disappeared down the hallway towards the cloakroom leaving Mercy to make her much familiar way towards her Aunt. As she stepped into the ornate wood paneled dining room, she saw her Aunt already seated at the far end of the long table.

The dining room was perhaps Mercy's favorite room in the house, decorated with glass paned cabinets and a long ornately carved sideboard, displaying fine pieces of china. The walls were adorned with oil paintings of tranquil pastoral scenes or family ancestors of ions ago. The huge, almost lifelike, portrait of Emily's grandmother presided over the fireplace mantle, a commanding presence that seemed to own the very essence of the stately elegance of the room. It was a matching oil done by the same artist who had painted Aunt Emily's grandfather, the ship captain, that graced the wall of the grand drawing room just through the high arches to the right of the dining room.

Mercy walked over to where her Aunt Emily was seated.

"Aunt Emily. How are you?"

Emily jumped slightly at the sound of her niece's voice, pulled from her thoughts. She had been staring out the window at the waves crossing the Wellfleet Bay.

"Oh, Mercy dear. I'm sorry. I didn't hear you arrive. I suppose you found me lost in my thoughts. I seem to drift away a little more these days. Memories can be fleeting things. At first, one can just be thinking of something and before you know it, you are travelling further and farther back. Don't you find it so?" Emily asked.

"That happens to everyone," Mercy insisted.

"Indeed, all the same, perhaps it's just a sign of age, of getting to a point where there is more to remember of days past than days ahead to anticipate," Emily suggested. Mercy wasn't sure how to respond. She understood but yet this wasn't the sort of thing she knew her Aunt to dwell on. For the most part, her Aunt had more or less always had a rather positive outlook towards things.

"I had a lovely walk on the way here," Mercy said, hoping to shift the mood back to a lighter subject. "The town is bustling. I suppose there is an increase in ships going into port as well before the first signs of the bay freezing."

Emily knew what her niece was doing and was willing to take the bait.

"Yes, I've been watching out the window. The town does seem to grow more every year. Even heard Mr. Dilts at the horse livery is thinking of buying an automobile. Going to use it as a taxi he says. Imagine that, Wellfleet with a taxi service. What next?" Emily laughed.

Miss Emily turned around in her chair to face the table, motioning for Mercy to take a seat. She reached for the silver teapot and poured out a cup of tea for Mercy and another for herself.

"Are you hungry, my dear. I believe there's some soup warming on the kitchen stove. Care for some?" Emily offered.

"I'm actually quite fine. I had a late breakfast. Was somewhat occupied at the house before I came here," Mercy said, hoping instead to get to the matter of their visit.

"I'm sure you have been. *Occupied* that is," her aunt agreed.

"Perhaps we can just get to the reason you asked me to stop by. Truthfully, it was a bit unexpected and I was concerned. Is everything all right? It seemed urgent that you would send a note requesting I come the very next day. I assume there is something of importance?" Mercy asked, knowing full well that there was.

Emily studied her niece's face, a slight smile escaping from the corners of her mouth.

"we are much alike, you and I. Right to the point it is then. I understand you have taken in a young girl and she being with child."

Here it finally comes, Mercy thought. Her Aunt Emily had found out. If not Garrett, perhaps Doc Harrington, perhaps any number of others in their small world. But once again her Aunt Emily was ahead of things.

"Yes, her name is Addy. I found the poor thing wandering the old stone ruins up on the bluffs. Heard crying at first. Couple of nights. Was beginning to think I was hearing the ghost of Goody Hallet," Mercy said.

"Oh, that old tale," Emily scoffed, trying to appear casual as if they were just discussing a lost pet or something.

"Anyway, I finally got up enough courage to take a lantern and go have a look for myself. Came across the poor child, cold and shivering, just standing there, staring out to the sea below. Pitiful sight. I couldn't just leave her there. Took her home, sat her down by the fire, gave her some warm broth. Wasn't until I coaxed her out of her wet over garment did, I see she was pregnant,"

"I understand she's but a young child herself," her Aunt said. Mercy sensed she knew a lot more than she was letting on.

"Yes, maybe sixteen. Least ways that's what she told us," Mercy confirmed.

"Us?" Emily repeated.

"Yes, Garrett and I," Mercy answered.

"Oh, it's *Garrett* now is it? Not Doctor Harrington? How interesting. We'll leave that for later," Emily said. "Right now, I'd like to hear more about this young girl, this stray as it were, that you apparently have taken in."

"She's not a *stray.* She has family," Mercy insisted, her tone becoming defensive.

"Then why hasn't she returned to them. Do they not want her?"

Miss Emily knew the answer even if Mercy did not explain. The girl was a child herself, unmarried, carrying a baby of a man who obviously hadn't been willing to take responsibility. Emily knew only too well how *society* viewed such situations.

"It's complicated," Mercy offered.

"I'm sure it is Mercy. But do you think it wise to meddle in any of this? I know where your heart is surely.

But the reality of it...well...it's cause for thought. Why is this so important to you that you would complicate your own life. Haven't you had enough to worry about already?"

"Do you mean losing Henry?" Mercy asked.

"Well, yes, certainly that's part of it," Emily acknowledged.

"Or do you mean that my own mother gave me up for adoption and I've lost the two other people in my life that gave me everything I wouldn't have had if they hadn't taken me in?" Mercy said, the emotion so raw in her voice as to leave no doubt how deep the hurt lay.

Emily tensed, seeing the tears welling up in this young woman she loved. She felt her chest tighten. Her own strength to hold back the truth quickly wavering. She had long thought of the coming of this very moment. It was time, perhaps way past the time, she thought.

"Mercy, I never meant to abandon you."

Mercy didn't understand. Heard her Aunt speaking but the words somehow didn't register.

"Did you hear me, Mercy? I never wanted for it to be this way. I wasn't given any choice. You must understand that," Emily whispered, her trembling hands reaching out to take hold of her daughter before her.

"I...don't understand. Are you saying the woman who gave me up is *you*? You are my...*mother*?"

Mercy felt like she was suddenly suffocating. Her chest pounded as her mind grew numb by what it was trying to process.

"Why?! Why?!" she heard herself screaming inside herself in what seemed like a disembodied voice.

Emily tried to somehow find the words. She had formed a thousand ways over all these years of explaining what she was now finally revealing and now nothing seemed the right. She could not even begin to find a way to answer her daughter. She had envisioned this day, this reckoning, a thousand times and now, now that the moment was upon her, she had no idea how to navigate such fearful waters.

"You have to understand, I wasn't given a choice. I was but a young girl just as you are now. I knew nothing of the *consequences* of love, only the beauty my careless heart envisioned. He was so charming, so attentive. I thought I knew what love was, that it couldn't be something that could bring harm," Emily pleaded with her to see.

Mercy could only listen, frozen in place. She had always known from the time she was old enough to understand that her mother and father were not those who had brought her *into* the world. But she knew them as the parents who brought her *up* in the world. When they were lost in the island ferry sinking, she mourned their loss like any child would parents. But she had Henry in her life by then and had his strength to help her through. And she had her *Aunt Emily* as well, though she knew she was not blood but just a family friend who it seemed had always been there for her whenever she needed her.

"Please, I have never abandoned you. I have been right here all your life. I had to do what was best for you. I gave you to your parents because I loved you. Your adoptive mother and I had been friends since childhood. You know that. Your parents couldn't have children. They had tried and tried. But to no avail. And so, when I got into trouble as I did, my own father sent me away to avoid the scandal that would surely follow and it was decided you would be given to the only two people who I felt deserved you and I could still be in your life. Times were different. Even more so then today. An unmarried woman with child would be an outcast from society, her child a bastard without a surname."

Emily tried to explain. Her heart was beating so fast she thought she would collapse. She continued to hold on to Mercy's hands, afraid if she let go Mercy would run from the room.

"But all these years? Surely you could have found a way...some way to tell me the truth," Mercy asked. There was no harsh anger in her voice, just a soft anguished pleading.

"How many times I had wanted to do just that. But I promised your mother, my friend, that I would not destroy the relationship she had with you merely for my own benefit. As far as you were aware, your birth mother had not been able to keep you. That much was the truth," Emily offered.

Mercy looked into the old woman's eyes. She saw the pain, slowly allowed herself to even understand.

"And your mother and father gave you all the love they had to give. I did not hand you over to strangers. I was always there to be sure if they needed help, I provided it. Just as I have done now with you these several years since their passing,"

Mercy sat, still dumbstruck, taking all of it in. It was so much. Too much. But she had always loved her Aunt. She had always felt a special bond towards her. Perhaps now, for the first time, she truly understood why. She was unable to feel anger. She looked at the aging woman in front of her, saw the tears, the trembling figure before her and her heart nearly broke from the image.

"It's okay. Somehow, I suppose I do understand, mother," Mercy said in a hushed voice, trying to comfort the woman, who just minutes ago she had only thought of as her aunt. At the sound of the word, mother, Emily Wescott lost all remaining composure and allowed herself to let go of the weight she had carried all these many years. She began to cry openly, her sobbing chest heaving up and down in the chair.

Mercy put her arms around the woman, offering her as much comfort as she capable of giving at the moment. She had always loved her aunt but she wasn't all that sure how that may have changed in the last few minutes. She, herself, needed time to take all of this in. And yet here, now, she somehow found herself giving solace to a woman that had just confessed a terrible secret kept hidden all these years.

"Please, we're fine, you and I. I just need a little time to process all of this," Mercy said, trying to reassure her.

"If I could have changed anything. If I could have told you sooner, when you were younger, oh how I now wish I had. But after your mother Rachel and your father William were lost, I couldn't share the truth with you then. I feared it all would have been too much for you in your grieve. Then, in time, it just seemed so much harder for me to find the words."

"So why now? Please, I am so very glad you did. Don't misunderstand. But why now?" Mercy asked.

Emily studied her daughter's face, saw the confusion, saw the anguish fresh in her eyes.

"Because I somehow believe you feel obligated to give a home to this young girl you have taken in simply because you, yourself, had been adopted. And that's not a reason alone to make such a commitment to someone when your own entire life lays ahead of you," Emily said.

"I won't say that's not part of it. But it's not all of it. I just can't turn her out with nowhere to go, with no family to accept her. Whatever the circumstances were that you, my own mother, faced, that forced you to give me away, I don't want her facing the same thing. Surely, you more than anyone, must truly understand that. It's a decision that would be taken from her, made by the authorities, by the State. Not by a mother as it should be. If living with me, sharing my home and table, can prevent that, no matter the added hardship, what else am I to do. What would any Christian woman do? What would *you* do given the choice? A choice I now understand you never had?" Mercy asked.

Emily looked at her daughter, feeling prouder of her than she had ever been. Here, before her, was a young woman with miles of wisdom already earned.

"That is why I wanted you to come and see me. If I felt it was time to reveal one terrible truth, long overdue, it is only right that I offer help on another situation," Emily said.

"I'm not sure I understand," Mercy questioned.

"This home was built for a family. It has many rooms. I have been blessed with things I would have never had on the modest pay of a school teacher. This house needs the sound of laughter, of young people, of children. Let me give you and that young charge of yours that much. I know it can't make amends for the past, but it may help make the future right."

Mercy felt as though the weight of a thousand stones were being lifted from her. It would be the answer to all her problems, to Addy's problems. But Mercy also realized it might be more than her mother could deal with. She was advancing in years and didn't possess the energy and strength perhaps needed to watch over a teenager with child in tow.

"I can't let you do that...Mother," Mercy said, despite the desire to say just the opposite, "You're not a young woman anymore."

Miss Emily's eyes widened, a look of indignation flashing across her face.

"Oh, is that so, young lady?!"

Mercy realized a moment after the words left her mouth that they had been a mistake.

"I can still put the fear of God into folks half my age and make the strongest man, woman, or child run from my approach if I've a mind to. In that you should have no doubt!" Emily assured her. Mercy smiled. She certainly now knew where her own defiance came from.

"Besides, you and that young doctor of yours, where do you think that's going. You will want a life of your own, likely with him, I dare say soon enough no doubt," Emily insisted.

Mercy blushed at the thought.

"Oh mother," Mercy exclaimed, finding the term much to her liking, "You are terrible. Neither of us have talked of anything of the sort."

"There's no need to. I don't know everything but I've certainly seen my pairing off of young people in my life. It's nature, pure and simple. But we will talk of such things again at another time. Right now, I need you to go home and think about what I have said. I don't see it as an option. I'm certainly not offering it as a decision that needs to be made. As far as I'm concerned, it's already been made. You should see it that way too. Bring this young girl to see me. I gained a daughter back today and am ready to replace the spot you left as my niece with a new one!"

At that, Mercy lost whatever composure she may had been struggling to hold on to and again threw her arms around her mother, kissing her on the cheek.

Chapter 19

Though it had been but a few weeks, to Addy it seemed as if a lifetime had passed since she had come to live with her new family. First, in the safety of Mercy Daniel's cottage along the bluffs and now these even more amazing days with Miss Emily. The memories of the loveless days with her father, then the wandering alone, seeking shelter wherever it could be found, now seemed distant memories. At times, she even began to wonder if they had truly ever happened. To be given a home, one so beautiful as Halcroft House, and the care of a woman, who had so quickly become like a mother of her very own, convinced Addy that maybe there were miracles after all.

There were clean sheets on her bed which itself was as soft as any she had ever known. Clean, pretty dresses awaited her in her very own closet, which itself she believed was as big as her father's entire house. It was outfitted with shelves, racks with hangers, and even a miniature crystal chandelier to illuminate the interior.

Truly, she thought not even a princess could boast a better wardrobe.

Meals of every imaginable taste and delicacy served as she was waited on in a room of such grandeur and size she never thought could exist. And in the midst of all of this, Addy grew larger, healthier, closer to her time. Doctor Garrett attended to her with weekly visits. There was to be a "Christmas baby" he smiled, which only made her happier than she felt she deserved to ever feel.

But despite all this, one morning as Miss Emily and her young charge sat sharing breakfast, Addy found herself still doubtful, still wrestling with the same question that had persisted from the very moment she had been told by Mercy of the decisions being made for her. Afraid to ask, for fear it would suddenly become all too clear, afraid not to ask for fear if she wasn't somehow constantly reminded, it might turn out that all of this was to be only a brief stay until the baby arrived and nothing more.

"Miss Emily?"

"Yes, my dear, what is it?" Emily asked, seeing that look again on Addy's face and almost instantly knowing. She put her tea cup down to focus on the young girl.

"I...it's just...I still don't understand..."

"My dear child, what is there to understand. It's all so very simple, young lady," Emily interjected, certain of the question and with a desire to quickly push away Addy's fears.

"You see, I needed someone, someone just like you to share my days with. I once had a daughter. Well, truth is I still do. But I gave her away when I was a young woman not much older than you. This is my chance to make amends for that, though honestly, I truly wasn't given a choice. So, God sent you to me and now we have each other. It's not all that hard to understand, now is it," Emily smiled, reaching out and grasping Addy's hand reassuringly.

Addy jumped from her chair, throwing her arms around the older woman in a strong embrace. Miss Emily felt herself sinking limp into her chair. Of everything she had done for this young child, of everything she might do for her in the future, at that moment, it all seemed far more a gift to herself, Emily Wescott, than she might ever have hoped to receive. God does indeed work in mysterious ways she thought.

"Now, now, enough of this my child. Your breakfast will be cold. Promise me we will not have any further words on why we are together. Let us both agree that it's simply a matter of two people who needed each other and found a path to one another."

Their moment together was interrupted by the sound of the great door knocker being hammered against the front door. They both could hear the footsteps of Aldon Barlow going to answer it. A few seconds later, Mercy appeared in the archway to the dining room. She was bundled up in a heavy coat, her cheeks rosy red from the chilled air outside. She had a wrapped bundle of pretty pink floral paper under her arm.

"Well, this is indeed a surprise," Miss Emily said smiling. She now had the two most cherished people in her life in the same room. Daughter and granddaughter as she now saw them both.

Mercy entered the room, giving a hug to Addy and lightly kissing the top of Miss Emily's head, who reached up to caress the side of her daughter's face.

"And what have we here," Miss Emily asked, certain they were intended for Addy.

Mercy placed the package in front of the young girl, bidding her to untie the string that held the bundle together. Like a child at Christmas, Addy beamed with excitement as she worked the knot and peeled back the beautiful wrapping paper from Jacob's Mercantile Store. As the folds fell away, several fine garments were revealed. She lifted the first one up, holding it to the light. It was made of a white fabric with delicate flowers embroidered in a line along the garment's collar. To Addy it appeared to be a sleeping gown. But this was not mere cotton sack cloth as she had long been used to but a finer fabric, she was not familiar with. She looked up at Mercy with questioning eyes.

"It's silk, sweetheart. A dressing gown for you after the baby arrives. You will want to be comfortable but nicely dressed when your visitors come to pay their respects to the new mother and baby," Mercy said. Miss Emily nodded in approval. She was enjoying every moment.

Addy lifted up the next garment. In fact, she noticed there were several similar to this one under it, small, almost doll size.

"And those are for the baby. Have to be sure she will be warm," Mercy said.

"Or he," Miss Emily quickly said, "You never know."

"Just as long as it's healthy," Mercy added.

Addy leaped up from her chair, throwing her arms around Mercy. She had never known such happiness. She wanted to tell them but every time she tried the words somehow didn't come. Words weren't nearly enough she thought. She twirled around the room, holding the dressing gown up against herself, dancing like a young ballerina for the amusement of Mercy and Emily. She danced about the room to the music playing in her head and heart that only she could hear.

After a while, she began to feel tired. She felt dizzy from all the excitement. Felt a warm sensation overtaking her deep from within her. She plunked down in her chair, her face flush from her sudden exertion of energy. She looked up at Mercy, who now had a look of concern on her own face. Mercy was staring down at Addy's waist. A wet spot of red had started to form on Addy's day dress.

Addy followed Mercy's eyes to the spot, then looked quickly at Mercy and Emily, seeing their expressions, growing scared.

"What is that?!" Addy demanded to know.

Both older women knew something was wrong. Bleeding at this stage of the young girl's pregnancy was never good.

"You come with me," Mercy insisted, taking Addy by the hand and walking her slowly towards the stairs. She was trying to be as gentle as she could be but she knew she had to get Addy laying down and then get on the phone quickly with the doctors.

"You're okay," Miss Emily assured her, as she followed both of them up the stairs. She yelled out to Aldon to call Doctor Harrington immediately. Aldon answered, asking which one.

"Either one! And be quick about it. Tell them the child is bleeding and may be going into labor," Emily called back down to Aldon as all three women ascended the stairs. Aldon, who was now standing at the bottom of the stairs, quickly ran off to phone Doctor Harrington. It was the older Doc Harrington that answered.

"Doctor, you've got to come quick. The little girl, she's starting to bleed. Miss Emily said you best get over here right away," Aldon insisted. He waited for Doc Harrington to answer but the line went dead while he was still holding the phone.

It wasn't but what seemed a few minutes before there was a great knocking commotion at the front door. Aldon quickly swing the door open, revealing both Doc Harrington and Garrett breathlessly standing before him. No words needed exchanging as both men hurried past Aldon and climbed the stairs.

"Mercy?" Garrett called out.

"Up here, down the hall," Mercy shouted, the panic in her voice telling Garrett it was something serious. He and his uncle proceeded quickly down the long dark hallway towards the sound of Mercy's voice.

Garrett was first to enter the bedroom, followed by his uncle who was already quite winded from the rush over from their office. What they saw was indeed cause for alarm. There, sprawled out on the bed, lay Addy, the blood beginning to truly soak her undergarments and bedsheets. Mercy had managed to get the young girl's day dress off but daren't proceed with jostling her any further for the reminder of her garments.

Garrett walked quickly around to the far side of the bed as his uncle leaned down on the near side to feel the girl's pulse and forehead. She was slightly warm to his touch but not alarmingly so, though he noticed her pulse was elevated, possibly from being scared from all the other worried looks around her.

"Best let us have a look. I'm sure it's nothing. A little bleeding, especially this close to full term, isn't unusual," Doc Harrington assured the others, though he knew it wasn't something all that common. He opened his black bag and started to lay out some of his instruments.

"Miss Emily, perhaps you can have the kitchen staff bring up a large bowl of hot water. Going to need to sterilize a few things."

Miss Emily pulled the summoning cord hanging down from the bedroom wall to alert the kitchen she needed help but Aldon, who had been standing outside the doorway all the while, answered her.

"On my way," Aldon said, quickly traversing the length of the hallway and down the great stairs. Doc Harrington gently lifted the hem of Addy's slip, offering a reassuring smile while keeping eye contact with her to help calm her.

"Mercy, would you please give me a hand here," Doc said, motioning for Mercy to help remove the rest of Addy' s undergarments below her waist. Miss Emily pulled a chair over along the head of the bed and took the young girl's hand, comforting her.

"You are going to be just fine, my dear, just fine. Don't you worry. Doc Harrington has been delivery babies for as long as anyone around here can remember. Couldn't ask for anyone better and here you are with two doctors to look after you," Miss Emily assured her, patting her hand to reassure her.

Aldon and one of the housemaids returned a few minutes later carrying a huge bowl of steaming water and a stack of clean white towels. Doc Harrington placed his medical implements in the water. Using a pair of tongs to lift each one out after a few minutes, he laid them out on a cloth he had spread on the night stand next to the bed. He poured a bottle of rubbing alcohol into the bowl of water and rinsed his hands before donning a pair of surgical gloves. He handed a second pair to his nephew telling him to do as he had.

"Now, you just relax young lady. This won't hurt you a bit. No different than all the other check-ups you've had," Doc Harrington insisted.

He slowly began his examination, carefully inserting a speculum to gain a better look at what might be the source of the bleeding. He noticed immediately that her cervix had already begun expanding, showing clear signs of the onset of labor. Then he found the problem. Her uterus was blocked, likely from the placenta having shifted. The bleeding had been caused by that internal event and there was now a clear danger that the fetus might not be receiving the minimum blood flow from its mother.

Doc Harrington looked up at Garrett, knowing he could likely now see it as well and would know what it meant. Though still young to the practice of medicine, he was sure his nephew had witnessed enough births at Boston General to have likely run into this condition.

"What do you think, uncle?" Garrett said, knowing only too well the answer.

"Not sure we can wait. She's near full term as it is, shy one or two weeks at most. Best not risk it," Doc Harrington said in a hushed tone, trying to keep Addy from hearing his thoughts.

"Here?" Garrett asked, referring to what both doctors knew would have to be a cesarean birth.

Doc Harrington thought it over. Such a procedure was quite common, especially when there could be issues with a vaginal birth. But such things were normally conducted in a hospital with all of the needed tools and facilities ready at hand. To do so in the bedroom of the patient was turning back the clock a hundred years or more.

"No, too risky. She's only just started bleeding. Maybe less than an hour ago. But I'm not pleased with the idea of sitting her up in my car and go bouncing down the highway," Doc said. "I can have Aldon bring around the Packard. Plenty enough room to lay her out in the back seat," Miss Emily suggested.

"That will have to do. Less than ten miles anyway. Pretty short trip. Garrett, while we get the car ready, call the hospital. Tell them we are on our way. They'll need one of the surgical rooms prepped. Tell them I think it's a placenta previa case," Doc instructed him. Garrett started immediately for the door, Mercy following right behind him.
Doc Harrington called after her.

"Where are you going young lady?" he asked.

Mercy turned around, looking a little surprised at the question.

"To get my hat and coat, what else?" she replied. Doc started shaking his head.

"Not sure that's a good idea. Garrett and I will handle things from here."

"You don't seriously think for one moment I'm leaving this young girl's side, do you?" Mercy insisted. The forcefulness in her tone clearly suggested it wasn't a point open to debate.

"Well...okay. But we'll need your help then to get Addy down to the car.

Garrett returned to the room a moment later, informing them that he had called the hospital and that Aldon had the car waiting at the front door, the motor of the immaculate shiny black 1940 Packard running with the heater turned on full. Together, Garrett and Mercy lifted Addy from the bed, supporting her on each side as they made their way down the hall to the stairs and the front door below. Doc Harrington and Miss Emily were right behind them.

"You make sure you call me, Lee," Emily said, one of the rare times she referred to him as such in the company of others.

"Yes, of course, of course. It will be fine. We caught it in time. We said there'd be a Christmas baby in this old house. Going to keep my promise," Doc assured her even though he, himself, still had some concerns. Bleeding was never a good thing and the baby was, as near as he could tell, still a few weeks early.

Bundling Addy up warmly in several blankets, they eased her into the back of the massive automobile. She laid down with Mercy climbing in next her, resting Addy's head on her lap. Garrett took the wheel with his uncle sliding into the front passenger seat. They worked their way down the narrow winding road from Wellfleet out onto the mid-Cape highway. From there it was only a short ride before they were pulling up to the front door of the Cape Cod Hospital in Hyannis Port. A team of orderlies with a wheeled stretcher greeted them, helping to lift Addy on to the cushion and rolling her into the hospital. Addy grew even more anxious once inside. She had never been in a hospital before and the smell of antiseptic, the strange green tiled hallways, and the bustle of people rushing about in white coats seemed like another world to her. But as each nurse came to help, their soft soothing tones easing her fears, Addy felt herself growing calmer. She now seemed the focus of so much attention. She liked that, made her feel special like Miss Emily did.

Addy watched as a man dressed in what to her appeared to be a buttonless, pullover gown, the kind she had only seen women wear, approached her and Doctor Harrington. By the way the two greeted each other, she could tell they must be friends.

"Addy this is Doctor Boyd. He's going to help us with the birth," Doc Harrington said. Doctor Boyd extended his hand, taking Addy's with a reassuring grip.

"A pleasure to meet you, young lady. I hear we need to get you prepped for your big event. Do you have any questions before we do?" Doctor Boyd asked. He had the same smoothing tone as Doc Harrington.

Addy looked up at Doc Harrington, eyes questioning.

"Oh, you will be in excellent hands, young lady. Doc Boyd here is an expert at bringing newborns into the world. But never you fear, Doc Garrett and myself will be right there assisting," Doc promised.

He still didn't want to scare Addy by talking about the need for a cesarean birth. They would give her something to put her in a twilight state to numb any pain while still awake when they handed her the newborn to hold.

Addy settled down, letting Mercy take her hand as they wheeled the stretcher down the hall and into the prep room just outside the operating room. A nurse entered, asking who was the primary physician. Garrett stepped forward.

"Good then, I just need some information Doctor," the nurse said matter-of-factly, as though it were just another routine event she had attended to a dozen times that day.

Garrett answered her questions as best he could though for the most part, he, nor anyone, knew the answers. Date of birth, any known illnesses, allergies. Nothing Garrett could really provide other than blood type and approximate age. Then the nurse disappeared as quickly as she had appeared, off to help with any last-minute items.

As soon as the surgical staff had finished prepping Addy, they wheeled her into the operating room. Mercy, still at her side, started to go with her as well but Doc Harrington gently touched her arm, signaling that for her it was as far as she could go. She let go of the young girl's hand, giving her a reassuring smile.

"Everything will be fine. You have the best doctors anywhere. I'll be right out here waiting," Mercy promised her, as the double doors closed behind her.

Once inside the sterile looking pale green room, Addy's eyes began darting back and forth, taking in the strange surroundings. But Doc Harrington and Garrett were there, right beside her. It helped ease her fear. The attending nurses lifted her gently from the stretcher to the white clothed covered table in the center of the room. She found herself under the bright lamps hanging above her. A nurse rubbed her arm with a soft pad of cotton and what felt like a cooling wetness as the alcohol swab cleaned a spot on her inner arm. She felt a slight pricking sensation as another nurse slid the point of a needle under her skin. They taped it down and connected a clear thin tube which began to provide a dripping flow of clear liquid traversing down into her arm. Then another nurse, standing on her other side, inserted the needle of a small syringe. Almost immediately Addy felt a warm sensation come over her as her whole body began to relax. She felt sleepy. She stared up at all the movement around her, as though she was witnessing it all without being a part of it. The nurses then positioned a screen across her midsection, blocking off her view of her lower half.

"How do you feel Addy? Comfortable?" Doc Harrington asked.

She looked up at him, unable to focus her eyes on his familiar face. She tried to answer but found it difficult to speak. She seemed to only be able to mouth the words, just nodding, a slight smile forming on her lips. She felt giddy, as though she didn't have a concern in the world.

"Good, I think we can proceed, Doctor," Doc Harrington suggested.

Doctor Boyd, sterile gloved hands raised, approached her from the foot of the table. He picked up a scalpel and proceeded to make a fine incision across Addy's lower abdomen. A trickle of blood followed behind the cut, increasing as he went slightly deeper. One of the nurses kept pumping up and releasing the valve of the blood pressure cuff tightly wound around Addy's arm.

"How is she doing?" Doctor Boyd asked.

"One-thirty over eighty, Doctor," the nurse answered, keeping a steady eye on the gauge.

The doctor continued, cutting past the outer wall of her uterus until only a slight further incision would reveal the baby. Here it grew more critical, the need for precision ever more important to avoid harming the child with the point of his scalpel. As he proceeded, the shifted placenta that had started to detach itself from the wall of the womb, blocking the birth canal, came into view.

Just then, the bleeding seemed to quickly increase, well beyond what any of the three doctors present would have expected. They could see that the placenta had ruptured and blood was beginning to pump out into the womb rather than into the baby as it should have been. Doctor Boyd looked up at the blood pressure meter, could see by the expression of the nurse working it that something was wrong, very wrong.

"Doctor, its falling. Her pulse is dropping as well," the nurse said, a slightly alarmed tone in her voice.

"No time to waste," Doctor Boyd insisted, "Have to get the baby out while we set up a transfusion. We need to stem the loss of blood quickly. We're losing her!"

Doctor Harrington was already in motion. He grabbed one of the sacks of whole blood they had laid aside just for such emergencies. It was a match to Addy's blood type based on the information Garrett had provided in the prep room. In just a matter of seconds, Doc Harrington placed another needle into Addy's other arm and started the pump. The flow of blood was immediate. Meanwhile, Doctor Boyd worked quickly to widen the opening, gently lifting the baby from its mother's womb. He held it slightly aloft, allowing his colleague, Doc Harrington, the honor of cutting the cord. With his pending retirement, it might well be his last.

Doctor Boyd carefully felt for the rest of the cord tracing it back until he could feel the place where the perforations had caused the internal bleeding. He worked quickly to suture the tear. The flow of blood began to ease until it finally appeared to stop all together. If he didn't locate the source, he knew that even closing up the incision in Addy's womb she might still bleed to death. Within a few minutes they were relieved to see Addy's blood pressure starting to rise. Her pulse also slowly improved though Doctor Boyd thought it remained a little weak. They would have to keep a close eye on it but all three doctors felt Addy was likely now out of any immediate danger.

As Doctor Boyd worked to sew the incision in Addy's abdomen, Doc Harrington and the nurse began to quickly wipe the birth fluids from the baby, clearing out the infant's throat with a small suction bulb before he gave the child a smart little smack on its bottom. The baby's reaction was immediate and quite indignant. Her wailing cry filled the room.

They wrapped the pink little infant in a soft blanket and Doc presented daughter to mother. Addy stared down in amazement at the small creature she now held in her arms, tears streaming down her eyes. It was a miracle she thought, an absolute miracle. She looked up at Doc Harrington and Garrett, trying to say something. But they didn't need words. They knew. Though there would likely be difficult times ahead, nothing could dampen this moment in all of their lives.

"So little lady, what will we be putting down as far as a name on her birth certificate?" Doc Harrington asked.

Addy didn't hesitate for a second. She had long thought this part over and knew the answer.

"Emily Mercy Hawthorne," she declared happily, "That is if you don't think they'd mind?"

Doc Harrington and his nephew looked at each other, both nodding their heads in approval.

"Why, I believe they will be absolutely delighted," Doc Harrington assured her.

"Well, how about we get you over to a room to rest a while," Doctor Boyd suggested, motioning to the orderlies on standby just outside the door.

As they wheeled Addy down the hall to recovery, Garrett stepped away to go retrieve Mercy who had been forced to find a seat in the Waiting Room. He also had a call to make to Miss Emily, who he knew would be sitting by the phone anxiously waiting. Since it was still early afternoon, he suspected he would be heading to Wellfleet to fetch Miss Emily back to the hospital. It would be the customary few days of hospital stay for Addy, especially with her condition and he knew for certain, the grand lady herself wouldn't be put off with a wait of even a day. Certainly not once she heard the child had been honored with her namesake.

Chapter 20

As the last snows of winter slowly melted away, the Spring of 1945 blossomed with a fresh sense of hope in the world. News from Europe was encouraging. The Allied armies, having gained a foothold on the beaches of Normandy, France in June the summer before, were continuing to advance across Europe. The German armies were being pushed farther and farther back into their homeland as the Russians continued to advance from the West and the American and British Allies from the east. It would not be long it seemed before Berlin fell.

In the Pacific, the Japanese grew even more desperate as the Allied Forces recaptured island after island towards their goal of invading the mainland of Japan. Reports continued of kamikaze suicide air attacks on American fighting ships. Rumors of atrocities being conducted against civilians and prisoners of war alike persisted as the Japanese army retreated back across the very islands they had seized just a few years earlier. The last few outer islands of Iwo Jima and Okinawa were falling to the Allies; the final island strongholds before mainland Japan itself. Bombing over Tokyo and other Japanese cities night and day by Allied bombers had now brought the war to the very doorstep of the Japanese population.

On the American home front, rationing of gas, tires, food, and clothing was starting to ease even if only a little, helping to further fuel an economy that hadn't quite shed the long lean years of the Great Depression. Many of the more severely injured servicemen were beginning to make their way home from the military hospitals in Europe and the Pacific. But the troops still fighting held their course. Daily reports of plans for a final push in both Europe and the Pacific filled the headlines of every newspaper.

But to Mercy, the news of the returning soldiers and sailors only served to remind her that Henry wouldn't be one of them. Gone now almost a year, just one of the thousands upon thousands of casualties of the war, he wasn't going to be one of those youthful young men that would return, albeit older than their years would have made them.

She had made her peace with that reality months ago. As she knew only too well, she wasn't alone in such grieving. She had no right to feel unique when other families had lost so much more. The papers had dozens of such stories, none more well-known now as the Sullivan brothers and a poor mother who had lost all five sons to the war in the sinking of a single ship.

And with more and more time spent in the company of Garrett Harrington, she refocused her life now on the possibilities of that blossoming relationship more so than the fading memories of another.

As each weekend approached, when they both could take a moment for themselves from the labors of the week, her feelings towards him only grew deeper. She knew in her heart that God had blessed her, despite her troubled beginnings. True, she had indeed lost loved ones, she thought, but she had been given a gift all the same. She had found her birth mother, been given a sister in the form of Addy, and the new baby, Emily Mercy, was a blessing to them all. And most of all, to heal her wounded heart, she was rediscovery love again when God had brought Garrett into her life.

Mercy believed that all such blessings stemmed from the kind acts of the heart. In her case, she believed it had been through having been drawn to the mournful sounds of a child wandering the dreary ruins atop the bluffs of Wellfleet and in her refusal to simply turn away. Bringing Addy into her home had somehow led to discovering that her own mother had always been close by. Addy had been given the blessing of a child. All of them in turn had been given the further growth of a family of women who took strength from each other. And now, into their midst, had come a young doctor who was discovering a place among them that he had not known in the vast sea of people in a city such as Boston. It was almost more than she felt she could ask for, all too good a life when all around them lives were being destroyed by the ravishes of war. At times, it seemed to produce a mixture of emotions that in many ways frightened her.

***

Garrett arrived exactly at seven o'clock on Saturday night, just as he always did. It made Mercy smile to herself when she thought about how punctual he always was, quite the opposite of her. He had promised her a night of dancing in Hyannis Port down Cape. There was a special tavern she loved with a small but adequate enough dance floor and though he wasn't the first *beau* who had escorted her there, she knew if things continued to move along as they were, he might well could be the last.

The two had gone there once before. Good food, a nice dance floor, a jukebox with all the right tunes. It had been Mercy's suggestion then as it was now and Garrett took no issue with it though he knew the place certainly had to hold other memories of other nights for her. It was only natural, he thought, that it being one of the few places of its kind around for miles, Mercy would have visited the establishment in prior days. It didn't trouble him. If Mercy felt any connection still to Henry, it wasn't obvious to him when they were together. She had always given him her full attention, making him feel as though he, and no one else, was the center of her world. He believed that was all any man could ask for. He had no expectations that she would completely erase Henry from her thoughts and memories.

As they sat, sipping their drinks, making small talk about the things they had done the past week, they heard the sound of an argument coming from a far-off corner of the big room. The disturbance seemed to emanate from along the end of the bar. The tavern was known to get a little loud at times, especially on Saturday nights when the local fisherman finished their week out on the rough waters and came into town to let off some steam. But for the most part, Rocco's Tavern was a family place. It was only towards the later hours of the night did it become a place for singles.

From the far side of the tavern, the noise of tables being shoved, and chairs going over broke the otherwise peaceful sound of people enjoying their meals and drinks. Garrett and Mercy watched as a number of tough looking men, the bouncers the owner paid to keep peace, headed quickly over towards the source of the commotion.

"Maybe we should leave?" Mercy suggested, showing some concern. It was something she hadn't recalled ever seeing there.

"No, It's fine. Rocco's boys will sort it out quick enough," Garrett said, "You saw the size of those guys. Wouldn't want to be on their bad side, that's for sure."

And just as Garrett had spoken, the noise ended suddenly, the sounds of scuffling now only that of the two bouncers and the clearly inebriated customer being dragged between them, heading quickly towards the door. The trio passed the table where Garrett and Mercy were sitting. Mercy tried not to look up at the man being firmly escorted past them but as the bouncers approached, she caught a look at the face of the man they held upright between them. She quickly reached across the table, grabbing Garrett's hand. He looked at her then followed her eyes up to the man being hustled past. It was Addy's father, Charlie Hawthorne. Hawthorne saw them both as well. He stopped, trying to yank his arms free from his escort.

"Well, now, what do we have here? If it ain't young missy and her boyfriend. Fancy that," Hawthorne grinned, his words slurring from the overabundance of whiskey.

"That'll be enough now. Let's go," one of the bouncers said, grabbing Hawthorne's arm firmly again.

"Ah, come on. These are my friends," Hawthorne insisted, "Ain't that right?"

He leaned down as he spoke, his whiskey soaked breathe washing over Mercy's face. She reared back, disgusted.

"You know this man?" the bouncer asked, certain they didn't.

Garrett shook his head.

"In a manner of speaking though I wouldn't exactly say we're *friends*! What are you doing here anyway Hawthorne?" Garrett asked, "A bit out of your territory, no?"

"Oh, territory is it? Well I didn't know I had such a thing. Always sort of gone where I please. Besides, got business hereabouts," Charlie said, a broad grin cracking open across his face, revealing several missing teeth.

"Business?"

"Yeah, business. Bet you'd like to know. Well, you will. Soon enough," Hawthorne assured him.

"Come on. Time to go. You've bothered these nice folks long enough now."

The bouncer gave the drunk man a hefty shove towards the door. Hawthorne nearly fell over from the force. He turned his head back laughing.

"Oh, we will be seeing each other again. You and that fancy dame what's got my dear daughter living up there in that big house on the hill. You might think I didn't know about that. But I do," Hawthorne said, as they opened the door to toss him out.

"What does he mean?" Mercy said. She had hold of Garrett's hand, squeezing it tightly.

"Now don't let that old fool scare you. He's a harmless old drunk. He comes around here again we will let the police handle it. He has no rights when it comes to Addy. She's practically a legal adult anyway, can make her own decisions," Garrett assured her.

"Well, I guess you're right. He is just a thoroughly awful man," Mercy insisted.

"I have a thought. How about I stay the night at your place. Can keep an eye on you. Now that Addy and the baby are with Miss Emily, your living alone," Garrett suggested, a devilish look in his eye. Mercy let go of his hands long enough to give them a playful slap.

"Oh, I'm sure you'd love that. And I'm sure you'd love the gossip that would spread like wild fire across Wellfleet about a certain unmarried girl *entertaining* a gentleman under her roof all night with no one else home!"

Garrett was enjoying this.

"Well, I suppose I do know how we could fix that. I mean any talk of indecency," Garrett hinted. They had been seeing each other for a number of months now. He had been accepted by most everyone else in the town, including Mercy's mother, Miss Emily.

But Mercy wasn't going to let things go that easy, that unspoken. There were things that had to be said.

"I swear I don't know what you mean Mr. Harrington. For such an educated man you do sometimes surprise me with your ramblings. Whatever do you mean by 'fix it' sir?" Mercy asked, pretending she certainly had no clue, demanding he explain himself.

"Oh, I see how it is," Garrett smiled, knowing, of course, he had no choice but to play along. But if he was ready to truly talk about where he saw their future taking them, he knew this was not the place nor time. Not in the din of a noisy tavern, the sounds of patrons clinking glasses and bawdy laughter filling the air.

They continued with their dinner and their talk returned to other things. Addy and the baby, who would already be three months old the first of April just a few days from then. Both Garrett and Mercy agreed that the young mother and her child had settled in well with Miss Emily, who herself had never seemed happier. Mercy knew that Miss Emily had spent a lifetime teaching young children, but had never known the joy of raising her own, not even Mercy her own daughter, whom she watched grow up at a distance, mandated by a need to keep a dark secret. Now, as she lived out her sunset years, it had all come around; reconnecting with her own child, helping to raise another and her child. If God took pity on those he loved, Mercy was content in believing that God had truly shown her own mother his love.

Chapter 21

The first of April 1945 dawned a gray and cloudy day. The rains that had begun the evening before continued to wash the lingering snows of winter away. The sea air that blew in from the East offered a hint of the spring warming to come shortly. News had reached home that the Russian and Allied armies in Europe had entered Berlin and Germany was all but a defeated nation. Talk of a final surrender filled the front pages of every newspaper.

Miss Emily put down her newspaper when she heard the sound of someone knocking at the front door. She listened as Aldon Barlow opened it to greet whomever had come calling. But quickly, the sound changed from a peaceful greeting by Aldon to that of a louder confrontation. Whoever it was insisted he be allowed to see the lady of the house. She heard Aldon advising the stranger, a man by the sound of the other voice, that he was to wait there at the door. Miss Emily then heard footsteps approaching quickly. Aldon appeared in the dining room doorway, his face red with irritation. But before he could speak, Miss Emily saw another man, a stranger appearing next to Aldon, who turned quickly to confront him.

"Sir! I told you to stay at the door!" Aldon insisted, starting to reach out to take hold of the man, despite the stranger being somewhat larger in size.

"It's okay Aldon. I'll handle this," Miss Emily said, trying to keep her composure. She wasn't about to be the least bit intimidated by this strange disheveled looking creature, certainly not in her own home.

"Perhaps I should call the constable," Aldon said, staring hard at the man. He wasn't going to be intimidated either.

"If it becomes necessary, we will most definitely do so," Miss Emily assured them both, "Will it be necessary...I'm sorry I don't believe I caught your name sir?"

"Oh no madam. Certainly not necessary, I can assure you. My name is Charlie... Charlie Hawthorne."

Miss Emily stared back at the uninvited stranger. Addy's father. But she didn't let on that the name had any real meaning to her, though she knew his sudden appearance was no mere coincidence.

"Mr. Hawthorne, is it?" Miss Emily repeated, not a hint of concern in her voice, "Well, then perhaps you would care to have a seat. May I offer you a cup of tea?"

"Tea? Oh, wouldn't put you to the trouble. Not much of a tea drinker myself. Perhaps something a little stronger? If'n you have it, of course."

Miss Emily offered an insincere smile. No doubt something a little stronger. No surprise there, she thought to herself.

"Aldon, perhaps you'd be so kind as to fetch a glass of...*something stronger*," Miss Emily asked, leaving it to Aldon to make the choice.

Charlie Hawthorne grinned, taking a chair at the table, appearing to settle in to make himself quite at home. He looked around at the ornate furnishings, oil paintings, and the lavish table settings.

"Quite a nice place you got her madam. Quite nice indeed," Charlie said, nodding his head reassuringly.

"What can I do for you, Mr. Hawthorne. If it's work you've come to ask about, I'm sorry. I don't believe I need anything at the moment and frankly, I employ tradesmen

201

from right here in Wellfleet. I don't believe I've seen you around here before," Miss Emily said, sensing Charlie wasn't likely here looking for any work.

"Well now that's right nice of you to suggest some odd job here or there but that's hardly the reason for my visit. I'm here for my daughter. I believe you know her, Addy Hawthorne? Believe she's taken to living here, ain't that right?" Charlie said.

Aldon returned with a glass of whiskey, plunking it down in front of Charlie with no attempt at politeness.

"Why thank you Jeeves," Charlie said sarcastically, eyeing what was a little less than a half-filled glass, frowning back at Aldon to register his disappointment. He emptied the half glass of liquid in a single swallow, before turning his attention back to Miss Emily.

"As I was saying, I do hope my sweet child is doing well here. Thought it might be best to come see for myself, you know, being her father and all. I've got a responsibility."

If he thought he was being convincing in the role of a concerned father, no one else in the room was fooled.

"Oh, you should have no fears on that front, Mr. Hawthorne. I can assure you Addy is as well cared for as she might be anywhere," Miss Emily offered. She somehow believed that wasn't the real reason for the man's visit but before she could say more, Aldon interrupted.

"How much?" Aldon asked flatly.

"Sorry? I'm not sure I take your meaning, sir," Charlie feigned ignorance.

"Oh, I think we understand each other, Mr. Hawthorne. Let me speak plainly then. This is a shake down. Nothing more. You have no interest in your daughter. I believe you made that plain to others in this family some time ago. So, you happened to hear about your daughter's living arrangements. Not too shabby you thought and now you figure you can cut yourself in for some of it."

Charlie Hawthorne forced back a smile. He actually appreciated being able to dispense with all the small talk.

"I don't see a problem with that, do you," Charlie asked, giving up any further pretense as to the purpose of his visit.

Miss Emily herself had suspected it was something like that. She realized Aldon would see things as they were with this dirty little man.

"And so, you haven't come here to claim your daughter nor your granddaughter have you then," Miss Emily asked.

Charlie didn't answer right away. He wanted to see where this would go next.

"You didn't answer my question," Aldon demanded, fighting back the desire to grab hold of the miscreant sitting smugly in front of him, sipping Miss Emily's whiskey, while polluting her home with his very presence.

"Well, I wouldn't think a thousand would be too much to expect for the loss of my daughter's affection and, of course, her care of our household. Someone had to keep the place tidy and meals on the table for when I got home from a day of hard work," Charlie insisted.

"You mean a day of laying around some gin joint, soused," Aldon corrected him.

Charlie didn't answer. He just sat looking at the old woman to see what she had to say.

"That seems like a quite a lot of money," Miss Emily suggested.

"One hundred," Aldon quickly said. "And believe me that's the best offer you're going to get other than my offer to call the local Constable and have him come by."

Charlie straightened up in his chair, eyes scanning both Miss Emily and Aldon.

"Well, I'm not the sort of man to argue over money though I got to say you value my dear daughter a might on the cheap," Charlie assured him, "Cash though. Don't take much stock in checks. Too easy to cancel if you know what I mean."

"That's going to be a problem. It's not as if that sort of money is just sitting around in a drawer somewhere. I will give you forty dollars now and you come back in a couple days, say when you are finished with the jobs you got around here, and you can get the rest?" Aldon suggested.

Charlie mulled it over in his head a moment, trying to figure out where there might be a snag in the plan. But walking out of here right now with fifty, and a promise of more in a couple of days, seemed like his best and only option. He wasn't going to fall for accepting a check and he knew if he pushed it much further he might find himself facing the police. He could easily enough check things out when he came back before stepping into a trap he thought.

"Okay, I guess that will work," Charlie said to Aldon, holding up the empty glass in a failed attempt at getting a refill. He put it down and stood, facing Miss Emily.

"Ya gotta understand madam. I ain't trying to do no hold up here. Times are tough and I just figure seeing how you helped out my kid and her baby and all, you might see your way clear of extending a little help to me. It's only the Christian thing to do. I know you see things that way," Charlie said, sounding almost honest for a second. Even Miss Emily felt herself softening a little.

"But two days, that's all!" Charlie insisted, his tone betraying any plea for genuine sympathy. Aldon hadn't been fooled in the least. He'd known many the likes of Charlie Hawthorne in earlier times, in an earlier life.

Hawthorne pulled his worn hat over his head, bending down the brim in a gesture of farewell. Aldon took a few bills from a small roll of money he kept in his waist coat pocket for deliverymen and messengers, handing them to Hawthorne. Charlie started for the dining room door, followed closely by Aldon.

"Oh, that's okay. I know the way out," Charlie said, not wanting to find himself alone with this other man, who he somehow sensed wasn't a mere peaceful gentlewoman's butler. Aldon let him go but stood in the doorway to the hall watching to be sure Hawthorne went straight out.

Once the man had left, he returned to Miss Emily.

"He will be, back won't he?" Miss Emily said flatly.

"You mean for the rest of the money?" Aldon asked.

"Yes, certainly for that. But I mean after that. He's not going to go away that easy, is he?"

"Oh, now don't you worry. It'll be fine. A man like that one usually just take the table scraps they can scoop up and then clear out. He's no grifter," Aldon assured her.

"Grifter?" Miss Emily asked, truly unfamiliar with the term. It sounded like something out of one of those Damon Runyon novels.

"It's someone who...well...never mind just a term I heard once somewhere for lowlifes. Like I said, he may not even come back for the rest of the money. Probably figures he got away this time. Won't be so lucky if he sticks his neck out again," Aldon assured her, hoping it would ease any concerns she had.

But Aldon was seething with anger from the mere fact that this beloved woman was even the slightest bit upset by the whole thing. He was just glad that the visit had gone unnoticed by Addy who had remained upstairs, hopefully still sleeping.

Chapter 22

Every day, every morning, it was the same routine. The Japanese guards at the Ofuna prisoner of war camp in Japan, stormed into the crude bamboo shacks that served as the prisoner's barracks and rousted them awake, shouting for them to form a line outside for the morning roll-call. Those who hesitated, even momentarily, were quickly clubbed. The POWs, many of them mere skeletons, rose to their feet the best they could to avoid the bamboo sticks each guard held, hobbling out into what was already the oppressing heat of the scourging tropic sun. The prisoners were a collection of soldiers from many services; American, British, Australians and French. Some were taken prisoner from army units overrun by Japanese land forces. Some were downed flyers from planes shot down in air combat and others, like Henry Gates, had been scooped up out of the sea following the sinking of their ships by marauding Japanese submarines patrolling the waters off the Pacific Rim islands.

The camp had been intended only as a transfer station, where the newly captured could be interrogated, often brutally if they resisted questioning, before being shipped out to labor camps. But many of the prisoners had now been there far longer than expected. And for most, their fate was unknown by the countries they served. Even their names had been withheld from the Red Cross since Japan itself had never agreed to the terms of the Geneva Convention, which required all nations involved in the war to report on the whereabouts and conditions of prisoners they held.

The Captain of the prison guards, a man the POWs had come to call Pug for his obese size and wrinkly, short muzzled face, much like the breed of dog of the same name, waved his bamboo stick, threatening to strike any man who didn't stand upright in line. He, like most of the other guards, viewed the prisoners with contempt for having allowed themselves to be taken captive. They believed all such prisoners were inferior to Japanese soldiers, who had sworn to die at any cost for their Emperor. Such filth and cowards, Pug believed, should only be dealt with in a manner befitting their lowliness. He had no more compassion for them than he would a mosquito bothering his flesh, swatting at them at the least little irritation.

Henry Gates and the others had learned to steer clear of this one in particular. They had seen how his anger, once provoked, only ended in severe physical punishment.

"Stand up," Pug screamed in broken English at the disheveled line of men in front of him. He was one of the few guards who spoke English, though poorly at best. Many of the other guards either didn't know the English words or simply refused to speak the language of their worthless prisoners.

Another guard paced briskly up and down the rows of men, counting them as he went along. Though they were miles from any civilization, surrounded by swamps filled with venomous snakes and other creatures, the guards were meticulous about keeping an accounting of all their charges. Escape without outside aid would be near impossible. Yet, some had still tried. And all who did had failed, only to be recaptured and dragged back to the camp. Then, after a mock trial by the camp officers, the escapees were summarily executed in full view of the rest of the prisoners. Over time, further escape attempts grew rarer.

"You go now. Eat," Pug yelled, his face attempting a smile as though he was bestowing an act of kindness on them all. But other than perhaps providing the most modest of nutrition, and even that protein coming mainly from the maggots and worms that infested the spoiled rice they were fed, it was hardly a meal even the starving would rush to claim. Henry, like many of the others, found sustenance through bribing the guards with items they had either secreted with them into the camp upon their capture or tiny items they crafted from the materials they could scrounge from the scrap pile within the fenced camp.

But not every guard was like Pug. The prisoners had found that some of them could even be mistaken for almost being human. One in particular, a thin wisp of a soldier with a boy's face the prisoners had named Kilroy, routinely turned an unseeing eye or deaf ear to things. He never used his bamboo rod though he would raise it in a simulated threatening gesture when other guards were close. But before long, Henry and the other prisoners understood it was all an act and eventually risked trying to draw the young guard into their confidence. Slowly and cautiously, Kilroy became one of their trading conduits for food and other items. It was these scraps, added to their meager rations of mealy rice, that often meant the difference between life and a death by starvation for many of the prisoners.

As the months dragged on, Henry held on to the hope that if he just somehow endured, he might once again see his home, his people. But he also knew he was slowly changing inside. He began to see the world around him as a cruel one, where caring for others, even for himself, had consequences. He was slowly retreating into a world absent of all other emotions save one; survival. And so, every night, as the sun set and the prisoners were returned from their work detail to their barracks, Henry lay down on his bamboo reed mat, grateful that another day had passed. And as the months of existing in the hellish existence he endured, he let go of thoughts of home, of all other memories, even of Mercy Daniels. These things all now seemed so very long ago and distant. Hope, he found, was a dangerous thing.

Chapter 23

Charlie Hawthorne sat by himself at a table in the corner of the Barnstable Tavern. Lately, he always sat alone since there was no one else that knew him who would share his table. He had burned too many bridges with his drinking, lying, and cheating those who he might have once counted among his friends. But he didn't mind it at all, actually preferred it that way. To him, friends were just people who when you most needed them would be nowhere in sight anyway. They couldn't be counted on to fork over as much as two bits for a beer when you were down on your luck.

But tonight, he didn't need any friends to pay for his drinks. He was plenty flush as he saw it. A twenty-dollar bill in one pocket and the remains of another he had folded tightly in his shirt. Even Bill the bartender, who lately insisted on seeing coin before he'd pour Hawthorne a drink, was impressed when Charlie eased the edges of the bills out for a peek. He didn't want to produce the greenbacks in plain sight for fear those he owed drinks or money to who might be in the tavern would descend on him like vultures.

He had arrived at the tavern early enough to get a table for himself since the place always filled up with a crowd on Saturday nights. But now, as closing time approached, he found himself pretty much alone again in the near empty place, save Bill the bartender and a couple of other men he didn't know, sitting at another table across the room.

"Hey old man, how about another shot and beer. Service a bit slow here tonight," Charlie called out to Bill behind the bar. Bill put down the towel he was using to dry freshly rinsed glasses and reached for a shot glass. Bill reached over to the bottom shelf for the bottle of the cheap house whiskey that Charlie usually drank. But Charlie saw him and quickly called back out again.

"Hey not that cheap shit you old bastard. Like I told you when I came in, top shelf only tonight. You know I got it covered."

Bill put the bottle of house whiskey back and reached up for a better grade of whiskey. Then he filled a beer mug from the tap and brought the drinks over to Charlie's table.

"Seventy-five cents," Bill said, before he put the two glasses down on the table. Charlie stared up at him, pulling out a dollar bill and tossing it rudely on the tray in Bill's hands.

"Keep the change, you old bastard. More coming from where that came from," Charlie grinned, revealing a smile of more than just a few missing teeth.

"What'd ya do, rob a bank?" Bill asked, knowing even if the old drunk didn't have the talent for it, he'd probably given it more than a thought at some time or other.

"Nah, better than that. This deal don't got no bank guards!" Charlie broke out in laughter, pleased with himself at his allusive reply.

The bartender payed him no mind, certain wherever the money came from it wasn't from hard work.

"Better finish up. Closing time soon," Bill reminded him. He walked away toward the only remaining customers sitting at the table across the room and repeated himself. The two men raised their beer mugs in polite acknowledgment.

But Charlie had always been a man who kept his own schedule. Certainly, when it came to work and now as he sat enjoying the taste of good whiskey. He got up and put a nickel in the juke box like it was the middle of the afternoon and picked out a tune, an old Muddy Waters blues song, one of his favorites. As the music started, he returned to his seat amidst the glaring eyes of Bill the bartender.

"You're out of here when that's over," Bill told him. Charlie just waved him off. But he knew Bill would toss him out on his ass if it came down to it. Had before.

"You know, Billy boy. Best be careful otherwise I might take my business elsewhere."

Bill only shook his head. "Oh, you're killing me here with promises."

Bill continued putting up the glasses from the rinse water, stacking them in a neat line. He began wiping the bar top, dumping ash trays as he went along. Finally, the song ended. Charlie slugged down the rest of the whiskey from the shot glass and the few remaining sips in his beer mug. He stood, trying to find his balance for a moment on shaky legs. When he finally did, he was satisfied that he had achieved that perfect high. Still able to put one foot in front of another, although with some concentration, but as he liked to put it; *feeling no pain.*

Then in one final act of defiance, rather than bring the glasses over to Bill as most other patrons did at the end of the night after Sally the waitress had gone home to her five kids and no husband, Charlie just walked away from the table towards the door. He tossed a nickel on the end of the bar with a flare of a wealthy man.

"You'll get them, right old man?" Charlie smiled. Bill let it go. It wasn't worth an answer. Charlie walked past the table with the other two men, leaning down and *whispering* in anything but a hushed tone.

"Best be getting out of here boys before ole Bill here gives you what for! Watch him, he's a mean one!" Charlie broke out in a fit of laughter, appreciating his own sense of humor as he always did. One of the two men nodded. Both started to rise, taking their glasses toward the bar.

As Charlie stepped out into the cool Spring night air, he inhaled deeply, trying to clear his head. He stumbled a moment, taking the few steps across the wooden porch to the stairs. He halted before descending, fumbling through his coat pockets, searching for his pack of cigarettes. He found the slightly crumbled, near empty pack in his inside coat pocket and popped one out into his mouth. Then he started patting down the outside of the coat looking for a book of matches. They weren't so easily found and as he stood there, unlit cigarette in mouth with a growing sense of the need to relieve himself around the side of the building, he started cussing to himself. Charlie was the type of man who found that swearing always helped whenever something wasn't right with him.

It was then that he heard someone offering him a light and the flicker of a low flame appeared beside him.

Charlie turned, seeing the face of the man. It was one of the two men he had seen still inside the tavern when he was leaving. He leaned in, catching the flame on the tip of his cigarette. But before he could even mumble as much as a thank you, he felt the wind in his lungs rushing out of him from a sharp blow to his stomach. He started to collapse, his knees buckling. But as his legs began to give out, he felt himself being sharply hoisted up by another man who appeared to his right.

"Oh, no Charlie, can't have you falling down, not just yet," the man said, calling him by name as if they knew each other. They dragged him down the steps and across the gravel parking lot, towards the wood line on the far side, away from the dim bulb of the tavern's single porchlight.

Charlie started to call out for help but received yet another blow to his mid-section to quickly silence him. They held him up as he tried to catch his breath.

"Look what do you want?" Charlie managed to gasp, "I got some money if that's what you want?"

"Nah, we don't want your money, Charlie," one of the men said.

"Then what? I ain't never met either you guys. You don't got no grievance with me," Charlie pleaded.

As they continued to drag him across the open lot towards the dark, the lights of an automobile, parked at the edge, flickered to life. A shadowy man stepped out of a long, black, shiny Packard sedan. Charlie couldn't make out the man's features, hidden by the bright beams of the headlights.

He tried to break free from his captors, yelling for help. He watched the dark stranger approaching. He could now make out it was a finely dressed man in a long overcoat. The two men let Charlie drop, amused as he crawled desperately towards the dark figure, pleading for salvation.

"Mister, you gotta help me. These guys are crazy. They got the wrong guy. They must think I'm someone else," Charlie swore, wiping away the blood that was coming out of his mouth from the two sharp blows. The dark figure in the long coat looked down at the sniveling man at his feet, shaking his head.

"No Charlie, you see we have the *right* man. Don't you worry about that. Stand him up."

The two men jerked Charlie up on his feet. He felt his head spinning and a fresh coil of pain gripping his stomach.

The dark shadow figure brought his face closer to Charlie's so he could let the frightened man see him a little clearer. It was then that Charlie Hawthorne realized he knew the other man, had seen him before, recently. A look of fear and recognition washed over his expression.

The dark man could now tell Charlie had at last made the connection.

"Yes, Hawthorne. It's me, Aldon Barlow. I believe you weren't expecting to see me again for yet another few days. But you see I thought we needed to talk. You ran off so quickly the other day. We didn't have a chance to finish our little conversation," Aldon Barlow said, reaching up with his leather gloved hands to dust the dirt off of Charlies shoulders and straighten the collar of his jacket. This display of concern didn't provide Charlie with any real comfort. Aldon hadn't meant it to.

"You see Charlie, I'm not *exactly* who you think I am. Maybe that is where you made your first mistake. Oh, and I can promise you, it *was* a mistake. You trying to shake down Miss Wescott like you did. Just how serious a mistake? Well, that's what we're here to talk about," Aldon assured him.

"Listen, I...didn't mean no harm...honestly, I didn't. Just thought I could use a few dollars, that's all," Charlie insisted.

"So, you figured my friend, a dear kind lady who has done more for your daughter in just the past few months than you have ever done for her for her entire life, that sweet woman owed you something, is that how you figured it, did you?"

Barlow's voice quickly changed, now sounding like a hissing snake.

"Hold him up," Aldon Barlow said as he reached inside the pocket of his long overcoat. With a quick, fluid motion, he produced a knife. At the push of a button, Charlie could see the thin blade of shiny steel flick to life. The two men gripped Charlies arms so tight he thought his bones would snap. They stood him up roughly, until the toes of his feet barely touched the ground.

"Please, I ain't looking for the rest of the money. I swear. And I only spent a couple of bucks of that what you done gave me. It was all just a big mistake," Charlie pleaded.

"Yes, exactly...a *mistake*. That's what I said, didn't I," Aldon Barlow agreed, "And what do we do when we make mistakes in life, Charlie?"

"I don't know, fix em?!" Charlie offered, trying to find any words that would appease his captors.

"Sort of Charlie. You see, when people make mistakes, they pay for them, some even get punished for them. Now ain't that right? That's what we've got courts for, ain't it?" Barlow said. But Charlie knew it wasn't a question needing an answer.

"Please...," Charlie continued to beg.

Barlow reached up, patting his gloved hand in a gentle motion on the side of Charlie's face. Charlie began to sob, now growing even more afraid.

"Only you see, I ain't no Judge, no jailer. So, we've got a situation here, now don't we?" Barlow suggested, waving the knife blade slowly in a tick-tock motion back and forth in front of Charlie's face.

"Let me ask you, how much of that money I gave you got left in your pocket there?"

Charlie reached down slowly into his pocket pulling out the folded bills, showing them to Barlow in his trembling hand.

"Give them to my friend here," Barlow said, "Now how much more you got?"

"That's it. I swear. That's everything," Charlie said, carefully reaching down and turning his pants pockets inside out to reveal nothing in either of them. Barlow shook his head with a look of disappointment.

"Now see, that's what I mean by we got ourselves a situation here," Barlow repeated.

"I don't understand. I gave you everything I had. Maybe five, six bucks short. And I can get that for you, I promise!"

"Yeah, but that's what I mean by a *situation*. That's only going to cover returning the amount you stole from my friend. And we do agree you *stole* it right?" Barlow demanded. Charlie nodded his head.

"That's not going to cover your *fines*," Barlow said.

"Fines? What fines?" Charlie asked. He had been following along up until then. Now he was getting confused.

"Well, sure Mr. Hawthorne. You been on the bad side of the law before. You pays your fine or you spends your time in jail. Simple. But like I said, there ain't no fucking jail, now is there?"

But before Charlie could answer, he felt the hands around his arms tighten even further as Barlow brought the tip of the steel blade to the side of Charlie's face. He sliced Charlie's cheek open causing a gushing wound, the blood quickly flowing down his neck into the collar of his shirt. Charlie let out a scream in pain but Barlow only covered his mouth with his gloved hand to muffle the sound.

"Ssshh now, it's over, that's all. Just a little reminder for you to see in the mirror every morning so you remember not to fuck with people you don't know," Barlow whispered in his ear, motioning for the two men to release Charlie. The one man gave him a final shot to his gut, forcing Charlie to his knees.

"Now if I ever see you anywhere near Miss Wescott, if I ever so much as hear you talking to anyone about your daughter and her baby, I swear to the Devil himself, tonight will seem like you got invited to a picnic! I don't need you to answer that you understand, I know you do," Barlow said.

The three of them got back into the shining black Packard, leaving Charlie crumbled on the ground in a heap of his own blood.

As Barlow started the car, his companion held the folded money out for Aldon.

"Keep it for you troubles," Barlow said, putting the great automobile into gear.

The man peeled off a few of the bills, handing the rest to the other man in the backseat.

"No trouble at all, Mr. Barlow. Always enjoy working for you," the man assured him, taking a cigarette from his pocket, and lighting it with a flick of the metal lighter he had used to light Charlie's cigarette with. In the dim glow of the dash, the neat row of filed notches on the side of the lighter's case appeared like the teeth of a saw.

Chapter 24

Mercy thought it a bit odd that church bells began ringing on a Thursday morning, and all the more so being it was still well before noon. But the sound that they produced all at once, coming from every direction, told her it was something more than a wedding or fire. All across Wellfleet, and from neighboring towns, the sound of bells, fire whistles, boat horns and anything that could make noise seemed to fill the air.

She stepped outside her cottage door and looked out across the sand dunes towards town. She saw a multitude of cars driving up and down Main St. and could hear the drivers blowing horns. People were emerging from their homes and businesses, shouting to each other, some waving flags in a state of immense excitement. Young boys raced up and down the streets, lighting off firecrackers in what to Mercy looked like a mid-day Fourth of July celebration. But that had been over a month ago.

She ran back to the house, quickly closing the front door and then hurried down the sandy path across the dunes towards town. Whatever it was that was happening she started to feel a sense of excitement filling the air as she grew closer to Main St. She could hear yelling and cheers from the small crowd of people that had quickly begun to gather outside the town hall. People were arriving in such great numbers that the road was already jammed with cars, motors left running, doors open, drivers and passengers flooding the town square.

Mercy tried to grab hold of Mr. Parry the town druggist as he raced passed her, still wearing his white smock. Mercy yelled at him, asking what all the commotion was about.

"It's over! It's all over! The Japs have surrendered," Mr. Parry yelled as he kept running towards the crowd, "The announcement just came over the radio!"

His words grabbed hold of her, her heart leapt with the same overwhelming joy that was gripping everyone else. Over three long years and it was finally over. Germany had surrendered four months earlier. Hitler was dead. Now this. News had come a few days earlier that a secret weapon, a powerful new type of bomb, had been dropped on Japan and a few days later, another. And now, the enemy had surrendered.

Mercy started to run along Main St, caught up in a swarm of people racing towards the town center and then she saw her mother out on the front porch of the great house, Addy holding the baby, the rest of the household staff standing next to her. They were waving their arms at Mercy, beckoning her to ascend the steps, to share whatever had stirred the town to such a frenzy. She raced up the long granite steps towards them.

"My dear, what on earth?!" Miss Emily shouted, losing her characteristic composure.

"The war! It's finished. It's all over. The boys will be coming home finally," Mercy shouted in excitement. But her own words caught her up short, a feeling of sudden sadness swarming over her a second later. Everyone but Henry she thought.

Miss Emily saw the sudden change come over her daughter's expression, the look of joy becoming one of pain. As Mercy closed the few feet that separated the two women, Miss Emily threw her arms around her daughter, embracing her, guiding her towards the front door.

"Oh, what blessed news. Come, we should at least have a toast. No more gold stars, no more mother's sons lost," Miss Emily said, trying to find the good in all of the tragedy that the nation, the world, had been plunged into. They went into the house and Miss Emily asked Aldon to fetch some champagne.

"This is indeed a day for celebration. And nothing is better for a celebration than champagne. I don't care if it the middle of day!" Miss Emily insisted.

They went into the dining room as Aldon quickly headed for the wine cellar. He had put aside a few bottles of their best vintage for just such a time as he knew must one day surely come.

"Enough for everyone," Miss Emily called after him.

As they waited, they saw Doc Harrington's car coming up the long, curved driveway. He sat in the passenger seat, Garrett driving. The car came to a lurching halt as Garrett jumped out and ran around to the other side to open the door for his Uncle. As the older man started to step out, Garrett reached in to take his arm but Doc batted his nephew away, obviously signaling he was more than able to get out by himself.

"Go on, get. I'm fine. I'll meet you inside," Doc smiled. He knew his nephew wanted to be first to share the news, though somehow Doc had a feeling they already knew.

Garrett stepped quickly towards the door. He didn't even bother to knock. He knew it would be unlocked at this time of the day and he wouldn't need an invite to enter.

"Miss Emily? It's Garrett and Doc. Where are you? Have you heard the news? It's finished," Garrett yelled down the hall as he quickly made his way towards the dining room where he imagined the others might be. As he neared the great archway, he was surprised to see Mercy step through it, rushing towards him. She had her arms out, flying into his embrace.

"Oh Garrett, isn't it great news?! Everyone is so excited. Have you seen the town? Everyone is racing around down there. I've never seen such excitement," Mercy insisted. She couldn't help herself. She kissed him, not on his cheek but full on his lips. He pulled her in tightly, his strong arms wrapping around her tiny form.

"I love you Garrett," she whispered, surprised by her own words.

Garrett eased her back slowly, but kept his firm hold. He looked at her, knew immediately what his only response could be, should be.

"And I love you, Mercy Daniels. I believe I started falling in love with you from the moment I first saw you," Garrett said, embracing her tightly again, and this time pressing his lips against hers, feeling like he never wanted to let go.

Chapter 25

For most everyone, life slowly returned to much as it had been before the war. There was again plenty of food and new clothes available. Gasoline, oil, and tires for automobiles became plentiful once more. War time ration cards got stuffed away in dresser drawers as keepsakes or tossed out altogether. As the service men began returning home, first a mere trickle and soon a flood, they cast off their military uniforms for civilian clothes. The work force also changed from largely women and old men to young men. Women went back to their domestic life, swapping pants for dresses, though having become accustomed to the former, their wardrobes would forever after include both.

In Wellfleet, the fishery and canning factories began to hum again at full production, lights burning around the clock. And the fishing fleet came back out of mothballs where many of the boats had been stored due to lack of men to work them. The town wharf buzzed once again with activity. Parades were organized and they seemed to become nearly weekly affairs. Politicians gave speeches, calling for everyone to remember the brave and wounded. And, of course, to be sure to come out to the polls to vote for them in November.

For Mercy it was a time of growing happiness. Addy was safe with her mother, Emily. The young girl's father, Charlie Hawthorne, for some reason had never returned to trouble them again. Emily Mercy was growing bigger every day and had taken her first steps. She already seemed to be talking, though in a language that only she alone understood.

For Mercy and Garrett, their time together only produced stronger feelings and more shared memories. There were fewer and fewer days when she thought of Henry now, his face fading in her thoughts. Even if she took a moment to sit quietly and recall the time they had spent together as young people in love, experiencing for the first time that feeling that two lovers share, she found it more and more difficult to bring the vision of his face back to her. She had not wanted to believe others when they told her she would learn to get over it, to somehow be at peace with her loss and move on. How could she, she thought. He was the love of her life. And yet, with Garrett now in her life, she began to realize that perhaps her belief of Henry being the one and only had been wrong.

But now, as thoughts of Garrett filled up the once empty places in her heart, she understood. She would lock away the memories of *her* Henry, keeping them in a special place, but locked away nevertheless. She began to think of thoughts of Henry as almost a betrayal of the love she now felt for Garrett. Perhaps, she thought, what she had felt for Henry was after all just the inexperience of a once youthful heart, overtaken by emotions never felt before. Now, as she had matured, had managed to deal with the trials of life that the war, that responsibilities like Addy and the baby had placed her in and of the discovery of a mother she had always known but saw as someone else, Mercy was no longer a naïve child herself. What she believed had been true love with Henry she began to see as something less when she felt Garrett near her. In a strange sort of way, she believed that God had redeemed her from her pain and sorrow, had a plan for her that she herself might not have understood.

And there were other changes that all of them were dealing with. Doc Harrington and Miss Emily had grown older, aging so much more in what seemed like such a short time. The day of Doc's retirement was looming closer with the passing of each day. He no longer made many house calls, leaving his nephew Garrett to attend to that part of their now shared practice. Though he kept his office hours, they, too, had become fewer. For Doc Harrington, everything was falling into place as he had planned when he first invited Garrett to join him.

It was, for Doc, a bittersweet time though. He had been the town's only doctor for over fifty years, had presided over the birth of a great majority of the people and in time over *their* children. But the time was nearing when he would step aside and leave things to someone else, another Harrington, who had quickly earned the respect and trust of Doc's *extended* family.

As for Miss Emily, she also felt the passing years beginning to take their toll. As she approached her eightieth birthday, she realized it was perhaps time for making certain arrangements to ensure that when she was no longer here to oversee their well-being, her family was provided for. She knew she had much to be thankful for. She had herself been well provided for by a caring family now departed. She had a daughter, Mercy. She had what she felt was a grand-daughter in Addy and a great-grand daughter in her namesake, baby Emily. She would not leave this world the final heir to a bloodline descending back through the ages. This, more than anything, was her greatest comfort. She believed this was *her* sign of God's redemption for what she may have failed to do right in her own youth, when she may have failed

Mercy though she was but a frightened girl herself, unable to do as she may have thought she ought to do.

She would see to their comfort. They would not have worry or have concern. The fine house that her ancestors had left for her, the estate that sustained her against the trouble of the world, the wars, the depression, the life she might never have had on a school teacher's earnings alone, this would be her legacy to them.

And as she could well see, there might soon be a son-in-law added to the family. What she had witnessed Mercy suffer in the loss of Henry, what she was powerless to help in, she would now share in the joy the two young lovers were certain to take to the next stage of their lives. And with God's help, Emily thought, she would be able to share a few precious years in that as well.

As for Garrett, he kept busy, taking over more and more of Doc's practice. Once fairly much an unknown to most, merely a summertime visitor to a few others at best, he had now quickly developed a devoted following. Perhaps it was his good looks and charming bedside matter that attracted some, certainly the younger women of the town, or perhaps it was his bringing newer ways of treatments and medicine that impressed many of the others. But any concern Doc might have had that his young nephew wouldn't be accepted into the community, itself often reluctant to accept change, no longer worried him. There would be a *Harrington* to keep his own namesake alive. Doc took comfort in that.

But Garrett wanted more than the acceptance of the townspeople. He wanted Mercy. Not just her acceptance like any other but her love, her heart. And as their days together grew in number, a mutual understanding of what each wanted, grew as well. He often found himself day dreaming of how he would ask her, imagining the perfect setting, the right time. But then it had occurred to him that she might not be ready. She had given her heart to someone else and that loss was likely still all too fresh he thought. He would have to bide his time, allow her to fall in love with him as he had already fallen in love with her.

Then on one particular evening, after sharing dinner, they drove up to the top of the bluffs overlooking Wellfleet Bay to watch the sunset. It had become one of those rituals they both enjoyed together. A time at the end of the week when they could spread a blanket out on the dune grass, open a bottle of wine, and just enjoy the solitude that surrounded them. Below, the harbor lights shimmered, reflections of the incandescent beams dancing on the water. A soft breeze embraced them both. At first, they just talked, sharing the events of their week, a little conversation on the news from outside their world. Then, as the wine and coming on of the night served to relax them more, they just lapsed into silence, a time when just the touch of each other's hand spoke more than words. He put his arm around her, drawing her closer to him. She found herself surrendering to the feeling, growing less and less aware of the borders they were to politely maintain with each other. Had he dared to touch her in a more passionate way, she knew she might likely accept it, would welcome the intimacy. But he never did. She knew it was not his nature to break that trust. Though they were alone, she always felt as safe with him as if they were in a crowded room. And yet, perhaps ever so slightly, she wished he would indeed break those bounds and just take her, there and then, abandoning the constraints of *polite society.*

From the years of war, of loves lost, of so many young men never returning, their generation had learned that sometimes seizing the moment might be the only chance they would have. Their generation would now never return to the ways of their parents and their grandparents. Decorum be damned had in many ways become their outlook on life now.

Garrett poured a little more wine into her glass and handed it to her. She willingly accepted, the sweet red nectar slowly working on her own inhibitions. She rested her head on his shoulder, looked up at him, studying every facet of his face as it became memory.

"Have you ever wondered if two people can find each other not by accident but by fate," Mercy asked, staring out into the distance.

"Do you mean like what the poets say, *kindred souls?*" Garrett said.

Mercy nodded her head on his shoulder.

"I suppose some believe in such things. I like to think it might be so," Garrett offered, "But what would trouble me is if two people *are* supposed to be together, that if by their very birth there is somehow some other spiritual connection, what if they wander the earth their entire lives never finding each other? Or worse, what if one finds that other soul and then loses that person?"

Mercy listened, not all that certain where Garrett was going with this. Surely someone could have more than a single person in their life that they could fall in love with. There, sitting close to her, was certainly evidence of that very thing. Yes, she had loved Henry. She would have married him, settled down with him, raised children. But whether it was God's will as she had been taught to believe, or merely fate, as others accepted as their explanation, he was gone and she had found a new love to fill her heart. Having been granted such, twice in one lifetime, was to her a miracle in itself. She had her answer. Yes, there were soul mates in this troubled world and not always just one chance at finding them.

Mercy felt a chill take hold of her. Garrett felt her tremble. He took the edge of the blanket they sat on and pulled it up around her shoulder despite the still warm evening air around them both. Perhaps it was just the sea breeze beginning to come in off the water as the last muted rays of sunlight faded on the horizon she thought. But to her it felt like something else, a cold feeling from within her when recalling Henry that had just passed through her.

"Maybe we better head home," Garrett suggested, though he would have preferred to stay just as they were, snuggled together in the growing darkness. Below them the soft roll of the waves, lapping softly against the shoreline, was the only sound.

Mercy looked up at him, nodding her head slowly.

"Perhaps," she said, her tone far from convincing. Garrett could tell they both were reluctant to move.

"Oh, come on now, there will be many more evenings like this if you want them," Garrett said reassuringly, hoping she would agree.

Mercy pressed her cheek firmly against his strong shoulder, the only response really needed.

"Promise?" she asked nevertheless.

Garrett gently lifted her chin upwards towards him. He kissed her softly. Then again even more deeply. She had her answer.

239

Chapter 26

Mercy often received morning phone calls from her mother during the week, most of the time for no other reason than to just check in with each other. But her mother sounded different this morning when she asked Mercy to please come to the house as soon as possible. When Mercy tried to press her on the reason, her mother merely insisted she come at once. Nothing wrong, she had promised, but she wanted to see her.

So, Mercy wasted little time dressing and hurrying down the path towards town, climbing the brick steps up to Halcroft House where an equally silent Aldon Barlow greeted her at the door.

"What in the world is this all about, Aldon?" Mercy asked as he closed the door behind her and led her down the hall towards the small sitting parlor across from the dining hall. As she entered the comfortably furnished room, she saw her mother seated on the couch, and next to her, Addy in one of the large stuffed chairs. But it was not until she had proceeded further into the room did, she notice a young man in a blue uniform occupying another chair close to young Addy. He was holding baby Emily Mercy, tickling her chin and making eyes at her to the baby's giddy delight.

"Mercy, I would like to introduce you to Ensign William Thames," Miss Emily smiled, motioning with her hand towards the young officer. But the name didn't mean anything to Mercy. At least not at first. Then his first name, William, struck a chord.

"Billy? Addy's *Billy*?" Mercy questioned.

Addy jumped up excitedly, throwing her arms around Mercy.

"Oh, isn't it just wonderful! He's come home, home to me, home to all of us! I knew he would!" Addy exclaimed, she hugged Mercy then quickly moved to Billy and their child. Mercy was dumbstruck. She had not expected anything like this.

"I...well...I honestly don't know what to say," Mercy admitted.

"I pretty much said the same thing earlier this morning," Miss Emily admitted.

"I went looking for Addy and heard from some people in Yarmouth I could find her here. But you can only imagine my surprise when I was introduced to my daughter of all things," Billy smiled. "I can't even start to thank you for all you have done. I sent letters but she said she never got them, not even one."

"I can only imagine what her father did with them," Miss Emily insisted.

"But it's all right now," Addy said, looping her arm around Billy's.

"It must have been terrible for you Billy. Being so far away from home. The war. Not knowing what had happened to Addy. Not knowing you were a father," Mercy said.
"There were some tough days, that's for sure. So many shipmates I'd known that were lost. German U-boats took quite a toll on our ships. I never knew when it might be the one I was on. Maybe it was a blessing I didn't know about the baby. It sure would have made my time at sea all the harder. I was missing Addy bad enough," Billy admitted.

"But that's all over now, isn't it, honey," Addy said, pulling herself in closer to Billy.

"Yes, and I've told him he is more than welcome to stay here, with us," Miss Emily assured them.

Billy smiled, shaking his head, but his expression revealed something else.

"That would be great, but just for a little while. I'm just waiting for new orders then I'll have to ship out again, at least for a little while. The Merchant Marines is my life now. But it's a good job. Good money. Many guys raise families on the pay," Billy insisted. "Besides, I don't know what else I could do. Maybe work the fishing boats but it's not something I ever felt I was cut out for and honestly, it's a lot riskier."

Addy, however, wasn't sure she liked what she was hearing. She thought she had lost him, no word all this time, and now after he had finally come home to her, he was already talking of leaving again so soon.

"But you just came back," Addy said, "You can't leave again, leave me and your daughter?"

"It's not like that, Addy. I'll probably be home more than away. We load up, ship a load out to some other port and return. A few weeks, maybe a month at most. The war is over. No one is trying to sink ships anymore. I have to make a living for us, for the baby. It's all I know how to do right now. The Merchant Marines is a good life for many families. And I'll know you and the baby are safe here. Isn't that right Miss Wescott?" Billy said, hoping for some support.

"Of course, it is. My grandfather, and his father before him, made their living from ships. It's an honorable trade. A good and fitting one," Miss Emily reassured Addy.

"Well, we don't need to settle everything right this minute," Mercy suggested. "Surely, you two will want to spend some time together and we can watch the baby anytime you both want to sneak off for a moment."

Addy thought it over. Mercy and Miss Emily were right. There was time now to work everything out. It wasn't perhaps the worst solution to things. She knew Billy wasn't going to simply stay living with her and Miss Emily forever. He was a man, a father. They would want to plan to be married. All the things she had thought of since she was young girl.

"And besides, we have a very important birthday to plan for," Miss Emily reminded them all. Addy would be turning eighteen in a few weeks. She would become a woman in her own legal right. It was an age when she could now be fully and legally able to do as she wanted, no longer a ward to her father or anyone else.

"Oh my, that's right. I'd almost forgotten," Mercy said, realizing as well that it was significant in another way. Her father no longer could hold legal claim to her, to her assets, to anything that Addy might own, though both Mercy and Miss Emily had often wondered why Charlie Hawthorne had indeed never returned for the rest of the money he had tried to extort from Miss Emily. Perhaps Aldon had been right after all when he said Charlie would realize that there was more risk than reward in pressing the matter. Anyway, all that would be in the past for sure once Addy turned eighteen.

"Why don't you gather your things from your berth on the ship and bring them here for a while?" Miss Emily suggested, "We have plenty of rooms and I'm sure any one of them would be more comfortable than a ship's hammock."

Billy appeared to be thinking it over. It did sound like a welcomed change.

"As long as it's not any imposition mam?"

"Not in the least," Miss Emily assured the young officer, "This old house has too long lived with shadows and the stillness. It's time we brought a little life back into it."

Chapter 27

Following Captain Garrett Harrington's wounding in France, leaving him with a slight limp in his right leg and no longer eligible for active duty, he had asked to remain in the medical reserves state-side where he felt he could still be of service. Upon his return he had devoted much of his time at Massachusetts' Boston General, administering to the wounded veterans returning home. When he received a call from his uncle that he needed him to begin taking over his medical practice in Wellfleet, he had requested re-assignment to Mid Cape Hospital in Hyannis Port. Although the war was now over and his enlistment term near finished as well, he knew there was an overflow of patients being redirected there and could still be of help managing the care of the hospitalized veterans. There was also an Army Corp of Engineering installation nearby with a hospital unit and injured servicemen also ended up there for emergency treatment. So, the army granted his request. *Captain* Harrington was assigned to work at the hospital several times a month on an *as needed* basis to supplement the fulltime staff.

For Garrett it had not only been a way he could be of continuing service to his country but it helped ease his feelings of guilt that he had been home in the safety of America while many of his generation had still been abroad facing the real danger of the enemy.

He travelled to the hospital several times a week, working long hours between hospital shifts and managing the patients of Doc Harrington's practice. But he found a balance that still allowed him to spent time with Mercy and the others.

Towards the end of September, with the war in Europe and the Pacific finally over, service men began streaming back home in ever increasing numbers aboard ships, both military and civilian liners, the latter commandeered by the Government as troop transports. The ports along the northeast from Boston to Philadelphia and the west coast from San Francisco to San Diego became swelled with soldiers and sailors returning to their families. Among these were countless wounded, rotating back from overseas hospitals or released from German and Japanese prisoner of war camps. Men with physical wounds as well as those with no visible signs of injury but wounded none the same in mind, spirit, or from disease. Some so thin and wasted, Garrett wondered how they had even survived the passage home. Men laying in hospital beds with blank stares into a world that they alone had seen, could still see, their days racked with anxiety, their nights filled by nightmares beyond description.

As the Autumn of that year wore on, the numbers only increased. Many patients originally destined to Boston Mass General soon had to be diverted to other facilities just to manage the overload. First, they were taken to other hospitals in nearby cities until even those strained from the load. Then to smaller hospitals, many in the direction of where the patients would eventually be released for home. So, Garrett and the staff at Cape Cod Hospital, saw the roster of Cape Cod men growing. Men from towns and smaller villages up and down the Cape. Barnstable, Yarmouth, Eastham, Provincetown and even Wellfleet.

And each time he made a visit, as he checked in on newly arrived patients, Garrett would make a note to contact their families just to help reach out either in addition to the notices being sent by the military or in case they had perhaps not gotten to that serviceman's family just yet.

It was on one of these visits that he came across the names of several mid-Cape men from towns like Eastham and Wellfleet. But as he went over the list of the newly arrived his eyes stopped short on one name in particular. *Lieutenant Henry. S. Gates*, U.S.N.

Garrett stared at the name, re-read it, ran his finger along the print as if doing so would ensure him it was truly there. Next to the name there was a room number. 141 South Wing. It was the Intensive Care Unit. He dropped the clipboard down at the nurse's station, causing one of the RNs on duty there to quickly look up into the wide-eyed stare of Doctor Garrett.

"Doctor, is everything okay?" she asked, seeing that clearly it wasn't.

Garrett looked at her, grabbed the clipboard again, held it towards her, pointing to the name.

"When did this man arrive?" he asked, "I don't recall seeing it a few days ago when I was last here."

The nurse was still unsure why he was acting the way he was. New patients arrived all the time. There was nothing unusual about new names being added every day let alone a few times a week.

"He came in yesterday with another man. Both navy officers. This one though is in bad shape, poor thing. They said he had been a prisoner in a Japanese POW camp for over a year. Nothing but skin and bones. Couldn't walk on his own. They have him on..."

But before the nurse could finish, Garrett was already halfway down the hall, moving in hypnotic steps towards Room 141. He passed other doctors and patients, several who called out to him. But he did not respond; unhearing, unseeing. He came to the doorway of Room 141 and stepped in. There was no one else there. He wasn't sure what he would find. He had never met the patient in Room 141, never met the man listed as Henry Gates but Garrett had never been someone inclined to accept mere coincidences. A naval officer, heading home to Wellfleet by the name of Henry S. Gates. It could be no other than Mercy's fiancé. His heart sank. He had to be sure but he knew if it were indeed true, he also had to quickly tell Mercy. No matter what it meant for them, he couldn't keep such a thing from her, not even for a day.

As Garrett stepped further into the room, he eased back the privacy curtain that had been pulled around the patient lying in the hospital bed. He lifted the patient chart from the hook on the foot of the bed, scanned more of the information found on it. Saw the words, *"liberated from Ofuna prisoner of war camp, Japan. Serial # KAH091959"*

In front of him, stretched near lifeless on the bed, lay little more than a skeleton. The man's cheeks and eyes darkened hollows. The bones in his arms, hands, and fingers protruding under a yellow drum taut layer of skin. Connected to him was a transfusion bottle of plasma dripping down as though it were the sands of an hour glass slowly ebbing away.

Garrett leaned down towards the man in the bed, spoke softly into the man's ear.

"Henry?"

The man seemed to respond, his closed eye lids moving slightly at the recognition of his name.

"Henry Gates?" Garrett said again. And again, the man in the bed seemed to respond. His lips appeared to move as if trying to form words. Suddenly Garrett knew it had to be Henry Gates, a ghost returned from the dead. It was all too impossible, unbelievable. Garrett leaned down again, and quietly dared to say another name.

"Mercy Daniels"

At the sound of the words, the man in the bed grew more animated than he had been since Garrett stepped up to his bedside. It was as though that name in itself somehow stirred Henry from his coma-like state. For Garrett it confirmed it. Here laying before him was Mercy's lost young man. And Garrett realized that as this man was now found, it was he, Garrett Harrington, that was now lost.

As Garrett stood there, unable to move, unsure of exactly what to do next but knowing there was one thing he had to do, to tell Mercy, a nurse entered the room, surprised to find Doctor Garrett there. She quickly recognized him and knew he was not assigned to the Intensive Care Unit. Doctors held reign over the patients.

But nurses, especially Head Nurses, held reign over the hospital, floors, wings, rooms and all.

"Excuse me Doctor, may I help you?" the nurse asked. Her tone suggested it was more of a demand than a question.

"This patient. Do we know where he comes from?" Garrett asked, still refusing to believe it was who he dreaded now that it might be. The nurse studied him, unsure what the doctor meant.

"He arrived yesterday. He came in from one of the transport ships on the West Coast. Then by hospital train across country," the nurse said matter-of-factly as though such things were common knowledge to anyone who worked there.

"Why Doctor? Do you know this patient?" the nurse asked, still unsure what the young doctor's particular concern was.

"I believe I may. But there is no family listed here on his chart," Garrett said, lifting the clipboard back up again from the hook at the foot of the bed.

"Well, that would probably be because there was no immediate family, no next of kin listed on his service record," the nurse said, her voice becoming a little more edgy. She had many patients to attend to yet. Now this young doctor stood before her and seemed to have nothing better to do with his time than question her about things she didn't have the answers to herself.

"Doctor, may I suggest, respectfully, of course, that if you have any information concerning this patient that you think may be helpful you go see the administrator and offer it. I'm sure the patient's family would appreciate it. He may have a wife, a mother, a sweetheart waiting for some news."

The word *sweetheart* struck Garrett hard. Yes, a sweetheart. The same woman he himself had fallen in love with. The woman he had planned to ask to marry him. And now, here, before him, was the very man she had once pledged her heart to, her life to.

The nurse could see the troubled look in Garrett's eyes. Sensed this was not just another one of a hundred patients the hospital was filled with

"Doctor? Are you all right?" the nurse asked, pulling Garrett back from his thoughts. He looked at her, a blank stare in his eyes. He slowly nodded.

"Yes, thank you nurse. My apologies. I am keeping you from your duties," Garrett said. The nurse resisted confirming that he indeed was. Instead she returned to the hallway and continued to push her cart of medicines further down the hall to each room. But she kept a watchful eye on the doorway of Room 141, expecting to see the young doctor emerge at any second. Eventually,

Garrett turned and left the room. He headed down the opposite side of the hospital to the Administrations Office. He knew he really didn't need anything more in the way of proof. He realized now that Henry Gates had somehow survived the sinking of his ship, had been captured by the Japanese, reported as lost in action, had somehow survived the depredation of a Japanese prisoner of war internment camp, and now miraculously had returned to the world of the living.

He wasn't sure how he was going to tell Mercy. He only knew it had to be him who did so. If for any reason, someone told her first and she were to discover he had already known, whatever chance he might have with her now would likely be destroyed. He would simply have to trust that the love they had developed for each other might somehow survive this news. He also knew that although he had planned to propose to her the next time they were alone, he probably now had to wait. It wouldn't be fair to do so before she found out the truth about Henry Gates.

Chapter 28

Garrett wasn't exactly sure just how he would go about breaking the news of his discovery in the hospital to Mercy. In the end, he decided that it would be better if he shared it not only with Mercy but with her mother at the same time. He knew Miss Emily would be able to help her daughter deal with the sudden realization that Mercy's fiancé had quite literally returned from the grave. And in a way, almost selfishly he thought, perhaps Miss Emily would offer support to them both that what they had found in each other was still something to be kept alive.

So, he had called Miss Emily first. Told her he had something important he wanted to share with them both. Asked if he might come over that morning and would she ask Mercy to be there. When Garrett arrived, he found Miss Emily, Mercy, and Addy with the baby in the dining room, just finishing some breakfast and tea. Both women were smiling in anticipation of what they could only imagine was Garrett's intention to *pop the question* right there before them both. But after Garrett sat down, politely refusing coffee, the grim look on his face told them at once that they had been wrong about the purpose of his meeting with them.

Garrett studied their faces, searching for a way to begin. But he realized there was no easy way to say it other than just tell them all the truth.

"Mercy..." Garrett began, reaching out to take hold of her hands, "I've seen Henry."

The words didn't register with Mercy. She didn't understand.

"What do you mean you have *seen* Henry?" Mercy asked with a look of utter confusion, "Like you had a dream about him?"

Garrett shook his head.

"No, Henry Gates is alive. I saw him at the Cape Hospital. He was brought in two days ago and I saw his name listed on the new arrival charts yesterday when I went there for my weekly rounds."

Mercy snapped her hands away, staring at Garrett in disbelief. No, she thought, that's not possible.

"Henry died in the war. I got the letter. You must be mistaken. That's all. You are just mistaken. It has to be someone else. A mix up. Yes, that's it, a mix up," Mercy insisted. She looked at her mother, looking for some sort of agreement. It had to be a mistake.

"He's been in a Japanese prisoner of war camp. He survived the sinking of his ship. All hands were not lost as the Navy had believed. Those prisoners were kept captive without any communication to the outside world. Not even the Red Cross knew all of the names of the men in those camps."

Still, Mercy wouldn't let the truth settle in. It was all just too incredible. She had accepted the loss. Had grieved and then simply learned to move on. She had found Garrett. They had fallen in love. She was waiting for him to ask her to spend the rest of her life with him. And now...

"No, you are mistaken, it isn't so," Mercy repeated, as if doing so long enough would make it all go away.

"I think you need to go down to that hospital, see for yourself Mercy," Miss Emily finally said, "It's the only way."

"I will take you if you want," Garrett offered, "Of course I'd understand if you want to go alone."

Mercy looked into Garrett's eyes. She could see fear in them. She knew what he must be thinking. Where did he now fit in all of this?

"Yes, I know. But I won't go alone. I want you take me Garrett?" Mercy said.

"Of course, I will. He's in intensive care at the moment. He's been through a terrible ordeal. He's going to need time to recover, gain his strength. That's the physical part. But there simply is no way right now to tell how much other damage he has suffered. These men have been put through hell. Tortured, starved, extreme deprivation. He will need those that know him, that care for him, to surround him every step of the way back to life," Garrett insisted.

Mercy realized he sounded like a doctor now. That there was no other emotion revealed other than that of a caring human being.

"Give me a moment with my mother," Mercy asked of Garrett and Addy. They both understood.

"I'll wait in my car. Take your time. I made sure I had no patients scheduled for this morning. I'll drive you there when you are ready."

Addy stood up as well, cuddling Baby Emily in her arms. "I think she's probably hungry. I'll be upstairs feeding her if anyone needs me," Addy said, wishing she could do more but realizing she could not.

Once everyone had left the dining room, Mercy turned to her mother. Before she could find the words, Miss Emily spoke.

"You will know what to do, daughter. I believe that. And even if you aren't sure, God will tell you. You must trust that,"

"*Momma*, I'm frightened," Mercy said, her words caught the older women with some surprise. She had never heard Mercy call her that. *Momma.* She felt her heart sink at the sudden realization that there was nothing she could really do but be there for her daughter. She couldn't even begin to imagine the emotions running through her daughter. A young man she had once planned a life with, a man whose death had taken the very spark of her life away only to be rekindled by another young man, now found herself torn between the past and the present.

    ***

Though the ride over to the hospital was a short one, no more than thirty minutes, Garrett and Mercy spent it in what seemed to both of them an eternity of silence. For her, she was lost deep in questions and thoughts of what had happened, how it had happened, what would she find. For Garrett it was the sudden realization that things might never again be the same, not for him, not for *them.* The woman sitting next to him now wasn't only his. How would he deal with that feeling? He wasn't sure. Only that there was a growing sense, a fear in him, of an undefinable sense of loss.

He parked the car in the staff parking lot and walked around to the other side, opening the door for her. She got out and to his reassuring comfort she took his hand as they walked together through the entrance reserved for medical staff. Inside, they worked their way past the commotion of doctors, nurses, orderlies, and patients. The bustling activity that swarmed around her seemed to only add to her apprehension. It was very much a foreign place to her. A number of the medical personnel greeted *Doctor* Garrett as he led Mercy through the long hallways and corridors towards the intensive care unit. They passed through double pale green doors into a sudden vacuum, absent of the noise they had left behind on the other side. Here, the quiet of the space seemed to rush back in around her. Hushed voices, murmurs of pain or labored breathing began a new assault upon her senses. There was a feeling of foreboding that closed in on her. She was suddenly aware these were those desperate souls whose fates might no longer be in the firm grip of those who tended to their pain. That maybe all that they clung to was a God who might not in the end hear their prayers.

As Garrett led her down the corridor, she stole quick glances inside the doorways they passed. Patients laid in beds, some wrapped in bandages that covered portions of their bodies, others connected to a menagerie of clicking and whirling machines pulsating in near lifelike heartbeats. Others patients, simply lied there, staring blankly with unseeing eyes, no longer aware of their surroundings.

Finally, Garrett stopped outside Room 141, a handwritten name plate adorning the wall next to the doorway. It read *Henry S. Gates.* This couldn't be happening she thought. It had to be a mistake. *Her Henry was dead.* The words formed in her mind but she just couldn't comprehend their meaning. *Her* Henry. She felt herself letting go of Garrett's hand, involuntarily but somehow with an understanding that frightened her. For a moment, though her feet remained frozen in the spot where she stood, she knew that inside the room her past waited for her.

"Go in Mercy," Garrett said in a whisper. She looked at him, seeing him in a way she had never before. How could he be so calm, so understanding, she thought. Doesn't he realize.

"You come in with me," Mercy said.

"I'll be right here. You go in and see. I may have been entirely wrong," Garrett suggested, though they both knew otherwise.

Mercy slowly stepped through the doorway, moving trancelike towards the bed, towards the partially pulled back privacy curtain until the foot of the bed, and the man lying in it, came into her view. She ventured slowly, her eyes following the form covered in the bed sheets until they locked on Henry's sleeping face, his eyes closed, his expression almost serene. She gasped, the tears slowly clouding her vision. There, laying before her, was a man she had given up for dead, had grieved for. Yet there he was now all the same. A resurrection.

"My God, it's him!" Mercy heard herself saying inside her head. "It can't be him"

Again, the words repeated over and over in her mind as though she was hearing the voice of someone else. She stepped towards the side of the bed, impulsively reaching out, gently brushing his hair away from his forehead. Touching him again after all this time brought a flood of emotions washing over her.

She reached down, taking his hand, wrapping her fingers around his. She felt him responding to her, his fingers tightening around her hand. She leaned down, softly whispering his name into his ear.

"Henry, it's me," Mercy said.

She felt him grasp her hand in response. Though his eyes remained closed, the muscles of his face reacted. She could see there was recognition, something familiar to him that he was reaching out to in his darkness. She gently ran her other hand down the side of his cheek, caressing his skin. Again, the muscles in his body responded.

Garrett entered the room, standing next to her. He just watched, his thoughts a troubled mixture of a concerned doctor and now a doubtful lover.

"There is nothing physically wrong with him, no wounds or other injuries we could find. It was obvious he had been mistreated. But the real problem was one of simply having been nearly starved to death. Rickets, malaria, lice. The Navy doctors started patching him up as soon as the Marines liberated the camps and starting bringing these boys back. They got him as far as San Diego where he spent time in the hospital there, before they thought he might be strong enough to survive the journey by train home. He'd been in Boston General after that until they moved him here a few days ago," Garrett said, telling her everything he had been able to find out from the Hospital Administration.

"But he hasn't woken up?" Mercy asked. Garrett shook his head.

"Not that they know of. They said they found him and several other prisoners pretty much in the same state. I was told a few of them didn't make it back state-side. There was simply nothing to be done. He's one of the lucky ones," Garrett insisted, his voice offering the hope that he knew Mercy must be needing right now.

"Lucky ones," Mercy repeated.

They both fell silent, Garrett allowing her time to take it all in. She reached over to his hand, took it in hers, somehow communicating what words might fail to do at a moment like this.

"Now what happens?" she asked.

"It's really a wait and see situation. The doctors, the staff here, they've done all that can be expected. They've got him on fluids, he's starting to show a little improvement in weight, no infections other than the bouts with malaria, which frankly he may have for most of the rest of his life. So, the rest is up to time," Garrett offered.

"And God," Mercy quickly added. Garrett shook his head slowly.

"Yes, and God," he reluctantly agreed.

Chapter 29

As the weeks wore on, Henry's health continued to slowly improve. He had finally emerged from his coma, aided by continued feeding and medication. Before long he took his first feeble steps out of his bed with the help of the orderlies and not long after, was walking again by the aid of a cane for support. He was anxious to take his leave of the hospital, knowing they could certainly use the bed for others returning from the war with more serious conditions.

But he had no immediate plans for his return to peacetime society. Before he had left for the war, working on the fishing trawlers had been what he felt most suited for as a mean to earn a living. He loved the sea. It was part of most any New Englander's life. When it had come to going into the military, he felt there was no other choice for him but the Navy. Already age thirty at the time of his enlistment, it wasn't as though he needed to be concerned about being drafted into the army. There had been little worry about that. He was well above the age of the average of the more desired eighteen to twenty-three-year-old draftee.

In fact, it had been this very point that had caused Mercy and he to part on disagreeing terms. She had insisted there could be other ways to serve his country right here at home, without risking his life on a foreign battlefield. He had insisted he couldn't face those around them if he stayed home while others joined up.

But part of him knew the *other* truth. It was a chance to escape the doldrums of living in a small town and the often soul crushing day in and day out routine of working the sea. It might be his last and only chance to see some of the world before he settled down, married, and raised a family. He believed Mercy would wait for him. He believed that certainly shouldn't be too much to expect given the times. He had declared his intentions, she had accepted, though he realized that was before he revealed his intentions of joining the service, and he reasoned that a good woman would simply have to understand even if it meant asking her to put her life on hold as well.

Mercy came to see him at the hospital as often as she could get away. She brought him small presents of his favorite foods as well as socks and a scarf she had knitted for the coming winter chill. They sat talking and she told him of things that had gone on in Wellfleet while he had been away. She spoke of those that had passed away and of the new ones that had been born.

But there were things that neither seemed willing or ready to discuss. Mercy said nothing about Garrett. To Henry, he was nothing more than an acquaintance of hers, the nephew of Doc Harrington and someone who happened to also work at the hospital. And yet, Mercy felt a sense of guilt for not revealing more. But for reasons she understood and some she didn't she found she wanted to avoid even speaking to Henry about Garrett, referring to him as *Doctor* Garrett as if by doing so she could keep her world with one separated from her world with the other.

And yet she also discovered that strangely enough Henry never brought up their engagement. She no longer wore the ring he had given her and given the circumstances surrounding his reported death she imagined he could understand why she might have finally taken it off and put it away. But if he had noticed, he never mentioned it and frankly it troubled her.

As they sat during one of her visits, Mercy showed him pictures she had brought of Addy and the baby, who was now almost a year old. She held them out for Henry to see and when she spoke about them, he noticed how her voice filled with excitement and pride. It was if they were her own flesh and blood he thought, not once upon a time strangers.

"And here's one of little Emily playing with Miss Emily's cat. She loves that cat. Tries to call her *baby*," Mercy laughed, handing the picture to Henry to see.

Mercy flipped through more pictures in her hand.

"Oh, and I love this one. We gave her a bowl of chocolate pudding and she got more of it all over her face than in her mouth!"

Again, Mercy handed the picture to Henry who managed a smile. But he didn't seem to share the same level of enthusiasm as Mercy did with the candid photographs. And Mercy could sense his indifference. After a while, she stopped shuffling through the pictures, deciding that perhaps he was tired, perhaps he simply had had enough. But there was something else she thought. He seemed to drift away at times, as though a part of him was somewhere else, far off. She felt the change in him. He wasn't *her* Henry anymore. But she tried to push such thoughts away. No, he's just tired she told herself. No need to dwell on it. He'd already made such progress in his recovery.

"Have they told you when you are being released?" Mercy asked, putting the pictures away in her purse and changing the subject.

"Doctor Harrington thinks maybe in a week," Henry said.

"Oh, that's great news, isn't it?"

"Is it?" Henry answered sharply, his reply taking Mercy very much by surprise.

"Why would you say that. Of course, it's good news. You will finally be home again."

"Home? And just where is that? Back to that hole in the wall apartment at Mrs. Duncan's boarding house?!"

"But I thought you loved living there. You always said it had a great view of the harbor," Mercy insisted.

"I suppose," Henry said, his tone softening, "Maybe you could look into it for me. It'll perhaps have to do until I can figure something else out. Perhaps I'll see if I can get work on old man Crowley's trawler though winter's coming on so after the fall runs there won't be much work. Probably sign up for some of that veteran's disability pay but that won't last me too long," Henry added, sounding doubtful.

"It'll work out, you'll see," Mercy assured him.

Henry just looked at her, studied her face, shook his head.

"I see you still are the constant optimist, aren't you?"

Mercy felt it sounded like less than a compliment.

"I'm not saying it's all going to be easy," Mercy insisted, "But you have survived so much and come home. No need to over think it. You've already made such progress in your recovery. Surely that has to give you hope."

"I'm afraid we didn't have much use for *hope* with those Jap bastards. *Hope* was a dangerous thing in those camps. You woke up, survived another day, and were grateful when they'd let you alone long enough to sleep. I'd say there were a good number of men arrived there believing in God and wasn't long before them guards beat such thoughts out of them," Henry told her, his words etched with pain and anger.

Mercy reached out to him, placing her hands on his.

"Well, that's all behind you now," Mercy said trying to comfort him.

Henry stared back at her. "Maybe"

Chapter 30

On Saturday night, Garrett picked Mercy up at her cottage a little before seven. Saturday dinner dates had become their ritual. They looked forward to just being alone somewhere, share a meal, a bottle of wine or even two if they were feeling especially daring.

There was a small restaurant just up the coast near Provincetown that had a few tables and booths. A warm and inviting sort of place with table clothes and candles, a fireplace in one corner, portraits of sea captions and ships adorning the walls. One of those family run businesses where the owners greeted you at the door and made you feel welcomed every time you entered. Garrett thought it almost too perfectly contrived, as though it was the sort of place the owners envisioned was what the developing summer tourist trade wanted to find. But Mercy had declared it all "just so very divine." So, it had become their own special place. The place even came with its own bit of a quirky hostess, an elderly woman who they surmised might be the owner's grandmother. She strangely enough always inquired if Garrett and Mercy had a reservation though seldom when they arrived where there more than a half dozen people seated at the more than ample number of tables.

As they waited for their orders, Garrett poured them both a glass of wine. Mercy seemed to swallow it down rather than sip it. Garrett reached for the bottle and began to pour her another glass, this time a little more towards the top.

"You appear a little...thirsty," Garrett kidded her.

Mercy smiled politely back at him, offering no comment.

"Everything all right?" Garrett asked, sensing something a little different even as they had started off in the car from her house. She was normally more animated and talkative. This evening, she seemed a little distant, lost in thought.

"Oh no, everything is fine...just have so many things on my mind. I'm sorry," Mercy apologized.

"Care to share them with me?" Garrett offered, though he really didn't need her to explain. He already knew. Ever since Henry Gates had returned, she seemed different.

"Probably best not to talk about it," Mercy suggested.

"I'm not sure I agree, Mercy. Maybe talking about it is exactly what we *do* need to do."

Mercy looked at him, saw the concern in his eyes. She wanted to explain her feelings, to tell him she felt torn by the situation. But she loved him and somehow because of that she wouldn't say anything that could hurt him. She just needed time, time to sort things out. She knew there shouldn't be any confusion. Henry had made his decision. He had left her to pick up the pieces of her broken heart. But she ultimately had to live with his decision to go to war. She would wait for his return.

Then came the news, a telegraph from the War Department that he was lost at sea. She had also accepted that and slowly moved forward with her life; a life that Garrett had entered to make her feel happiness and love again. When she thought about how she now was being forced to revisit those two lives, the feeling of anger she had felt with Henry seemed to return all over again. But she also knew deep down that there was no denying that the flame she had once believed to have slowly gone out was now somehow persistently flickering back to life in her heart.

"I know it's about Henry," Garrett said, pushing aside any pretense that it was anything other than that troubling Mercy, "I know you have been to see him in the hospital many times. That's was only to be expected.

At first Mercy wasn't sure how to answer. She couldn't lie to Garrett. Yes, it was true that as time had gone on and Henry improved, she had made more and more frequent trips to see him. But she now felt as though Garret was accusing her of some wrong doing even though he said he understood.

"I just feel terrible for him, he was so ill," Mercy tried to explain, knowing that was only a partial truth. She was searching for something, for answers, and every encounter with Henry only seemed to awaken an earlier bond, which itself only deepen the feeling of indecision.

"I understand. It must not be easy for you," Garrett offered.

"Do you? *Understand*?!" Mercy asked.

She felt herself growing upset at just how *understanding* Garrett actually was being. At how reasonable about the whole thing he appeared to be. It would be easier for her if he did protest, did question her loyalty to him. But sympathy from him only made her feel more guilty for still having the feelings that were springing back to life in her.

"Mercy, I'm not sure what you want me to say? Do you want me to tell you I don't like you seeing Henry? That I *demand* you stay away from him? Though I may feel that, I don't believe it would be right for me to say such things. It's simply not my place to expect such a thing. Besides, I'm afraid that might only serve to push you away. All I can do is stand by and watch, wait until you deal with all this. Do I love you? I don't believe there is any question about that. Hopefully you already know that," Garrett said, taking her hands in his, looking into her eyes.

For Mercy, it only made things more confusing. Here was a man who could give her the life she had thought she wanted. Someone to share equally in all they did, all *she* wanted. Someone she had come to believe was a steady and stable man. The sort of man Mercy had once thought Henry was. But she knew something that no else, not even those closest to her did. Nor did she dare to tell them. Not her friends, her mother, no one. Certainly not Garrett. She hadn't lied when she said she understood why Henry felt he had to go away to war, that it was his duty, that it was what was expected of him. That much had been the truth.

But what she *had* concealed was that Henry had another *mistress* in his life. Not another woman. Had it been so she could have at least fought for him or let him go without guilt on her part. But there was something perhaps even more difficult to fight against. Henry was just not yet ready to take a wife, settle down, raise a family. She knew, even when he had proposed to her, there was still a part of him that had long yearned to escape the small fishing village they lived in. For her, such a place was all she ever needed. But for Henry, he wanted, he needed, to see more of the world.

When the war came, though he was nearly too old to enlist, he grabbed at the chance. He had broken her heart when he left. But he had made his choice. Yet despite the memory of the hurt he had left her to deal with, there somehow had always remained the love she had felt for him, with him. And it was that love, dormant as it might have been, locked up in the believe he was lost in the war, that was springing back to life inside her. And it made her angry. Not so much with Henry. He had paid the price for his misadventure she thought. She couldn't even begin to imagine what he had endured. Only now, were the survivors' stories being told of the inhumane cruelty, of the evil, his captors meted out.

No, she thought, her anger was with herself. Or perhaps it was more the *guilt* within herself. Here, sitting before her, was a man who had only shown her kindness, caring, support. He had stood by her side when she took in a stranger and her unborn child. He had also been there to support her in the sudden revelation that the woman she had long thought her aunt, not by blood but my friendship, had indeed been her mother. And now, she found herself torn between her love of two men.

The waitress brought them their food, but by now, neither had much of an appetite. They sat quietly, picking at their meals. Garrett ordered another bottle of wine, which they both consumed as though it were the sole curative to ease their pain. Garrett could find nothing more to say, his own mind slowly succumbing to the belief he might being losing her and there was nothing he could really do about it. Thoughts of proposing right then and there, of rushing her into his life, safe from any others, seemed the wrong thing to do. He felt a sickening sense that perhaps such a time may have even now slipped away. If only Henry had been sent to a different hospital, he thought. If only...if only. But such thinking would get him nowhere now, no relief. All he could do was watch and wait. And hope.

Chapter 31

Mercy had, for most of her life, sought the guidance of her *Aunt Emily.* She had always loved and respected her parents. But her Aunt Emily seemed to offer other opinions, other options when Mercy disagreed with the advice they gave even though she knew it was always intended for her best.

Now, with the understanding of just who this woman of wisdom truly was, Mercy had come to depend on her even more. And Miss Emily certainly knew what her daughter needed to talk with her about when she appeared at her door unannounced early one morning. She knew how her daughter was being torn between *two* loves in her life.

"Come in sweetheart, I've been expecting you," Miss Emily said, as Aldon Barlow escorted her from the front hall to the dining room. Though Mercy knew the way, she noticed how Aldon often liked to walk the short distance of the hallway beside her, exchanging pleasantries whenever she came for a visit. She sensed he somehow thought of her as his own child. He had always acted fatherly towards her, asking about her health, her work, what she was doing. Over the years they had grown quite close and she had long ago accepted him as nothing other than family.

"I'm sorry for coming here without calling first. I just needed to talk," Mercy apologized.

"Nonsense, child. You never need to announce your coming. This is your home as much as it is mine. Surely you must know that by now?" Miss Emily said, inviting her to take a seat near her. She poured a cup of tea for Mercy then refilled her own. She offered over a plate of Danish but Mercy waved them off.

"I'm not all that hungry, mother," Mercy said. The older woman more than understood Mercy hadn't come for a mere social visit.

"Must not be easy," Miss Emily offered. Mercy didn't answer knowing a reply wasn't needed. Tears began welling up in her eyes. Ever since she had learned of Henry's return, every night when she went to bed and every morning when she awoke, the same troubled feelings remained with her. When she was with Garrett, she felt guilt for no longer being completely certain of her feelings for him. When she was with Henry, she somehow felt she was betraying Garrett.

Back and forth her feelings tugged at her. She had no appetite, struggled to sleep, and had even grown unable to focus on her weaving orders, finding the mere act no longer satisfying. She felt as though she was just going through the moments of her days.

"I just don't know what to do. I had accepted the fact that Henry was gone. I had actually used my anger for his decision to leave to fill the void in my heart made by the sorrow I felt," Mercy admitted.

"I don't understand. Why would you have been angry at him. Like so many young boys, it wasn't really their choice to go to war," Miss Emily tried to reason.

"That's not entirely the truth. I never told anyone but it *was* his choice. At his age, Henry had no fear of being drafted. I'm not saying it wasn't right for him to want to serve his country. Just that there were other ways he could have chosen to do so. Henry wanted to leave here for other reasons."

"Well, I'm sure many men felt the same way. I suppose that's been true for all young men in every war. It's a chance to see things beyond their surroundings, experience things out there in the world. For most of us, we are born, live, and die within so few miles of our beginnings," Miss Emily offered.

Mercy nodded her head; she could accept that much. But she knew there was more.

"If that was all there was to it mother, I'd accept that," Mercy insisted.

"Then what more is there, daughter?" Miss Emily asked.

"He wasn't sure about *us*," Mercy confessed. "He never perhaps said so in words exactly but I always felt there was some question in his mind as to whether or not he was ready to, or even wanted to, settle down with a wife and family."

Miss Emily saw her daughter's pained expression and her immediate desire was to ensure Mercy that she was mistaken. But she could see in Mercy's face that there was indeed more truth than imagination to what Mercy was saying. It also explained other things. They had been engaged for well over a year before Henry left and in all that time, they had not announced a wedding date, had made no plans, none at least that Mercy had ever shared with her.

"Why did you not tell me, sweetheart?"

"Honestly, I was too embarrassed. And I kept hope alive that if he returned, and I prayed that he would, he would have changed. Changed his feeling towards marriage, changed his feelings towards me. I thought maybe going to war, seeing all the horrors I had heard told of, he would understand how blessed he was to just come home to me. And I didn't want the family to think he left because of me," Mercy confessed, tears now flowing steadily down her face.

Miss Emily reached out, wrapping her daughter in her arms, trying to comfort her. In many ways, she, too, understood what it was like to love someone who was distant from her. It might not be the same as a man who was ensure of himself as Mercy now revealed Henry had been, but she nevertheless knew what it was like to love a man she couldn't have because her family had not approved, especially under the circumstances in which her daughter, Mercy, had come into the world.

"Then perhaps there is no decision to really make. You do love Garrett do you not?" Miss Emily asked.

"Yes," Mercy answered, nodding her head.

"And you do believe he loves you?"

"I do. Very much I think," Mercy said.

"And have you spoken of marriage?"

"Yes, although he has not as much as asked me," Mercy insisted.

"Then perhaps the time has come to talk with him about that," Miss Emily suggested.

Mercy looked up at her, not sure what she was suggesting.

"But women don't ask man to propose to them, mother," Mercy said.

Miss Emily reached out, lifting Mercy's head up with her hand to look into her eyes and smiled.

"Perhaps not in so many words, but I assure you dear daughter, women have been getting men to ask that question for as long as the two sexes have existed. Poor helpless souls that they are, men just don't always know that what they thought they were pursuing had all the while been merely waiting to be *caught!*"

Mercy found herself slightly amused at her mother's words. It eased her feeling of helplessness. But she wasn't so certain that a proposal from Garrett would resolve her dilemma. After all, Henry had already proposed to her. She just wasn't sure now if he truly still felt as strongly about that as he once did. And if Garrett were to now propose to her, she couldn't be sure if it was something he had been on the verge of doing or was simply now doing more out of feeling of urgency to avoid losing her. She couldn't accept marriage with either on such terms.

"Have you ever been in a situation like this, mother?" Mercy asked.

Miss Emily smiled at her, patting her hands to comfort her. But the truth was she hadn't.

"No sweetheart, I have not nor can I say what I would do in such a situation," Miss Emily admitted.

"But you did love my father, did you not?" Mercy asked.

Miss Emily looked away for a moment, silent. Twice now in just a few months Mercy sensed her mother was still holding something more from her. But Miss Emily turned back to her daughter, looking deeply into her daughter's eyes.

"Oh yes, my child, I did very much love that young boy; your father. In fact, I still do very much. He is in my heart every day when I wake, every night when I go to rest." the older woman insisted. It was such an emotional response that Mercy had little doubt of its sincerity.

"Then how can I choose? Though they are different in so many ways, I believe they both are sincere in their love for me," Mercy insisted.

"Sadly, loving someone isn't always enough. It takes a strong bond between two people to weather the storms of a relationship, of a marriage. And there will be stormy times just as sure as there will be good times. But we sometimes get confused between feelings of lust and those of love. Lust is little more than the planting of the seeds of love. Lust is a passing moment in time. But real love? That is the true bloom of that seed. It's when you can let go of your own sense of self-preservation and replace it with self-sacrifice. When you grow to a point where there is no longer any separation in mind, body, and spirit between you and that other person," Miss Emily insisted.

As she listened to her mother's words, she pictured Garrett. Then Henry. She looked for a revelation, some epiphany to strike her. None came.

"Anyway, you will know in time. You have only to keep enjoying the company of both. Your time with Garrett is still fairly new yet and your time with Henry should focus on a renewal of the friendship you had. If one or the other cannot accept that, perhaps then you shall have your answer," Miss Emily suggested.

Mercy realized her mother was right. There was indeed no need to force a decision. She needed time to sort through it all.

"Thank you, mother. I do so love you," Mercy said. She stood to leave, bending over to kiss her mother on the cheek, just as she had done since she was a little girl. But for Emily Wescott, such moments had taken on a new feeling of closeness ever since the true nature of their relationship had been finally revealed.

Mercy started towards the hallway door from the dining room, surprised by Aldon Barlow, who just happened to be standing there in the hallway as though he had been waiting for her just out of earshot. He walked alongside her as she was leaving.

"Miss Mercy, if you don't mind me saying, you seemed a little...well...*distressed*, when I greeted you at our door this morning," Aldon said.

Again, this was something Mercy had noticed on other occasions. Aldon often referred to Miss Emily's house as his as well. But he had been in her mother's employ for as long as Mercy could remember. In fact, his being there was one of her earliest memories. So, she had really always thought it seemed only right he should see Halcroft as his home as well.

"You know if you ever need to talk about things, maybe get an old man's view on something, I'm always here to help," Aldon told her.

Mercy hooked her arm through the gray-haired man's arm, giving him a warm hug.

"I know that Aldon. You have been such a good friend to all of us these many years. To my mother and to me you have been like family," Mercy assured him.

"Is it Doc Harrington's son, Garrett, that troubles you?" Aldon asked, "Or your fiancé Henry?"

Mercy hadn't expected the question. But she knew it was pointless to feign ignorance at Aldon Barlow's question that her troubled look had to do with anything other than the two men. She paused just before the front door, turning to look at the man who had always held a place in her life. She did have a question she wanted to ask though she wondered if it might not be awkward for them both. Mercy hesitated but then asked it anyway.

"Tell me, have you ever been in love?"

Aldon smiled ever so slightly, though Mercy felt his face bore a slightly pained look. Mercy sensed there was something hidden deeper within him. She now felt ashamed for having pried.

"Oh, forgive me, I had no right to..." Mercy quickly started to apologize. But Aldon gently put his hand up to quiet her.

"A fair question, a fair one for sure. Yes, I most certainly have. You young people don't have an exclusive on love. I, too, fell in love once," Aldon confessed.

"And?" Mercy continued.

"And it was the most marvelous thing to have ever happened to me. That's all I will say of it. So, you, my dear girl, must search your own heart for your own answer. But as I am sure your mother just told you, in time, and likely soon, your heart will tell you what you need to know," Aldon assured her, opening up the front door for her.

As she stepped past him to leave, as she had with her mother, she leaned over and kissed him impulsively on his cheek. Aldon Barlow smiled warmly at the gesture. He closed the door behind her, standing for a moment, deep in thought. It troubled him to see Mercy this way, her usual bright personality dimmed by the indecision she was facing. It wasn't normal for him to just stand by, not being able to do anything. He had always fashioned himself as the family protector. He found no fault in Garrett Harrington. He was certain the young man had feelings for Mercy, though perhaps a little slow in declaring them in a way that left no doubt of his desires.

But Aldon wasn't as sure of what Henry Gates was truly about. Though he had overheard the conversation the two women had just shared, he was wise to the way of men, knew how some could race headlong towards relationships, towards marriage, while others sometimes shrunk from the vision. It wasn't his right perhaps to judge another man's actions but then this wasn't just any young woman who was involved.

He returned to the dining room to find Miss Emily staring out the window, her gaze seemingly miles away beyond the harbor below. She barely noticed when he stepped back into the room, taking a chair on the other side of the table near here.

"Not a good situation," Aldon said. Miss Emily only nodded her head slowly, continuing to look out upon the water.

"No...no it isn't," she agreed.

"And I imagine it's not easy for you either," Aldon added.

Again, Miss Emily shook her head in agreement.

"Nor for you either I assume," she said.

"No, it isn't. But then I've grown accustomed to keeping much of my feelings to myself all these many years," Aldon admitted.

Miss Emily reached out, laying her hand on his. She let it rest there. They both fell silent, watching the boats heading out of the harbor to the open bay on the morning run.

"I know. I have never forgotten that. You have had to bear witness to her growing up right before you," Miss Emily said, turning to look into his eyes. There were tears flowing down her cheek. He reached out and gently wiped them away.

"Perhaps it is time. She probably needs to know the rest of it," Miss Emily said quietly.

Aldon looked at her, thought about it. Yes, it might be something that needed to be done but he wasn't sure that now was the time.

"Not now. She's had so much to adjust to. We always said there would come a time, but not now. Later, when she's been able to get this behind her," Aldon suggested.

Miss Emily didn't say anything further. It was his decision. She had respected that right just as he had kept her secret from Mercy all these years.

Chapter 32

Garrett had not been himself the last few weeks and Doc had certainly noticed the change. While his nephew continued to keep up with all his appointments, both inside and outside the office, Doc could nevertheless see that the young man appeared to merely be going through the routine. Their conversations were suddenly limited to work, the patients, and only those things that focused on running the practice. Garrett had grown distant. Doc suspected he knew the cause but also believed that his nephew would talk to him about it when he was ready.

When, after several more days of this, his nephew's demeanor hadn't changed and he had not come forth with any explanation, Doc decided it was time to take the first step towards getting Garrett to open up. They had always enjoyed a closeness when it came to talking about anything and everything. The two had even talked about girls, when his nephew had first become aware of the opposite sex as being something other than childhood friends to play with on the beach, searching for pirate treasure or exotic shells.

As Garrett saw the last of their patients out for the day, Doc asked him to step into his office. He motioned for Garrett to take a chair across from his desk, As Garrett did, his uncle pulled a side desk drawer open and produced a bottle of whiskey, Jameson, his favorite, and two glasses. It was one thing Doc had found to be better than any truth serum ever devised. As his own Irish father had often said, "Never trust a man who doesn't drink. For sure he's hiding something."

Doc blew the dust out of both of the glasses. He poured out two healthy doses of the amber liquid, pushing one of the glasses towards his nephew.

"What's this?" Garrett said, "And it's not even Friday yet."

"Oh, the hell with that. The end of any day is always a good and just cause to sit back and enjoy a sip," Doc insisted.

But Garrett knew there was more coming. He had tried to appear as he always did, smiling, energetic. But it hadn't been easy, always that one thing that kept creeping back into his mind.

"How is Mercy doing? I haven't seen her around much these last few weeks," Doc asked, zeroing right in.

"She's fine. Been a little busy, that's all," Garrett said, trying to sound nonchalant.

"Must be difficult for her," Doc offered. Garrett nodded. He didn't need to have his uncle explain what he was referring to. They both knew.

"Amazing story. I know the boy, that Henry Gates. Good enough young man I suppose though I hadn't figured him for an enlistee. Some said at his age, near thirty I believe when he signed up, he certainly didn't have to," Doc said, idly twirling the whiskey around in his glass.

"Yes, I heard that but I suppose like so many of us, there was a little pressure all the same. What with so many joining up or even being drafted, hard for a young guy to stay out of it. People talk, you know how it is," Garrett suggested.

Doc Harrington shook his head in agreement.

"That's certainly true. Though no one around here would have said much about it I'm sure. Anyway, pretty much broke that young girl's heart Miss Emily said when he did leave. Then, of course, came that damn screw up from the War Department claiming he was dead. I've heard tell of a couple such cases. Can't even begin to imagine how those families dealt with that. I suppose getting their loved ones back makes up for it though," Doc insisted.

Garrett didn't reply. His uncle's words had perhaps hit on Garrett's greatest feeling of guilt. If he were completely honest with his uncle right now, he'd admit to one dark thought that he felt guilty for having. A part of him, the selfish part of him, actually wished Henry hadn't come home.

"Uncle let me ask you something."

"Anything, nephew," Doc said, though it didn't take much guess work as to what it was about.

"Should I just step aside?"

Doc hadn't actually expected the bluntness of Garrett's question.

"Well...I suppose that would depend."

"On what?" Garrett asked.

"Well, on whether you and Mercy have become serious enough about each other for you to think you had to make room for someone else in her life. Is that the case, son?"

Garrett had always thought it appeared obvious, at least to his uncle and Miss Emily. Even Addy knew about their feelings for each other. But Doc wasn't asking a question. He was making a point. Yes, he knew his nephew and Mercy Daniels had become close, more than friends, perhaps even *lovers* though respectable society didn't talk openly of such things.

"Sure, at least I thought we were, I mean that she was...serious about me...about *us*," Garrett assured him.

"Then I suppose you have as much right as the next man to hold your ground. Afterall, doesn't Mercy get a say in this?" Doc suggested.

"But they were engaged," Garrett reminded his uncle.

"True. Very true. But some say he made his choice to leave. And some even go as far as to say not strictly out of some patriotic sense of duty but perhaps because he was having second thoughts. Many a young man has gotten cold feet when they start to look at things in the wrong light. Marriage is forever or at least it ought to be," Doc insisted.

"Still, maybe I have no right to interfere," Garrett said.

"Nonsense, you have as much right as the next man to win that young girl's heart. As I said, don't you think that's her decision in the end anyway? If you have feelings for her, and I know you do, you can't just accept things as lost until she, not you, not Henry Gates, not anyone else, says it is so," Doc insisted.

Garrett thought it over. He felt his spirits lift a little, began to see it as he was being presented with a challenge. He could accept losing his heart over her but he'd be damned if he'd go quietly if there was even the slightest chance for him.

"But I'll tell you this, Garrett Harrington. If you've a mind to keep that young girl for yourself you'd best not be wasting any more time declaring it. Ever figure what she might be going through, torn between the two of you, not knowing even if she has a choice to make," Doc insisted.

Garrett knew his uncle was right, of course. Though he and Mercy had shared words on how they each felt for each other, even said they loved each other, he had never gone beyond that. He had never declared his love for her as strongly as a proposal confirms.

Doc pushed his desk chair back slightly, sliding one of the drawers open. He produced a small box and slid it across the desk top towards Garrett. The young man picked the small box up and opened it, revealing a sparkling diamond ring inside. He looked up at this uncle, eyes questioning.

"It was your Aunt's, my dear Mary's. I know she would approve. So, you truly now have no reason for any more delay. If you want that girl as your own you better damn well get to it!" Doc insisted.

Listening to his uncle, it did seem all that simple, Garrett thought. He had to declare his true feeling, his heart to Mercy. If nothing else, she would know his true intentions. If she chose Henry then at least he would not wonder for the rest of his life if losing her had been a matter of his simply not having let Mercy know how much he wanted her. He could live with her saying no, hard as that might be to take, but he didn't want to live with the regret of having done nothing. Then Garrett remembered it might indeed not be as simple as his uncle suggested. There was perhaps something more.

"But uncle, she's already engaged," Garrett reminded him.

"Is she? Does she wear his ring?" Doc asked.

"No, but she only took it off when she thought he was dead," Garrett insisted.

"And now, now that he's not dead, and after all this time, has she put it back on?"

Garrett realized she had not. He saw her hands in his mind. She wore no ring.

"Nephew, you are a Harrington, are you not? I've never known us to be a people of indecision. You won't get a chance like this again. I can attest to that. I've known many a woman in my life. Seen all kinds and I know this much about Mercy Daniels. She's one of the rare ones. Her heart is as big as they come. She's a gentle woman but one not to be trifled with. She knows her own mind. She cares for others around her in the most unselfish way. As to her beauty, well there's no need of

297

saying more," Doc said, swallowing the last of the whiskey in his glass.

"She's known her challenges, had her own struggles, and yet look at what she did for that young lost girl with child. No, my dear nephew you cannot look to find better. She's as right for you as my beloved Mary was for me. This I can assure you," Doc continued, the look on his face as convincing as Garrett had ever seen.

However, Garrett didn't need any more convincing. He knew his uncle was right. Mercy was different to be sure. And every time he was with her, he felt comfort, a warmth that when they parted seemed to leave him. He had certainly known a sense of lust with other women, a desire to know their closeness, the touch of their bodies next to him, a hand held, a lip kissed. But when he was with Mercy, he knew it was different. He knew that she was such a woman that no matter what of life's storms would befall him, she would be by his side. It was not a feeling he had truly known before. Gentlemen were raised to be the protectors. But his mother had perhaps forgotten to mention that a good woman, the right woman, could be a man's own shelter.

"I'll do it!" Garrett said to himself, not realizing he had spoken his thoughts out loud.

"Then it is done. Waste no more time, nephew. You go see that young lady and you ask her to marry you. You don't let a minute longer pass. Tonight. Or as God is my witness, I'll ask her myself!" Doc swore.

Chapter 33

With each passing day, Henry found that his condition continued to improve. He was now walking with only the most minimal need for his cane to steady him. His morning walks around the hospital grounds grew longer, no longer aided by the staff. The orderlies had left him to himself, certain their need to walk alongside him was no longer a necessity. The doctors had let him know he was pretty much ready for release any time he wanted. The only lingering pain he felt was the headaches that came mostly at night, so severe they would jolt him awake in the middle of his sleep. That and the nightmares. Bizarre and twisted fear filled experiences. Disconnected thoughts, places, and images. But he kept those to himself. He knew if he discussed them with anyone, especially the doctors, it might be a much longer time before going home.

He had been out walking for the better part of an hour one morning when he felt his legs growing weak again. He had been pushing it lately, each morning's walk a little farther. He decided it might be best to return to his room. Lay down. Rest again.

As he entered his room, he was surprised to find someone else already there, sitting in one of the chairs by the small table near his bed. The man's back was to him. He was looking out the window at the hospital grounds but upon hearing Henry enter, the man turned slightly to show his face, though he didn't bother to stand up.

"Good morning Henry, old friend."

"Mr. Barlow? Well, this is certainly unexpected. How have you been?" Henry asked, limping over to shake Aldon's hand.

"I believe the more interesting question is, how are *you*? I've heard your story. Quite an amazing one I must say. We are all so very glad you found your way back home," Aldon said, motioning for the young man to take a chair at the table. Actually, Henry had wanted to just lay down in his bed upon his return but somehow thought better it might certainly be rude of him to do so.

Yes, Henry agreed. They were "old friends" in a manner of speaking. Henry had visited Miss Emily's house many times in Mercy Daniels' company. But Mr. Barlow, as Henry had always called him, troubled him. Henry had always had sort of an odd feeling around the man as if there was more to him than simply a house servant.

Once when he was a just beginning to court Mercy, they had stopped by Miss Emily's house to let Miss Emily see Mercy's new dress she was wearing for a church social that night. Henry remembered how both women thought his brown tie didn't match his blue suit, a silly thing in his mind but important enough to Mercy that she insisted he march straight down to Aldon Barlow's quarters in the house and ask to borrow another tie. When he arrived at the doorway of Aldon's room, however, he found the room empty. Barlow was somewhere else about the house. He had thought to turn and leave. But fearing further scolding from Mercy, he quickly entered the room and opened the door to the armoire, expecting to find a collection of ties hanging amidst shirts, pants, and suit coats. He was sure Aldon wouldn't mind when he discovered it had been Mercy and Miss Emily's idea to borrow one. But to his surprise the cabinet was empty, not an article of clothing, nothing. Then perhaps out of sheer curiosity, Henry had opened a few drawers of the dresser in the room and found each of them to likewise be empty. He quickly left the room and never mentioned a thing to Mercy, simply telling her he really liked his tie and had bought it just for this dance. Thankfully Mercy let it drop. But it had always remained one of those odd things Henry connected with this strange man that no one in Wellfleet seemed to know much about other than he had been in the employ of the Wescott household for so many years.

Henry took a seat at the opposite side of the table from Aldon Barlow. He noticed what appeared to be a bottle of something wrapped up in aging yellow-brown paper tied up with string. Aldon eased the package across the table.

"Here, I brought you something. A welcome home gift. Twenty-year old Canadian Whiskey from my own private stock. Forgive the wrappings, it's the way all of them came back then," Aldon said.

Henry took the bottle and peeled away the musty smelling craft paper to indeed reveal a bottle of fine 1925 cask aged Canadian whiskey.

"I'm sure you will have to hide it from the staff and take it with you when you get out of here," Aldon whispered to the younger man as though they were sharing a secret only the two of them would hold.

"Thank you, Mr. Barlow, I appreciate the gift. Very generous of you. Yes, I will, of course, take it with me when I am released," Henry promised.

"And when might that be?" Aldon asked.

"Likely any day now I suppose. The Doctor said it's pretty much up to me. I'm sure they could use the bed for someone more in need."

"No doubt, no doubt," Aldon agreed, "And where will you be heading?"

Henry thought it an odd question. "Well, back home to Wellfleet, of course."

"Oh, yes, of course. Likely an apartment. Perhaps your old place?" Aldon suggested.

"As it turns out, yes, I've made arrangements to rent it again."

"And a job?" Aldon continued to ask.

Henry now began to feel they were having more than just a casual reunion; that he was somehow being interrogated. It was turning into something more than just two man who knew each other sharing a conversation.

"Well, I suppose if you must know, I've gotten a position at the fish processing plant. It's only temporary, of course, until I'm fit enough for a berth abroad one of the fleet boats. But I must ask, why all this interest, Mr. Barlow?"

"Oh, purely out of concern for you, Henry. Nothing more. Thought if you needed some assistance I could be of help. I have a number of connections and with jobs being at a premium, what with all the men returning home, sometimes knowing the right people can make the different," Aldon suggested.

"That's certainly generous of you. But I think I'll be able to manage," Henry assured him.

"And so how are you and Mercy getting along? Aldon asked, finally getting to the true purpose of his visit.

Henry studied the man for a moment. If it had been pretty much anyone asking, certainly a true friend, he wouldn't have found the inquiry all that odd. But again, coming from Aldon Barlow, it just somehow seemed out of place. He weighed his answer carefully.

"Mercy has been wonderful. Comes to see me several times a week. We talk. She's filled me in on all I missed here and I tell her about the war, though I dare say cautiously. There was much of that experience needs no repeating," Henry said.

"No, I can certainly imagine. Best a young woman like our Mercy be spared such stories," Aldon agreed.

Henry noted how the older man referred to her as "our Mercy." He had remembered him doing so on other occasions in the past. Again, it was just one of those things that sounded odd to him, as though Aldon had assumed a role in their lives beyond merely that of a house servant.

"That's good. It pleases me you both are getting along. I thought perhaps she might still harbor some hurt feelings about you going off to war. She struggled with that for many months I can tell you. Had Miss Emily quite upset as well," Aldon said.

"Yes, I understand that now. You do realize that it hadn't been my intention to cause anyone pain. It was just something I felt I had to do," Henry felt he was somehow defending himself though again he wasn't sure why.

"Oh, I understand, Henry. Truly I do. A young man needs to seek a little adventure before he settles down. Needs to see what's beyond the hills so to speak, else he could end up wondering what he missed for the rest of his life," Aldon assured him.

Henry thought about it for a moment. He knew that had certainly been part of it as well. Yes, he felt a duty to serve. Most men did. But there had been that fear that the world was passing him by, that he might spend his entire life living no more than a few miles in any direction from where he was right then. And even as much as he loved Mercy, it might not be enough. So yes, he knew Aldon Barlow was right. A brief adventure was all he saw it as, nothing more. She would understand, be waiting for him when he returned, just as countless other wives and sweethearts had waited.

But whatever had been his thinking, whatever had been the motivation behind his actions, he still didn't see it as any of Aldon Barlow's business.

"So, you are ready to come home then," Aldon said, "I'm sure you are anxious to get back to your old life. Get back to work. Plan your wedding with Mercy no doubt,"

Again, had it been anyone else, Henry might not have felt the question somehow invasive, even a bit out of line. He didn't answer. But it wasn't silence Aldon Barlow had come for on this question.

"I assume that is you plan, is it not son?" Aldon asked. Henry felt and ever-growing sense of irritation.

"We have things to discuss if that is what you are asking?"

Aldon Barlow grinned, seeing he was getting Henry to open up a little more.

"Precisely. Yes, you both no doubt have much to discuss. It will do you both good for sure. She has been under quite a strain these last few months, what with having to first accept losing you, learning to move on, cultivate, how should I say, other *interests* and then, like a ghost as it were from her past, you reappear. All a bit rattling for her I can tell you. And for Miss Emily I might add as I'm sure you can imagine."

"Yes, I can certainly appreciate what she has gone through," Henry said, wondering if Barlow could even begin to fathom what, he, Henry had endured.

"Can you?" Aldon asked.

Now Henry decided he *was* certain this man, Aldon Barlow, *was* irritating him. He decided to see just where Barlow was going with all this.

"And as to these other *interests*, what might *they* be, Mr. Barlow?" Henry asked, though he suspected he knew exactly the other man's point.

"Well, I'm sure you can appreciate that a young girl like Mercy, still very much eligible in life, having lost someone, would in time want to move on, would she not?" Aldon asked.

"And I'm assuming you are referring to Doc Harrington's nephew, what's his name?"

"Garrett." Aldon quickly offered.

"Yes, Garrett...Harrington."

Henry wasn't blind. He could see whenever Mercy and Doctor Harrington were together in his hospital room that they were more than casual acquaintances. He had seen the looks they exchanged.

"Well, it certainly isn't for me to say. But yes, I would imagine she has indeed developed somewhat of an *interest* you might say,"

"Well, as you say, it is all very intriguing. But I'm hardly concerned. Are you forgetting we are engaged?"

"Yes, there is that isn't there? I haven't forgotten. But are we certain she hasn't though? I don't recall having seen her with the ring on her hand, not for some time, and certainly not even now these several months you have been back."

Henry had finally had enough. There it finally was. This conversation, this little charade of a visit to see how he was doing, had gone on long enough. Time to end it.

"Mr. Barlow, you will have to excuse me. I had rather a long walk this morning and frankly I need some rest. So, if there's nothing else, I'll say my goodbyes and thank you for your visit as well as your concern," Henry said, standing to usher the man out.

Aldon Barlow rose slowly, not wishing to show that he was being hurried in any way by Henry's abrupt suggestion he leave. He lifted up his long black coat he had folded neatly over the back of the chair when he arrived and calmly eased each arm in to put it on.

"Oh, I certainly understand, Henry. I'm sorry if I overstayed my welcome. Was not my intent. Just enjoyed chatting again," Aldon said, extending his hand to shake Henry. Henry obliged.

Aldon started for the door but turned once more to face Henry as he neared the threshold.

"Actually, there is something I wanted to be sure we had an understanding on. My expectation is you will do right by Mercy. Stay or leave, you'll be sure to work this out soon. I'm sure we both agree nobody wants to see her continue on this way. She's not herself. And we *all* are concerned," Aldon Barlow said, "Enjoy the whiskey."

With that, Aldon Barlow disappeared down the hall. Henry stood a moment, turning over the man's words in his head. He wasn't completely sure but somehow, he believed they had been some sort of threat.

Chapter 34

As Henry's health improved, Mercy felt she could reduce her visits to once a week for an hour or so. She had let her work suffer from the constant trips to see him and she was getting behind. She also suspected he would be discharged any day now. He had already rented his old apartment back in town and the fish processing plant had hired him for an inside job until he felt he was ready enough to go back out on the boats. He told her he was glad to be home and looking forward to getting back to work but she could tell there was something else still troubling him. He didn't talk much about the war, even less about the prisoner camp and his experience there. She thought in time he might. But so far, he hadn't and she realized only he would know when he was ready, if ever.

She brought him another pair of wool socks she had made, the kind she knew would keep him warm if and when he did return to working the ocean waters of the bay and sea. If the weather was fair, she and Henry would sit outside when she came to see him so they could enjoy the sunshine and air despite the chill of oncoming winter. She was glad to see that Henry had learned to get around just fine with little more than the help of a cane. They both agreed that before long even that could be tossed aside.

Other than the occasional flare ups of malaria, which the doctors said would likely disappear at some point, he was returning to the physical condition he had been in before he left for the war. But the nightmares were still there. He didn't say much about them to her other than that they came almost every night and left him in an exhausted sweat when he awoke each early morning.

She tried to get him to open up about them, assuring him it was only natural to experience such things given what he had been through. She tried to encourage him to talk to the doctors but he had so far refused, suggesting he didn't need a "shrink" to certify him as crazy.

But Mercy noticed that even as Henry returned to being the same person he had been physically, there was something different. Certainly, in his mood, even in his smile, which seemed to only appear rarely and when it did, perhaps in response to some good news or something funny she tried to share with him, it seemed forced. The doctors said it was likely just some temporary depression brought on by the war. They could treat that they assured him. But Mercy sensed there was more. It was as if part of the Henry she knew had not come home, was still out there somewhere, waiting to find his way back.

They sat in the hospital garden, watching the wind whirl the first fallen leaves across the ground. Mercy remembered it had been the beginning of Autumn when Henry had asked her to marry him and then just a month later, he was gone. Off to Camp Peary in Virginia for basic training before being loaded up on a troop train west to ship out across the Pacific. She had kept the letters he had written her, filled with stories of all the new adventures he was having. Everything was new to him and his letters gave off the sense of excitement he was feeling. She would read each one several times, sharing with him his adventures through those letters. But as the weeks turned to months and the months rolled on, their arrival dwindled to one or two and then there were simply none. Her friends told her it was nothing to worry about. The military censors enacted greater and greater restrictions on communications back home for fear information about troop location and activities would leak into enemy hands people said reassuringly. But she had already begun to fear the worst even before word came from the government that he was lost at sea, his ship sunk by the Japanese with no survivors. She had kept all his letters all the same, at first planning to keep them for his scrapbook when he returned and later, after the news of his death, as a memory of a young man she had once loved and lost.

They sipped on the coffee they had gotten from the hospital cafeteria, each of them bundled up in warm coats. Mercy caught him up on her week, the new woven items she had sold, everything from placemats to blankets. Her weaving business had really started to grow she told him, hoping he would show interest. With so many customers ordering new things now that the war rationing had been lifted, she said she had even begun thinking about maybe teaching Addy the art of weaving on the loom so she could help out and earn some of her own money.

As she talked, she noticed that Henry only appeared to be listening, nodding his head every once and awhile, smiling as though he understood. But she felt he was somehow still off somewhere else at times. Then after one particularly long silence, he spoke.

"You know I had a visit yesterday from your old friend, Mr. Barlow," Henry said.

"Aldon Barlow? Here?" Mercy asked, not sure she had heard him correctly.

"Oh yes, was sitting in my room when I returned from my morning walk. No announcement. In fact, he seemed to have been able to even get past the front nurse's desk without so much as a call from the receptionist to see if it was alright."

"He never said a word to me that he was planning a visit. Well, that was certainly nice of him, wasn't it?" Mercy said, somehow sensing Henry didn't share that feeling.

"So, you had no idea he was coming here?" Henry asked.

"Me? Why would I?"

"Well, he seemed rather concerned about you. I just thought perhaps you had been talking with him," Henry suggested.

"No, not at all. I'll admit, Aldon has certainly always taken a keen interest in me. But I certainly don't make it a habit of sharing my troubles with him," Mercy said.

Then she remembered her having asked him about whether he had ever been in love before. And she realized he could well have also overheard her and her mother the other morning when she was visiting and talking about her troubles.

"What exactly did he say?" Mercy asked, her curiosity now rising.

"To be honest, it wasn't so much *what* he said but rather *how* he said it. I had the feeling he was warning me about something, about getting things settled with you," Henry admitted.

"Settled? I don't understand?" Mercy said, not sure she liked where this was going either.

"He said you've been upset a lot lately. Maybe not so sure of things anymore, sure of us."

Now it did start to add up, Mercy thought. And yes, while it was the truth, it wasn't something she felt Aldon Barlow, old family friend or not, had a right to meddle in. Though for all Mercy knew, her mother may have had a hand in this herself. Mercy had never known Aldon to do much of anything strictly on his own when it came to the business of the family, especially her mother.

"And what exactly did you tell him?" Mercy asked, herself now a little more than just casually interested in what the two men had spoken about.

"I told him we had things to work out. That there had obviously been a few changes since I had left," Henry suggested.

Indeed, there had been Mercy thought to herself. And yet perhaps nothing had changed or at least had gotten resolved between them. He left, he had his reasons, whether she had agreed with them or not. And she still questioned whether whatever had caused him to leave her wasn't perhaps still lingering deep inside him somewhere. Had his time in the military, his time as a prisoner of war, convinced him his life was here in this small town, here with her? Or was that yearning for something more, something distant and elusive likely to surface again.

"And what exactly are those things that we need to work out, Henry?" Mercy pressed him.

She knew it was time they talked. It had been nearly three months since his return and she had waited patiently while he recovered. But it was time. There were others to be considered. She couldn't, wouldn't put her life on hold again. She had done that once. She would not do it again.

"Well,...things. Just *things*. That's all," Henry answered, still seeming vague about what *things* in particular.

"I mean after all, I have to get established all over again. No money coming in other than a few dollars from Navy disability and that won't last long. How am I going to support a wife on that?

Mercy sat listening, silent. Letting him go on.

"I'll barely be able to cover my rent. But I'm getting better every day. The job inside the fish processing plant, that's just temporary. Once I'm able, I'll land a berth aboard one of the fishing boats and then you'll see. I'll be making good money then," Henry insisted.

Mercy continued to listen, only half convinced.

"I suppose you're right. But I don't remember any of this talk when we got engaged. Certainly not how much money you made. We loved each other you said and that was all we needed to get by. Remember?" Mercy reminded him of his own words.

"Sure, sure, I remember but honey, we were just two dumb kids then. That's what I mean when I say *things* have changed. I had to do a lot of growing up to survive, we both did. I'm just saying we need to plan things out a little more now," Henry insisted.

"So, we need to wait is what you are trying to say. Wait to be married," Mercy asked.

Henry nodded his head. Maybe she understood he thought.

"Yes, that's all I'm saying. Why rush into something until we are both ready. We are still young, there is time. I just want to establish myself a little more. I don't want you to have to keep working all day and night at that loom, weaving things for the people around here. That's not what I want for you," Henry said.

"You make it sound like its drudgery. I love my work. And the fact that I can make money from something I love to do anyway is all the better. I would have thought you knew that, you would support me in that. Are you saying you want me to give that up?"

"Well, I would have thought you would want to, of course. You'll have a house to keep, a husband to look after, maybe even a few kids of our own one day," Henry insisted as though he had it all mapped out for them both.

Mercy felt as though she were suddenly talking to a stranger. How could he have all these plans that they had never talked about, that didn't seem to take her own feelings and concerns into account.

"Are you having second thoughts? Is that it?" Mercy asked, trying to understand. Henry paused before answering. He studied her face but what Mercy saw in his was indecision.

"It's not like that," Henry finally said.

"Then what is it? You haven't been the same since you came home. You're...well...different," Mercy insisted.

"Is that what you think. Different?!" Henry said, his voice rising, "Well, I would think you'd be a little more understanding yourself. It's not like I haven't been through one of the most life changing of situations. I still have nightmares from those long, horrible months."

Mercy wasn't sure what to say. Certainly, she realized what a horrible ordeal it had been for him, for all of those in that camp. Like so many others, she was only just now beginning to hear of the stories, the atrocities, see the pictures in the newspapers.

Yes, she could understand it was an adjustment to find himself back home where everything seemed so orderly, calm, peaceful. But she still couldn't help the feeling that Henry was pulling back. He seemed distant and even now, after several months of being home, that hadn't changed. Maybe that's why she still just looked at the engagement ring sitting in the ring box on her dresser rather than put it back on. He hadn't once asked about it being absent from her finger.

"I'm sorry Henry if I've upset you. I don't mean to do that. I do understand. Perhaps it is best we speak no more of it for now." Mercy suggested. Henry nodded.

"Well, I'm sure you want to get some rest. Unless you want me to stay?" Mercy said.

"No, you're right. I'm sure you have work to tend to."

Mercy stood up and kissed him on his forehead, turning quickly to hide the tears starting to form in her eyes. She left him there, sitting in the garden, gazing off into the distance as though he were a thousand miles away. As she walked back to the hospital wing to return to her car, she paused a moment, fighting back the urge to return to him. She felt an overwhelming premonition of finality as she began to leave. She turned and went back to where Henry was still on a garden bench. He was staring off across the hospital grounds, unaware of her return until she spoke.

"Henry, some time ago, a few months after we had been seeing each other, you told me for the first time that you loved me, do you remember that? Mercy asked.

Henry slowly nodded his head.

"And do you remember what you also said? Long before you asked for my hand?"

Henry did remember.

"I said we should get married someday."

"And do you remember what I told you then?"

"Yes. You said I shouldn't speak of such things if I didn't mean it."

"Yes. And we didn't...speak of it again... for quite a while. In fact, not until you asked me to marry you. And then not but a week or so after, you told me of your plans to go into the service."

"I'm not sure what you are getting at. I did ask you to marry me and gave you a ring, which I might add I notice you are no longer wearing," Henry pointed out.

"That's not my point. I suppose what I'm saying, maybe even asking, is did you really mean it either time, the most important being the last?"

Henry paused, weighing his words. But it was a pause too long. Mercy had her answer. Whatever Henry was thinking now, whether the ordeal he had suffered through had convinced him one way or the other where he saw his future, Mercy knew then that he might never had truly been committed to spending the rest of his life with her. Perhaps he did realize now how much he loved her, how she would be good for him. But it was becoming clear to her that it probably hadn't been so back then. And what frightened her now was would it not be so again sometime in their future?

"Maybe I was wrong Henry when I said you have changed. That the months gone from here, and perhaps how the struggle you endured, caused that change. But I'm not so sure you have changed. Perhaps you never really were ready and still aren't," Mercy suggested.

"That's ridiculous. You know how much I care for you," Henry insisted.

"Care? I believe that. But caring and loving aren't necessarily the same thing."

"Well, if they aren't, I surely don't know what is."

Mercy could see by his expression, by the tone in his voice, that he was becoming agitated. There was no point going further, at least not at the moment. It would get them nowhere.

"I'm sorry if I'm upsetting you. That was not my intent. I'm just confused about things, about *us*," Mercy said.

She waited for him to say something, maybe even stand up, grab hold of her, and tell her she was crazy, over reacting. But he only continued to sit, looking at her, those eyes without emotion.

"You probably need your rest. We can discuss this again when you feel more like yourself."

She leaned down and kissed him again. But she couldn't somehow seem to shake that feeling, one of finality as she walked away. She headed back again towards the parking lot. She had another stop to make and it couldn't wait.

Chapter 35

Announced or not, Mercy didn't care, as she ground her car to a halt in front of Halcroft House and proceeded through the front door. She hadn't bothered to knock or wait to be admitted. She charged past the housemaid dusting the hallway furniture. She found the living room empty and the dining room as well but then caught sight of Miss Emily in the sitting room, working on her needlepoint. She entered the room in such a state of commotion that she took her mother by total surprise. Miss Emily literally jumped back into her chair.

"My dear, what in the world?" Miss Emily exclaimed. She had not been expecting Mercy.

"Mother, I just came from seeing Henry at the hospital," Mercy began breathlessly.

"Oh my, is something wrong?!" Miss Emily asked, fearing there was.

"Not with Henry. But he tells me he had a visitor yesterday."

"Well, that's certainly nothing to get all worked up over, is it?"

"I'm not so sure I'd agree. Aldon was the visitor," Mercy said.

"Our Aldon? Well that's a bit unexpected. Though I must say that was thoughtful of the dear man," Miss Emily offered. But she realized what was really on Mercy's mind because the same thought had just occurred to her.

"Now I wonder what they would have had to talk about?" Miss Emily said, "I hadn't thought they knew each other all that well."

"Actually, I thought you might know," Mercy said.

"Me? Why would I know?"

"It's been my experience that Aldon Barlow doesn't get himself involved in family matters unless you have asked him to," Mercy insisted.

"I didn't ask for his help. I'm really not sure exactly what sort of help I would have asked him for anyway. If you are talking about your situation, that issue is between yourself, Henry, and Garrett. I certainly care about you and realize you are struggling with it but I assume you will handle it as you see fit," Miss Emily said.

"And that is precisely what I plan on doing so I don't need any help from Aldon. He really had no right to interfere," Mercy insisted.

But Miss Emily didn't answer. She just sat quietly, looking back at her daughter. Then without a further word, she picked up the small bell on the table near her, ringing it gently. A few seconds later, they both heard the sound of footsteps approaching. Aldon Barlow appeared in the doorway, a questioning look on his face.

"Aldon would you please come in. I believe Mercy has a question for you," Miss Emily said.

"Indeed, and what might that be young lady," Aldo asked, entering the room and standing next to Miss Emily.

Mercy hadn't actually expected this from her mother. She hadn't wanted it to seem like an interrogation. But it now appeared to her as if that was exactly what her mother was doing. All the same, she wouldn't be intimidated.

"I understand you paid a visit to Henry yesterday?" Mercy began.

"Indeed, I did. Was good to see he was getting along so well."

Mercy was surprised Aldon seemed so matter of fact about it.

"I wasn't aware you and he were that close."

"I'm not suggesting we are. I just know how important he is to the family, especially to you. I sort of feel that makes it my *obligation* to look after him. Of course, if I have overstepped my bounds here, you have my apologies," Aldon offered.

Mercy realized she might have sounded as if she was accusing him of some other agenda.

"Well, it certainly was nice of you. But I don't think you had any *obligation* as you put it," Mercy suggested.

Aldon looked at her, then at Miss Emily. He measured his response carefully.

"In a way I do feel it is my obligation. Your well-being, your happiness, has always been the most important thing to your mother and I," Aldon said.

Mercy heard the concern in his voice, saw how his expression changed when she questioned his involvement. He sounded just as her adoptive father would when they had an issue. She looked at her mother and noticed she, too, had the same expression as well. Mercy felt an odd feeling take hold of her.

"Mother, is there something else you haven't shared with me?"

Miss Emily reached up for her daughter's hand but Mercy pulled away instinctively. She readied herself for whatever her mother was about to say.

"Please sit down, dear. I want to tell you a story, a part of my life I have also had to keep secreted away for many years," Miss Emily said, motioning to a chair next to her. Mercy sat down, waiting.

"As you already know, many years ago now, even though I was forced to give you to someone else, I still felt blessed that I was able to remain in your life and watch you grow," Miss Emily began. "But what you haven't ask me about is how I met your birth father and what happened to him."

"I thought if you wanted me to know you would tell me when you felt it was time to do so. Until then, I just assumed that you and he were so young he went on with his life. Maybe even married and has children of his own by now," Mercy said.

Miss Emily shook her head no. There was more.

"You see he was the son of a smuggler. In those days, during the prohibition of the twenties, a more common name for such men was rum runner. People enjoyed being able to drink and just because the government was making a vein attempt to appease a minority of a few who didn't, others were making quite a bit of money bringing whiskey in from other places like Canada and Europe. Honestly, few people thought the law made any sense and only saw that otherwise good people were being turned into criminals for making it or smuggling it in," Miss Emily said.

"But what does that have to do with you and my father?"

"Well, these men would take their boats out to what was known as Rum Row, a spot some three miles out to sea into international waters beyond the authority of the government and its agents, where they could meet up with larger delivery boats, load up their cargo, and make a dash for the shoreline before the Coast Guard cutters could catch them. Your father and his father often brought their illegal cargo into the harbors of Wellfleet and were they were offloaded and trucked inland for sale. These smugglers became involved with many of the men from around here, who also saw it as a way to make money. Again, you have to remember most folks thought it was a bad law and couldn't see the harm in what these rum runners were doing," Miss Emily insisted.

"I have heard the stories. I have heard of how they sometimes had to throw cargo overboard to avoid capture by the Coast Guard," Mercy admitted.

"Oh, yes. And sometimes all those crates of whiskey would wash up on the beach where the local men and boys would gather them in and hide them. Oh, and what parties they sometimes had, I don't mind telling you daughter!" Miss Emily grinned.

"I still don't understand how this involves you mother?"

"Well, you see that's how I met this young man who came to be a part of our little village. His father was one of those smugglers. Your real father was a handsome young man and just a bit bolder than most of the other boys his age around here. He took to following me when he saw me on the streets, waiting outside stores and such, until one day he just walked right up to me, told me his name, and asked me mine. At first, I wasn't sure I liked that or liked him. He seemed just a little ill-mannered and not all that well kept. He wasn't as refined as the other young men I was used to," Miss Emily admitted.

Aldon stifled a laugh, nodding his head in agreement as if he, too, remembered that young man.

"But after a while, I sort of got used to him following along after me and when he asked me to go to the Harvest dance, I found myself saying yes, though I knew your grandfather wasn't going to be the least bit happy about it."

"So, you didn't go I guess," Mercy said.

"Oh, just the contrary. I was starting to find myself a little more than merely attracted to that young man and nothing my father or anyone else had to say was going to stop me from seeing him. And I suppose we both eventually realized we were falling in love with each other. From there things just snowballed," Miss Emily said, a hint of sadness in her voice.

"But I don't regret a moment of it and after all look at what I was blessed with," Miss Emily said, grasping Mercy's hand.

Mercy thought it was a beautiful story, though bittersweet because her mother had been forced to live her life without the young man she had fallen in love with and had a child from.

"I'm so sorry things turned out the way they did, mother. You must have loved him quite a bit."

"Oh, I did. And I still do," Miss Emily said.

"But to lose him and never see him again?" Mercy added.

Miss Emily took her daughter's hand squeezing it tightly, locking eyes with her.

"Mercy, I never lost him. You see...he's standing right here, next to me, just as he has all these twenty-five some years," Miss Emily finally confessed, unsure of what would come next.

Mercy felt as though someone had just delivered a blow to her stomach. She stared up at Aldon Barlow in disbelief. She saw his eyes pleading with her to understand. He knew they both had lived a lie, she living as mistress of the house and he as her attendant. But they had never planned to hurt their own child.

"We had no choice, Mercy," Aldon insisted. He came around from behind Miss Emily's chair, moving closer to Mercy.

"Your grandfather nearly disowned your mother when he discovered what had happened between us and he swore he would have me arrested. He probably would have done so if it had not been for the fact that some of his own fleet boats were themselves involved in the smuggling trade," Aldo went on.

"Of course, I had to leave town for a while to avoid any scandal, to prevent the family from being disgraced," Miss Emily said.

"Love between two people doesn't allow for any leniency in such cases. Fortunately, I was only some seven months pregnant with you when the school term let out for the summer. I had been able to conceal it until then. I went to live with my friend, your adoptive mother, down Cape until you were born. Your grandparents just told anyone who asked that I was vacationing out of town that summer and no one thought differently. Doc Harrington would drive down every week to check on me and when the time came, he delivered you."

Mercy's head was still spinning from the sudden realization that in the short span of just a few months she had learned who her real mother was and now the identity of her birth father. That and the fact that they had been right here all these years, right in front of her, watching her grow up. She wasn't sure if she wanted to cry out of pity for the life the two had had to live or anger for having kept such a secret from her all these years.

"But I don't understand? Why couldn't I have been told sooner?" Mercy demanded.

Her mother and Aldon looked at each other. They had expected this very question for many years. There was no answer they knew of that would suffice other than the truth.

"I had promised your adoptive mother that until she, herself, decided to tell you, I would keep it our secret. It was the only thing I could do, the right thing, after she and your adoptive father gave you a home, raised you, and yet allowed me to be a part of your life. Any other adoption would not have worked out that way. Aldon and I were not married nor would my family allow us to become so. I could have accepted the scandal, the whispers and ugly talk, but I could not allow you to suffer from the same."

Mercy saw the tears welling up in her mother's eyes. She began to understand. It would have been no different even now. An unwed mother and a child born out of wedlock would be tainted with a stain even a good woman could not remove.

"And so, all these years, you and Aldon have shared a roof but could never live as husband and wife," Mercy said.

"No, not in the normal sense," Aldon answered, "But in every other sense. We have been blessed with each other's company and after your grandparents passed away, we were able to share a bed. I have kept my old room downstairs in the servant's quarters merely for appearances but truthfully, none of my possessions are in it. The other household staff come early and leave just after dinner is cleaned up so we have the house to ourselves,"

"It has been a good life, daughter. You need not feel any sadness for us. We have been happy and the love we have for each, the love we have for you, has been more than enough to sustain us all these years."

Mercy thought of Addy. It all seemed to fit now.

"And that's why you gave Addy a home. Because she was, in many ways, just like you both when you and *father* were that age," Mercy suggested, realizing she had just called a man she had known for many years only as Aldon as her *father*.

The sad look that had been etched upon Aldon's face softened. He had heard her as well and the weight he had carried for all these many years felt as though it had been finally been lifted from him. He was not a man given

334

to much public display of emotion but now it was all he could do to keep back the tears that fought to escape his eyes.

"Yes, in that young girl I saw myself. Scared, with child, her father who offered no support. How could I not have helped? It was God's way of asking me to show a kindness that I alone could understand more than most," Miss Emily insisted.

"And your visit to see and talk with Henry," Mercy continued, looking up at Aldon, "That was to..."

"I couldn't just stand by and see you struggling with all this," Aldon quickly added, "I know your heart is torn between Henry Gates and Garrett Harrington. I needed to know what Henry was thinking. He went away once. I'm a man and I know what he was truly feeling when he left to join the military. Certainly, I have no doubt it was partly because of a sense of duty. But he had long passed the draft age and even the age of those who typically volunteered," Aldon insisted. He knew there were other reasons, reasons men who sought adventure in their lives had always had.

"Has he said he is ready to be married," Miss Emily asked. Mercy wasn't sure how to answer. He had not. That much she knew. Miss Emily didn't need an answer. Mercy's eyes told her what she needed to know.

Miss Emily took hold of her daughter's hands once more, again tenderly squeezing them.

"He has been through quite a lot. Perhaps he just needs time," Miss Emily assured her.

Aldon didn't add anything to Miss Emily's thoughts. He wasn't convinced and his visit with Henry Gates hadn't changed his opinion. But as Miss Emily suggested, perhaps it would have to wait and Mercy would ultimately be the only one to decide what she wanted anyway. He would let things be for now, but he would be watching.

Mercy looked at the hands of the tall grandfather clock across the room. It was a little after eleven in the morning and she had promised Garrett she would be home by noon when he had called the night before asking her if she would see him. She had promised him she would though she wasn't completely certain what he wanted to speak to her about. Their last meeting had not gone well. She knew it was her fault. She was still unable to explain her feelings beyond what she had already tried to reveal. She knew he was confused. She was as well. So, she had had no choice but to leave things as she had with him. She couldn't bring herself to hurt him. No more than she felt she could hurt Henry.

"I promised Garrett I would be home by noon. He asked to speak with me. It's the least I can do. I owe him that much," Mercy said, rising to leave.

Miss Emily was still holding her hand, only letting it slip away after Mercy had leaned down to kiss her goodbye. Then Mercy found herself doing something that she had rarely done. She approached Aldon Barlow and wrapped her arms around him, quietly hugging him against her. Slowly, almost as though he was unsure of how to respond, he raised his arms and gently embraced Mercy as his *daughter* for the first time in his life. It was more than he needed. It had been more than he had ever hoped for.

Chapter 36

When Garrett had arrived at the office that morning, he had asked his uncle if he might take his lunch hour outside of the office even though neither man truly ever took what they would have considered a break from their patient schedule for lunch. They would merely find a moment to grab a bite to eat if the house keeper came down to the office with sandwiches or stop on the way somewhere if out on house calls during the day.

Doc Harrington told his nephew that would be fine with him, believing there was more than just lunch on Garrett's mind. All morning, ever since Garrett had come into the office, Doc sensed his nephew's thoughts were not on his work. His thoughts were somewhere else and he had a good idea where. A little before noon, Doc called Garrett into his office.

"There is only my old friend Mrs. Crawford out in the waiting room. And she's not about to let a youngster like you go *fussing about her*. I believe that's how she would put it," Doc grinned. "You go have your lunch now. I'm fine here."

As impatient as he had sensed Garrett was, he wasn't surprised when his nephew seemed hesitant.

"Are you sure Uncle. I don't want to leave you alone to handle the office," Garrett said, though Doc could tell there was a hint of hope in Garrett's voice that his uncle wouldn't object.

"No, I'll be fine. You go on now. I've been running this office by myself for more years than I care to admit and a couple of hours more by myself isn't going to make any difference," Doc assured him.

"Well, if you're sure," Garrett said, taking his coat down from the hook and throwing it on. He headed for the door even before his uncle could response.

"I'm sure. And *you* better be sure you give that sweet girl a kiss for me!" Doc called after him. Garrett turned to face Doc, a look of false denial on his face which quickly vanished. There was no trying to fool the old man.

***

When Garrett arrived at the little cottage along the Wellfleet dunes, he saw a thin wisp of smoke curling up from the chimney, jutting out of the roof. He grew even more anxious knowing she was already home, just as she had promised. He had somehow hoped she might be still out shopping or making deliveries before noon. Now he had no time to sit and wait, and most importantly sit and go over the words again he had been rehearsing in his mind, words that had been coursing through him in an endless stream of variations and possibilities all morning and the night before.

He parked the car and approached her front door. But before he could knock, the door opened and there stood Mercy asking him in. Obviously, she had been watching for his arrival, had heard the car coming up the sandy path.

"Can I get you some coffee, something to eat," Mercy asked, going through the motions of a polite welcome. But both knew it wasn't a meal he had come for.

"Perhaps some coffee, that's all," Garrett said, thinking it might delay what he somehow was dreading.

Mercy went into the kitchen to get them coffee. She had put the pot on when she got home and it was ready to be poured. She carried a small tray back out into the living room so they both could sit near the fire. Despite its warming effect, they both still felt a chill. They sat a while in silence, sipping their coffee, staring into the flame, the popping and hissing sound of the burning wood the only sound. Then Garrett turned to face her, summoning up all the courage he could muster and began.

"Mercy, you know I've made my feeling about you known," Garrett said.

Mercy felt the need to stop him. She didn't want to make him go through all that again.

"I understand but..."

"No, please. Let me just say what I have to say and then you can tell me anything you want," Garrett pleaded.

Mercy fell silent again, shaking her head in agreement.

"You know I love you. I have told you so. But what I have not told you is just how much I *need* you. How much I want to spend the rest of my life with you. I know you promised yourself to someone else. But if I don't let my true feelings be known, I may live the rest of my life regretting that I let this moment slip away."

Mercy could hear the sincerity in his voice, saw it in his eyes. She felt her heart beating hard inside her. She wanted to tell him it was all right, that she wanted him as well. But the words would not form so easily. Henry's image, his face, would not leave her. She again tried to speak but Garrett held his hand up, pausing her from doing so.

"Marry me, Mercy Daniels. I will love you like no other man could ever love you. You have my promise. You will never know a moment in your life where my love for you doesn't burn as bright as it does this very day. I need you in my life. Any success, any station I might achieve in life, would be hallow without you by my side," Garrett insisted.

But Mercy was unable to find the reply she knew he wanted. Two months ago, there would have been no hesitation, she thought. No obstacle. But now, as she sat listening to his words, looking into the face of a man she knew she, too, had fallen in love with, she continued to struggle with the reality she found herself in. She had also loved Henry Gates. She had believed he was the love of her life. They had shared a special bond.

But now, she found herself also in love with another man. She had always believed that true love, the kind that makes you ache when you are with that person as much as it makes you ache when you are apart, could only happen once in lifetime. She had believed she had found that with Henry. But such a feeling had come into her life again with Garrett.

"I need time, Garrett. Please, I just need time," Mercy heard herself saying, as though she herself was listening to words being spoken by someone else there in the room with them. She knew it wasn't fair to him. He expected more. They had come so far together in such a short time. They truly did have an understanding between them and now she was pushing away as if all these months had never occurred.

"Mercy, did you not hear what I said. I love you. I want you to marry me," Garrett repeated as though saying it again might somehow reach her.

"I know. I understand. I...it's just that..."

"That you still are in love with Henry Gates? Is that what you are saying," Garrett asked, unwilling to leave it unanswered.

He would wait forever he thought if in the end she would accept him. But this was different. He could see how she was torn between the two of them, a love she had once given her heart to and another she had been ready to.

"I just need time. It's all so overwhelming. Please understand Garrett. I don't want to lose you, truly I don't," Mercy pleaded.

"Lose me?! As what, your friend? Is that what you fear? I believe the time for such things has passed. I'm not here to force an answer sweetheart. But to suggest we might just go on living as just *friends?*"

She looked into his blue-gray eyes, saw the pain in them, knew it was her that had put it there. But still, she couldn't make it go away with a lie simply because she felt responsible. She was frozen in place. She loved them both.

Garrett could see that it was pointless to keep pressing her. He loved her, would do anything to make her see that, to make her say she would have him but he didn't want it that way. He couldn't accept a decision made from a desire not to hurt him. If she didn't want him out of pure love, then it wouldn't be right. It couldn't be forced.

"I said once before that I understood. Hard as it is for me to say so again, I do understand. I believe you will make up your mind when you are ready and I will do nothing to cause you further hurt. I will be waiting for you, for your decision. But until then, perhaps it would be best if we just spent some time apart. Maybe then you will come to understand what I have known for some time now," Garrett insisted.

"And what is that?" Mercy asked.

"That you want to spend the rest of your life with me," Garrett answered.

Garrett gathered his coat and hat. He leaned forward, kissing Mercy on her cheek. Mercy felt a coldness between them. As he headed for the door, she sensed a terrible need to reach out to him, to stop him. She felt if she didn't, it would somehow be the end for them both.

But she hesitated, believing it would only be the crueler thing to have him believe that her stopping him was the answer he was waiting for. Her head ached from all the indecision that continued to grip her day after day.

Perhaps Garrett was right. Perhaps she felt an *obligation* to Henry, perhaps even more so than the desire she had come to feel for Garrett.

She sat there, unmoving, helpless, watching him shut the door behind him. She remained still as she listened to the sound of Garrett's car grow distant.

Chapter 37

Ever since she had been a little girl, Mercy had attached herself to Doc Harrington as though he was the grandfather she never had. To her, Doc had always seemed the wisest person she knew. She loved her parents, always did as they asked. She had also always sought out the answers to questions young girls have from her Aunt Emily, never knowing she was actually receiving the advice of her own mother all these years. But sometimes, she felt that even these people closest to her didn't always tell her what she *needed* to know. As she grew older, she understood that was because they told her what they thought was *best* for her and not necessary what she needed to hear; the truth. But Doc always did. Maybe not what she wanted to hear but always what she *needed* to hear.

Every Friday afternoon, Doc Harrington gave his house servant and cook the night off at the start of the weekend. For as long as Mercy could remember, Doc and his wife Mary had their dinner at the Wellfleet House just a short walk from his front door. The tavern and restaurant had stood on the same corner of Commercial St and Bank St for well over a hundred years. Even after his wife had passed, Doc kept this ritual. He would arrive around five-thirty before the regular dinner trade began to fill the place, take his usual table at the back corner by the fireplace, order the same meal of fried New England, whole belly clams, breaded cod, and boiled new potatoes before opening the book he had brought with him to read while he ate. Mercy knew you could set a watch to this ritual so she waited until a little past six-thirty when she was sure he would be nearly done with his meal before disturbing him. She couldn't ask him to drive out to her house in the dark now that he was pretty much limited to daylight driving because of his failing eyesight. And she couldn't very well drop by his office and risk running into Garrett. It would have been the same thing had she suggested he meet her at her mother's house.

As Mercy stepped through the doorway of the tavern, she was immediately greeted by Mrs. Hartpence, the wife of the owner. Mrs. Hartpence often served as the hostess on Friday nights while her husband went down to the wharf to get first pick of the day's catch coming in for the weekend.

"Well, good evening Mercy. This is an expected pleasure," Mrs. Hartpence smiled, unaccustomed to seeing the young woman there, alone, on a Friday night.

"Good evening. Yes, I've come to see Doc. I trust I am not too late?" Mercy said.

"Oh no, he is still here, though he didn't mention he was expecting anyone," Mrs. Hartpence said.

"He isn't. I just haven't seen him in a while and had the evening to myself. I thought I would surprise him with a visit and as we all know, if it's Friday evening, we know where we'll find him," Mercy smiled, trying to keep the exchange brief without inviting questions.

"Let me escort you to his table," Mrs. Hartpence offered. But Mercy just waved her hand.

"Oh, that won't be necessary. Back room, rear table, near the fireplace," Mercy grinned.

"Yes, indeed. We might as well carve his name on that table or place a small nameplate on the wall," Mrs. Hartpence smiled good naturedly.

Mercy nodded and proceeded past the woman towards the smoky interior of the dark tavern room. Deep inside, she spotted Doc Harrington, his dinner plate and utensils sitting neatly at the edge of the small table waiting for the busboy to pick them up. He appeared lost to his surroundings; eyes focused on the pages of his book. He hardly noticed Mercy as she approached, only looking up when she spoke his name. His expression went immediately from one of surprise to pleasure as he motioned for her to take the empty chair across from him. As she sat, he closed his book and laid it carefully in front of him.

"Not exactly unexpected," Doc smiled.

"That I would find you here? Not really, you are pretty much a person of habit," Mercy assured him.

"Oh, that's true. No argument there. But no, I meant that you would eventually come to me. With your troubles, as they might be. Is that not the reason for your visit?" Doc suggested.

Mercy wasn't sure just how to answer him. Decided she would offer another reason.

"Must I only come to see you when I am ill of health or have some trouble. I might just want to spend some time with someone I hold so dear as I do you," Mercy explained. She knew better, however, to assume Doc would believe such an excuse.

"Well, that's very nice of you, I must say. Quite a treat for an old man such as myself to have the company of such a lovely young lady on such a pleasant night. But I confess I am just a little bit curious," Doc admitted.

"Curious?"

"Why yes. On such a beautiful evening, after you both have worked a long week each, I would have thought you would have plans with my nephew?"

"Well, it's not like we are attached at the hip," Mercy said, feeling a need to defend herself.

"No, certainly not. I can appreciate that. I'm sure, like anyone, you need a little time for yourself," Doc agreed. But he noticed now that her expression changed.

"Why? Has Garrett said something to you?" Mercy asked, alert for any answer that might suggest Garrett had shared their conversation of the other evening with his uncle.

"Said something? Why no, my dear. What would he have to tell me? At least anything more than I already can obviously divine on my own."

Mercy knew now that there was no longer any reason to maintain some sort of pretense as to the true nature of her visit. She had come to seek the guidance she had grown to depend on from this beloved man all these many years. She reached across the table, grasping his hand tightly, no other words being needed.

"You've come to talk to me because you have a problem. It's not a mystery. In truth, it's not all that complex nor is it unique. Simply put, you are in love with two men. Your heart is *divided.* You thought you had once met the man you believed you had been waiting for. One who would take you from the foolish dreams of a young child to the feelings of a young woman. Then, when that had been taken from you, you found a way to move on. Another young man came into your life and you allowed yourself to once again believe maybe, just maybe, love had twice found you," Doc said, his eyes soft with understanding.

Mercy fought back the tears welling up in her eyes. She expected that this wonderful old man would know such things, could say such words.

"And so, you have come to me to ask me for an opinion on what to do. Not because there are no others in your life who don't love you as much but perhaps *because* they do love you as much. And they only want what's best for you. But for that very reason they aren't able to tell you what you need to truly know. They only want you to be happy. And you believe given the situation, that's not possible," Doc continued.

"But I can't hurt either of them. Not Garrett or Henry," Mercy insisted, the anguish tormenting her face, tears rolling slowly down her cheeks.

"But that's exactly why what you are doing child is wrong," Doc insisted.

"I don't understand."

"You believe by choosing one, you hurt the other. And while I won't lie to you and tell you that's not so, what you fail to see is that as long as you see things only in that way, then *you* will never be happy," Doc suggested, "And isn't your happiness worth something? Isn't that, after all, the most important thing?"

Mercy listened to his words. She began to understand. There was no way she could move forward without having to leave one of them go. And no matter what she did, the truth was that the one she let go would certainly in time find another. Had she not herself learned that lesson?

"So instead of trying to choose on the basis of which one you would hurt the most, perhaps you should choose the one who you know deep in your heart will make you the happiest. After all my sweet child, it is *your* life is it not?" Doc insisted.

Doc's words quieted her troubled heart. Yes, he was right she thought. No matter her decision, one of them would be hurt but they would be alright. Their lives would not end. They would emerge with their future intact. She needed to listen to her heart and not her mind. She stood up and wrapped her arms around the old man.

"If you were just a little younger," Mercy said to him.

"If I were a little younger, I think my dear wife Mary might have had a thing or two to say about it," Doc laughed.

He watched her walk away, hoping he had indeed been of some help but not in the least believing that it would still be a simple choice. Yet he hoped it would be one she made with *her* at the center of the decision.

Chapter 38

That first Saturday morning of December dawned clear without a hint of rain in the crystal blue skies over Wellfleet. By a little before noon the temperature had risen to an unseasonable high of nearly sixty degrees. It was one of those days that promised to be everything a young bride could hope for as the sleek, black, polished Packard pulled up in front of the First United Church along High St. At the wheel was Aldon Barlow, about to be father of the bride. Mercy, in a white satin wedding gown, sat next to her mother in the rear seat.

Aldon eased the car to a stop and stepped out of the automobile. He was impeccably dressed in a fine gray pin stripped suit with ascot, vest, and long tail coat. He reached for the door handle of the Packard, opening it for the two women. He held his hand out to take Miss Emily's, helping her to step out of the car onto the sidewalk. Then he offered his hand to his daughter, Mercy, as she emerged from the grand automobile in perfect splendor. Her dress flowed down around the curves of her body, gathering in delicate folds of lace and velveteen as it trailed off behind her in an elegant train. Together, they all started up the steps to the church, Aldon on one side, Miss Emily on the other.

The groom and the rest of the wedding party, along with the guests, had all been waiting well before noon for the arrival of the bride.

From the road atop the hill that led out of town, he stood, watching Mercy and her parents disappear through the front door of the church. He stood there, committing to memory the scene he had just seen. There was no more need for discussion, no more need to win her heart. Time for doing either had passed.

He slid back into his car, his one piece of luggage laying there next to him on the front seat. He started the car's engine and began to drive off slowly. He wasn't in a hurry. He wasn't particularly certain where in fact he was heading. Perhaps Boston, perhaps farther. As he drove out to Route 6, heading west on the Mid-Cape highway, he watched the town of Wellfleet gradually disappear in his rearview mirror.

Henry Gates thought of the life that might have been and at least hoped would still be for the woman he once believed he would marry.

"Have a good life, Mercy Daniels," he thought to himself. In the end, he knew that was really all he ever wanted for her.

Made in the
USA
Middletown, DE